Also by Sanjida Kay

Bone by Bone
The Stolen Child
My Mother's Secret

ONE YEAR LATER

ONE YEAR LATER

Sanjida Kay

CORVUS

Published in Great Britain in 2019 by Corvus, an imprint
of Atlantic Books Ltd.

10 9 8 7 6 5 4 3 2 1

A CIP catalogue record for this book is available from the British Library.

Paperback ISBN: 978 1 78649 255 5
Export trade paperback ISBN: 978 1 78649 879 3
E-book ISBN: 978 1 78649 256 2

Printed in Great Britain.

Corvus
An imprint of Atlantic Books Ltd
Ormond House
26–27 Boswell Street
London
WC1N 3JZ

www.corvus-books.co.uk

To my family

—Midway upon the journey of our life
I found myself within a forest dark,
For the straightforward pathway had been lost.

Ah me! how hard a thing it is to say
What was this forest savage, rough, and stern,
Which in the very thought renews the fear...

I did not die, and yet I lost life's breath.

The Divine Comedy by Dante Alighieri

PROLOGUE

He stands on the edge of the cliff and stares at the drop below. It's early, around 5 a.m., and he's only had two hours' sleep. He blinks, rubs his eyes. The wind, skimmed straight from the sea, is cold, and he can taste the salt on his tongue. There's a pale-blue line where the ocean meets the sky: the first sign of the approaching dawn. He has a torch in his pocket, but it's of little use, faced with the dark expanse of beach below him. He shifts slightly and feels the earth give way beneath one foot.

He doesn't have long.

The tide is almost fully in, and the man who'd phoned him had said she was at one end of the beach. The caller was drunk; he said he was on his way home from the festival, although that in itself was suspicious, because no one lives at this end of the island, save for the Donati family and the people staying in the holiday house below their farm. The man was slurring his words – fear, combined with the alcohol, making him barely comprehensible. He didn't say which end of the beach. Martelli had driven here as fast as he could, radioing for the ambulance from the car. He offers a silent prayer: that she is above the tideline, that he can find her in time, that she's still alive.

The clouds shift; the line of light over the water turns to buttermilk, and he thinks he can see her. *Could be rocks or flotsam. Or a body.* If it is the English girl, she's lying stretched out on the sand below the headland, where this spit of land joins *il cavalluccio marino*.

He clicks the torch on and starts down the cliff path. It's treacherous in daylight, never mind at night: narrow, twisting and steep, stones breaking through the soil. He slips, thinks he's going to lose his footing. He can't see how far it is to the bottom. He slides, collapses back against the side of the cliff, grabbing handfuls of vegetation to stop himself from falling the rest of the way. Loose grit and pebbles slide from beneath his boots, and he can smell the sweet, sharp scent of thyme and wild marjoram where he's crushed the plants in his fists. It's momentarily comforting: his grandma puts them in her *rigatoni campagnolo*. But then his torch hits a rock on the shore and the bulb smashes. He's in darkness, his breath ragged in his throat. He pushes himself half-upright and scrambles the rest of the way down. His ankle throbs where he's grazed it. The paramedics are not going to be able to carry her up here on a stretcher, he thinks, and the tide is approaching so fast, he's not sure if they'll make it round the headland, either.

If she's still alive.

He runs across the sand, through crisp, dried seaweed and a ragged line of plastic bottles, Coke cans scoured clean, baling twine and polystyrene chips. The tourists can't reach this beach, so no one clears away the rubbish. She's on her side, one arm flung out, her legs at a disjointed angle. Has she fallen from the cliff? The rocks surrounding her are sharp as needles, erupting through the sand like prehistoric teeth. The foam-tipped edge of a wave creeps across the toes of her right foot. She's missing one sandal. Her white summer dress is rucked up, exposing her thighs, revealing part of one breast. He throws himself onto his knees next to her. Her dark hair is wet and covers her face, so he can't see what she looks like – if she is the missing girl. But he can see the blood: an uneven pool staining the sand, spreading out from the back of her head.

Where the hell is the ambulance?

His radio crackles, but there's no word from the paramedics. He gently touches her with the tips of his fingers, and she's cold, so cold.

Mio Dio.

He's never seen a dead body before and his stomach clenches into a tight fist. Briefly he brushes the crucifix hidden under his shirt and then slides his hand beneath her hair, feeling for a pulse.

PART I

JULY, BRISTOL

1
AMY

It's as if the day has gone into reverse. Amy puts on lipstick and feels like she's getting ready for work instead of a night out with her husband. There's something hard and smooth in the pit of her stomach; it's the shape of an avocado stone, but larger, heavier. She can't remember the last time she and Matt went out. Before, probably. Most things happened *before*. She scrutinizes herself. She's thirty-six, but she looks ten years older; there are hollows beneath her cheeks, and her face has concertinaed into those folds that athletes get when their body fat drops. She's never been thin before. She always wanted to be slimmer, but now that she is, she hates it. Misery skinniness might look good in photos, but it's unattractive in real life. Matt winces sometimes when they try and make love, as if he might break her or she'll pierce him with a hipbone. She tries a smile. It's what the self-help books say: *Smile and then you'll really start feeling happy!* She covers the place where her dress gapes across her chest with a scarf and tucks the lipstick into the pocket of her handbag.

Nick should be here soon, she thinks. He's late, but then he always is. She goes to check on the children. Theo is sitting up in bed, reading.

'How fast can light travel?' he asks, without looking up. Although he's only eight years old, it feels as if he's been obsessed with space his entire life.

'Oh, I know this one! Seven times round the Earth in one second.'

The upbeat voice she tries to use with the children sounds fake and brittle, even to her.

'How many stars are there in space?'

'As many as the grains of sand in the sea.'

He rolls his eyes. 'Wrong.'

'Okay then. Seventy thousand million million million.'

'Seventy sextillion, you mean,' he says, but there's a grudging note in his voice.

'I've been revising.' She gives him a kiss. 'Night, love. You remember Uncle Nick will be looking after you?' He nods. 'Fifteen more minutes and then put your light out.'

She peeks into Lotte's room. There are pink-and-purple unicorns spiralling across the ceiling from a night-light. Lotte, two years younger than Theo, has been in bed for longer and is already snoring softly. Amy touches her forehead with the back of her hand. She feels hot, so she pushes the bedcovers down a little and worries whether it was sensible to let her wear a long nightie. She switches the night-light off, remembering, as she always does, that it isn't Lotte's.

Ruby-May's bedroom is opposite. Amy stands in the doorway. The room isn't quite dark: the curtains are open slightly and a street light shines through. She can see the curve of Ruby-May's new bed. Her youngest daughter was delighted that she didn't have to sleep in a cot any more and she was now officially a big girl. Amy resists the urge to draw the curtains fully closed, but she can't help going in and sitting at the end of the bed. It's so low down, her knees are almost level with her chin. She picks up Ruby-May's doll, Pearl, and sets it on her lap. Its hard, plastic hands poke into her ribs. On the shelf opposite is Ruby-May's Beatrix Potter collection; it was Amy's, when she was little. Lined up in front of the books is a set of Beanie Boos, with large eyes that glitter in the muted light. There's a thin bottle of gin tucked behind *The Tale of Peter*

Rabbit, but she resists that urge too. She listens for her daughter's breathing, as she does every night, and then stretches her hand across the Peppa Pig duvet cover.

Ruby-May slept tucked in a tight curl, like a fern frond before it unrolls.

She touches the spot where Ruby-May's toes would have been.

She can't imagine anything more soulless than a child's empty bed at night.

Matt used to make her leave their daughter's room, but he's given up. On her or on himself, she's not sure. Sometimes she still spends the night here, but every trace of Ruby-May's smell has gone. She glances at her watch and tells herself that she needs to make an effort. *We're going out, for the first time in over a year.* She forces herself to get up, to put the doll down, to hold back her tears. But instead of going to her husband, she slides *Peter Rabbit* and *The Tale of Mrs Tiggy-Winkle* forward and, with one finger, hooks out the bottle. It's a cheap one from Aldi and, over the artificial juniper, she can smell the sharpness of neat alcohol. She takes a sip and then another, and feels the warmth bloom across the back of her throat: a line, like a burn, running down her chest. One more and then she replaces the bottle and smooths the pillow. Her skin is so dry, her knuckles catch on the cotton.

In one month, it'll be a year. A year since their youngest daughter died. Ruby-May, the brightest jewel, her gorgeous girl. She'd always wanted Ruby-May to have her surname and not her husband's – Ruby-May Flowers sounds so much more romantic than Ruby Jenkins. She can't even bring herself to imagine the anniversary. It falls on the day before what would have been Ruby-May's fourth birthday.

I can't be here. I can't do this any more.

The books all say that time heals. But nothing can cauterize her pain.

♜

Matt doesn't look up when she walks into the sitting room. He's hunched over his laptop, catching up on work emails. Once, he'd have told her how nice she looked. She doesn't look nice any more, though, she thinks. Maybe it's not something he even considers any longer.

'No sign of him?' she asks, although it's obvious Nick hasn't turned up.

'No. Have you called him?'

She's already sent him one text and now she sends another, still trying for cheery and not as if she's blaming him.

'Just ring him,' says Matt. 'I've already had to pay a late fee to Uber.'

She goes into the kitchen where the signal's better and stands by the window into the garden. Nick's mobile goes straight to voicemail.

'Nick, I hope you're okay? We're ready! The reservation is... well, it's now. Can you give me a call, let me know you're on your way?'

She phones the restaurant and puts the reservation back by half an hour. She checks there are still Ubers in their area. Matt could always drive, if there aren't any when Nick finally turns up. She opens one of the drawers in the kitchen and takes a mint out from the packet hidden under the box of bag clips and bottle openers.

She stands in the sitting-room doorway and watches her husband. His hair has gone silver around the edges and there's the beginning of a bald patch on his crown. She can't be bothered any more. It's all so pointless. She's about to say they should just stay in, when Matt gets out his phone. He goes over to the window.

'Nick, mate. Where the hell are you? Get your arse over here.'

She joins him on the window seat. It's like a microclimate: cooler than everywhere else in the house. The sun is setting and there's a pink streak over Bristol's skyline. The room is scattered with bits of plastic – Lego and Octonaut figures, Sylvanian Families animals and a Playmobil zoo – which don't quite obscure the fallen glasses and dirty cereal bowls. She should tidy it up, but her bones feel weary.

'Shall we...'

'Yeah,' he says.

He goes into the kitchen and she can hear him banging cupboards, turning on the oven. He filled the freezer with ready-meals and packets of frozen vegetables when she lost the will to cook. He comes back with two glasses, a bottle of wine and a pack of tortilla chips.

When he switches on the TV, her sister's face fills the screen. Bethany's talking animatedly, her dark, glossy hair swinging. She's wearing navy nail varnish and skinny black leather jeans with a sheer blouse. You can see her bra when she leans forward and the studio lights shine through the fabric.

'Must have been her last one,' says Matt, turning up the volume.

Amy feels, as she does every time she sees her sister, a kind of cringing embarrassment: not because her sister is terrible – she isn't, she's good at what she does – but at the thought of being on live television, of having to say the right thing without stuttering, whilst somebody else is talking in your ear at the same time as you're trying to listen to a studio guest and make intelligent and witty conversation or read the autocue. She would hate it – the scrutiny, and the effort it takes to look like that: not a chip in her polish, not an eyebrow hair out of place. Bethany once showed Amy her Twitter feed after a show, and it was a deluge of comments about what she was wearing, how she looked and what the male viewers would like to do to her. Amy had been horrified, but Bethany had just shrugged.

'You should see my Facebook messages. Anyway, it means they're watching,' she'd said.

And now, of course, what she feels for her sister has become more complicated.

The doorbell rings and Matt pads through the hall in his socks to let Nick in.

'Nick Flowers, you're an hour late.'

'I'm sorry, mate. I was in the studio and lost track of time.'

'And you had your phone turned off?'

'Had it on silent. You know what Tamsyn's like.' He comes into the sitting room, shucking his coat onto the sofa, and hugs her. His stubble grazes her cheek. 'I'm really, really sorry, Ams. You can still go. I can stay as late as you like.'

She can't remember the last time he was here. She doesn't want to try. *Was it really almost a year ago?* He's met them in cafes, and taken the children to the park. But he hasn't been in their house for more than a few minutes. She guesses it's because he can't bring himself to walk past Ruby-May's bedroom, which she's left almost exactly as it was, one year ago.

'Matt's put something in the oven.'

'Lasagne,' says Matt. 'Do you want some, now you're here?'

'Guys, I feel terrible – making you miss....' He catches sight of Bethany. 'That's *The Show*, right?'

'It's an old one. We had it on catch-up,' Amy says. 'Did she ever tell you why she left and came back to Bristol?'

Nick sits on the sofa, and Matt hands him a glass of Merlot and tops up hers. Nick shifts uncomfortably. He must have been in touch with Bethany.

'You know what Bethany's like. She probably changed her mind about working on it. Or fell out with someone.'

'That's more like it,' says Matt, going into the kitchen. 'She never got on with that new girl, did she?' He hesitates and she knows he wants to say *The brown one*, but Sara knocked that kind of thing out of him. 'The one with the Scottish accent,' he says after a beat. 'Tiffany MacGregor or something.'

He reappears a couple of minutes later with a tray; plates of gloopy slices of lasagne and peas; another bottle of red.

'Thanks, Matt,' says Nick, passing a plate to Amy.

'How's work?' Matt asks.

'Same. Tamsyn breaks my balls on the days she wants me in the studio, but then I can go for a week without any work.'

'You should set up on your own. Take control of your life.' Matt shovels in a sloppy forkful of pasta. 'Do an MBA or a course on entrepreneurship. Can even do them online now.'

Her brother doesn't even bother responding to this. Once he'd have given Matt a playful punch and told him he'd got into photography because he wanted to be an artist – not a suit, like him.

She eats listlessly, hardly tasting the food, and after she's had a couple of bites, her stomach starts to convulse, as it always does at this point. Bethany is talking about holidays: apparently Croatia is the new destination; she raises her carefully groomed eyebrows archly. When was this filmed? May? It'll be the summer holidays in a week and Amy hasn't thought about where they'll go or what they'll do with the children, once they're off school. She sets her plate aside. Nick glances at her and frowns, but doesn't say anything.

Bethany's voice – low, husky, as if she's secretly smiling – tells them of Croatia's exotic azure waters and rocky coastline, but how you can still buy English classics – beer and chips – on the seafront. The camera (they must have hired a drone) zooms over the cliffs and across vineyards and lines of dark, conical trees.

'It's almost the... the – it's nearly a year since...' says Nick. 'I was thinking we should do something.'

It's as if her younger brother has said exactly what she was thinking.

'We could go away,' Amy says. 'Hire a holiday house and be away for... be away for—'

'A holiday?' Matt says. 'Really?'

'I can't be here,' she says. 'You know that.' Her voice rises.

The thought of being in this house, pretending to be cheerful for Theo and Lotte, fills her with a kind of panic. What would they do? Buy flowers, field condolences, all whilst trying not to think of her daughter as she last saw her, her lips swollen, her skin grey, her fingertips wrinkled...

Matt covers her hand with his own.

'And we can't go to Somerset.'

'No,' he says. 'Shall we talk about it later?'

'Italy. Italy would be perfect. It'll be sunny. It won't be remotely like here. The children will love it – they'll have a good time. Somewhere with a beach.'

'There won't be any flights or villas left,' says Matt. 'We've left it too late.' He's been eating mechanically. It's a new habit, to make sure he has ingested enough 'nutrients' to satisfy his doctor. He methodically spears the last of his peas onto his fork and takes a gulp of wine to force down the food. She can't be bothered to talk to her GP any more.

'No one will be able to reach us. I won't have to speak to anyone asking how we are.'

'We could get something online,' Nick says. 'Loads of people are letting their houses privately now, on Airbnb, that kind of thing.'

Matt reluctantly sets down his fork, as if he's accepted that he'll have to discuss Ruby-May's anniversary in front of Amy's brother.

'Do you mean the... the five of us,' Matt says, gesturing towards Nick, 'plus Chloe?'

Chloe, Matt's daughter from his previous marriage, is almost sixteen. Amy nods doubtfully. *She might not want to come.* Matt hasn't counted Bethany. Or their dad.

'I'll ask Sara.' Matt still sounds unconvinced. 'That's if we can find flights, and somewhere to stay, at such short notice.'

'It's in a month, not next weekend,' Amy says and Matt gives her a dull look. She never used to speak to him like that, and she wonders if Matt mentioning his ex-wife has set her off.

'What if,' Nick says, swallowing his pasta, 'what I meant was, what if we *all* went? The whole family. We should do something, you know, on the day. Together.'

He can't say the word, either. An anniversary has always been a joyful occasion: the anniversary of when she and Matt first got together, their wedding anniversary.

'*All* of us?' Matt asks again.

'It's not like we've seen each other much. It might help, you know?' Her brother clears his throat. 'I'm not sure how – well, how else are we going to get past this? We've only got each other, since Mum left, and Dad...' He tails off.

'Including Bethany?' Matt's lips are set in a thin line.

'I'll talk to Bee,' Nick says.

Matt glances at Amy to see how she's going to react. When she doesn't say anything, he picks up the plates and balances them in a messy tower, stacking them on top of the forks.

'Come on, guys. She needs to be there.'

Matt carries the debris from their meal into the kitchen. Amy squeezes her eyes shut.

'Amy, she's your sister. She's devastated by what happened. Have you even seen her?' Nick asks.

She shakes her head. 'A couple of times since the funeral. She thinks I hate her.'

'Understandable,' Nick says. They sit in silence for a moment. She doesn't know if he means it's understandable they haven't met up, or understandable that she can't bear being with her sister any more. 'I know what she's doing, from following her on Instagram,' he adds. 'You two were always closer than me and Bee. You can't let that go.'

He's right, of course. Her sister, who is thirty-four, is only two years younger than her. Nick was the baby of the family. He'll be thirty this year. The kitchen door slams as Matt goes into the garden. He used to love it: on fine evenings he'd potter about out there, mowing the lawn, digging over flower beds, scrubbing the algae from the patio paving stones. Now it's feral: a riot of bindweed and brambles; there are holes in the trampoline netting, and ash saplings have invaded the plant pots.

'And what about—'

'We can't leave him behind.'

'I can't, Nick.'

'It wasn't his fault.' Nick sounds like a robot. She's lost count of the times he's said that to her.

'I don't know how you can even say that. After what happened.'

He sighs. 'He's our dad. He's getting older. We need to look after him.'

'That's not the point. If he'd only accepted that it was his fault and apologized.' Nick looks down at his hands. 'No. There's no way he can come with us,' she continues. 'And don't even think about asking Matt. He'd kill Dad, if he turned up.' She takes a sip of her wine and rubs her eyes. 'It's a good idea to go away, though. I don't want to stay here with the kids on my own.'

The credits to *The Show* start rolling over Bethany, her male co-star and the new girl – Tiffany – who seems to have replaced her. Bethany is waving manically.

'Bethany Flowers,' Nick says in a faux announcer's voice, as if their sister were a movie star. And then in his normal voice he adds, 'I don't think she likes being on regional telly. Not quite the viewing figures. Do you want me to ask her about going on holiday?' He glances sideways at her. 'Assuming Matt agrees.'

Amy nods. 'He'll have to. I'll speak to Luca too.'

'Luca?'

'His family live in Italy. He might come for a few days, help with Lotte and Theo, so we can have a bit of a break, and then he could go and visit them. He should be with us anyway. He's almost part of the family, after all this time.'

Luca is studying for an MSc in child psychology and helps them with the school run when he's not at university. He used to look after Ruby-May while Amy is at work. Nick nods, although Amy wonders if her brother has spoken to Luca since last year. He might not even have talked to him when they were in Somerset for Ruby-May's birthday. The police had already arrived by the time Nick turned up. She can see the top of Matt's head silhouetted against the darkening sky. He's sitting on a broken bench just below them.

'You can ask Bethany. Just don't mention it to Dad. I should check on the kids,' she says.

'I'll go,' says Nick, 'seeing as I'm meant to be babysitting them.'

'If Theo is still awake, don't stay there chatting to him about spaceships,' Amy says. 'Or *Star Wars*, *Star Trek* or intergalactic space flight, in any way, shape or form.'

She watches Nick hesitate at the bottom of the stairs, as if bracing himself, and then he jogs heavily up. She goes to the window and stares down at her husband, wondering if they can resurrect this evening, maybe put a film on. Go to bed early and try and summon up some passion, or even some semblance of feeling for each other. She should go out to him. She wonders if he knows about the bottle of gin in the garden shed (that one's from Tesco and tastes even worse). But as if he feels her watching him, he returns to the kitchen, walking with the slow, stooped hunch of someone much older, and starts stacking the dishwasher. She's relieved she won't have to pretend, and pours another large glass of wine. She drinks it fast, without tasting it.

ONE YEAR AGO, SOMERSET

2
NICK

As far as I know, it happened like this. To my shame, I wasn't there when it mattered.

Of course you weren't! Bethany would interject, if she were here now. *You're always bloody late!*

They'd all travelled down on the Friday and I could have got a lift, but I was working. I planned to go that Saturday morning but, thanks to my catastrophic timekeeping, I missed my train. The next one left an hour later and stopped at every hole in the wall and that, I guess, is why I wasn't there when it counted. Still, at the time, I was pretty pleased with myself, because I'd found this toy unicorn with purple fur, massive sparkly blue eyes and a rainbow horn that I knew Ruby-May would love. I still have it. I suppose I should give it away, but I don't like to think of another child playing with it.

It was 15 August, the day before Ruby-May's third birthday, and everyone had gathered at Dad's. The Pines is a rambling farmhouse that our parents, David and Eleanor, converted years ago, and although it no longer has the land it came with, it still has a huge garden. It sits on the lower slopes of the Mendips in Somerset, the woods behind, green fields gently falling away in front of it. On a good day – and 15 August, with its clear blue skies, was one of those days – you can see over the tops of the seaside towns of Clevedon and Weston-super-Mare and all the way across the Severn estuary to Wales. It's where we grew up, Amy, Bethany and I.

That afternoon, Amy, my eldest sister, and her husband, Matt, drove to Clarks Village in Street. The Clarks factory, where they make their famous, sensible shoes, is there, as well as an outlet mall. They took their oldest two children with them, Theo and Lotte, so they could buy them a cheap pair each, ready for the new school term at the start of September. Amy wanted to pick up some extra things for the party too – she'd made the birthday cake and she had some sliced white for the children's sandwiches, but she thought she'd get a quiche, posh crackers and cheese, and sparkling soft drinks made out of insane combinations of fruit and flowers, which no one in their right mind should buy. At least that's what I imagine she wanted. I can't believe she would have given Ruby-May a bought cake back then, even though afterwards she couldn't manage to heat up a ready-meal. Or eat. They left Ruby-May behind. The toddler would have caused chaos in the shop, and as she was only going to nursery in the autumn, she didn't need new shoes.

Our middle sister, Bethany, had offered to look after Ruby-May. Bethany's good with children. She's a TV presenter, so you can imagine that her over-the-top energy, disregard for rules and ability to perform on demand goes down well with small people. So that afternoon, as I was inching across the countryside, Brean Down a gleaming Arthurian mound in the distance, *Blade Runner: The Director's Cut* playing on my iPhone, Amy, Matt, Lotte and Theo were in Street looking at shoes, and Bethany, Ruby-May and Dad were at The Pines. Dad is in his seventies now and is not as sprightly as he was. He spent most of the afternoon dozing on a wooden sun-lounger in the herb garden at the front of the house: it's a real suntrap.

I should mention at this point that they weren't the only people at The Pines. Matt's teenage daughter, Chloe, from his previous marriage, was sunbathing next to Dad. After a while, she grew bored and went indoors – to do her homework, she said, but she was probably attempting to hook up with her friends over the lousy

Internet connection. I found her half-empty glass of lemonade later, abandoned by the garden table, with a striped straw and a drowned wasp in it.

The only other person who was there that day was also inside. Luca – Amy and Matt's ad-hoc childminder. The master's degree he's studying for is in child psychology, although I'm not sure how relevant that is, but his ability to relate to kids is probably why Ruby-May loved him so much. Matt has to leave the house by 7.30 a.m., and Amy has a part-time job as a charity fundraiser, so for three days a week Luca took Lotte and Theo to and from school, and looked after Ruby-May. I guess he'd have taken her to nursery that September, if things had turned out differently.

I learned all of this later. At the time I wouldn't have known the minutiae of their daily lives and I'd never met Luca. I usually just turned up with sweets and caused chaos. That's what uncles do, right? Anyway, Luca was there to celebrate Ruby-May's birthday and maybe have a break from Bristol and enjoy the countryside. That morning he'd got up early and gone for a run.

At least, that's what the police told me.

Luca is tall and rangy, and I imagine him loping through the dawn-stretched shadows across the dew-soaked fields. He said he spent the rest of the day in his room, studying.

I say *his* room, although it was actually Eleanor's, our mother's. She used to paint there because it has the best light in the afternoons – it's at the front of the house, but at the far corner. You can see part of the herb garden from one of the windows, and glimpse the lines of thyme that she sowed in the cracks between the paving stones. Now it's the spare room: Dad painted it white, even the floorboards, and a rug covers the worst oil-paint stains. When the sun warms the wood, I can still smell the linseed.

I don't go in there much.

I'm procrastinating.

So, as I was saying, Bethany was playing with Ruby-May. They would have gone outside. Bethany doesn't like being cooped up or staying still. And it is an amazing garden if you're a small child and you're fearless, or haven't yet learned to be fearful. Bethany would have been tearing around the place: hide-and-seek in the orchard, singing and swinging Ruby-May on the rope strung from the large tree in the corner, racing across the lawn, mooing at the cows in the field at the end. She doesn't have the patience for imaginary games, so they probably avoided the wooden Wendy house with its teaset laid out ready for a pretend birthday party; and I can't believe she'd have gone near the ruins of the old cottage, after what happened there when we were kids. She also avoided the pond.

The pond is large, for a garden. In summer, when the water level dips, it still comes up to my waist. Our mother designed it: that August, the flags had finished flowering, but there were water lilies and dragonflies patrolling its borders. Eleanor used to sit on the sloping bank on a mossy bench and paint it. Once we were born, she refused to have it filled in, although Dad said a child can drown in just two inches of water. Maybe even then he didn't quite trust our mother's maternal instincts.

Dad had the local builder put up a low fence around the pond: it's high enough to deter a small child, and he installed a gate with a Yale lock on it. You need a key to open it. Eleanor hated it and stopped painting the water lilies. *No loss to the art world*, I thought, when I was younger. *It's not like she's bloody Monet.* But I know now that some artists still hold it against my father. It was all part of the story they told about him: how he tried to lock Eleanor up, hedge her in. Control her. *Make her look after her own children.*

That afternoon Bethany saw she had several missed calls. The phone signal is terrible at The Pines. Because she works in TV, there's no such thing as a weekend. The producers, the researchers, her agent all call her any time of the day or night. I thought it was an affectation back then. Bethany was working on a high-profile TV programme called *The Show*. Very meta. It was prime time, BBC1, but a new co-presenter had just been brought in, who was younger, bouncier, bubblier and mixed-race with a Scottish accent – the BBC was trying to up its diversity quota. Tiffany McKenzie. I thought Bethany was being an insufferable diva and didn't want to share the spotlight; I didn't realize what she was going through.

Sometimes, in the early mornings, it's as if there's a film projected against my eyelids: Ruby-May is a blonde blur, streaking through the orchard, her long hair stretched out behind her; the grass is preternaturally green, sun sparks off the red Katy apples and a cloud of rooks is flung across the sky.

Bethany woke our father and deposited Ruby-May on his lap. She told him to look after his granddaughter for half an hour while she went inside and made some calls on the landline.

It was more like an hour by the time she'd finished talking to her agent, the director of the shoot, the producer, the executive producer and then her agent again, to complain about what the director, the producer and the executive producer had said, and no doubt she also had to coordinate with her personal make-up artist, because *The Show* had axed hair and make-up during the latest round of cost-cutting.

The garden was unusually quiet when she went back out, blinking at the harshness of the sun after being cosseted by the dim light filtering through the mullioned windows into our dining room. She walked round the house to the herb garden and saw that Dad was still there, slumped in the sun-lounger, fast asleep.

There was no sign of Ruby-May.

JULY, BRISTOL

3
NICK

I'm walking to the studio when Amy calls. For once, I'm not late. I meant to get in early, though, to Photoshop the pictures from last week's shoot and catch up on invoices for Tamsyn. The low-lying mist over the river is rapidly being burned off by the sun. I pass Underfall Yard and head towards the marina. Tamsyn's studio is near Spike Island, an artists' cooperative, where my ex-girlfriend Maddison makes her hip screen-prints, and almost next door to a historic ship, the SS *Great Britain.* I took Ruby-May, Lotte and Theo there last year for one of my uncle-outings. Ruby-May loved it: she ran around the ship screaming, pretending to eat the fake jellies and occasionally getting lost by hiding in the cabins (I didn't tell Amy that part), but Lotte wasn't so keen, and she and Theo had nightmares for a week afterwards. There's a butcher's room with models of flayed animals strung from their heels, including a dolphin. The kitchen was swarming with stuffed rats and smelt of fish, and the neighs of a panic-stricken horse reverberated through the dark hold. Quite clever really, but I suppose living on a ship a few hundred years ago (I don't actually know when, I didn't read the blurb) was pretty grim. Amy had been annoyed: *What were you thinking, Nick?*

Amy tells me she's found a beautiful house, on an island off the coast of Italy, that's 'incredibly reasonable for August' and is big enough for all of us. It's got a swimming pool and it's near a quiet beach. There are direct flights to Pisa from Bristol, and then you catch a train to the coast and a ferry. She's got it all worked out. I'm surprised that Amy's found somewhere so fast, but I guess I shouldn't be, as she always used to be dynamic and organized. Before. I know it was my idea that we gatecrash Amy's holiday, but I'm not sure I can afford it. 'Incredibly reasonable for August' sounds like code for 'too much for a photographer's assistant'. I have to be there, though. I'll ask Tamsyn for some extra work or an advance on my laughable salary. I wonder whether Matt is happy, or at least not suicidal at the prospect of a holiday with the Flowers.

'Have you talked to Bethany yet?' Amy asks. 'I need to book it, if she's coming, or find a smaller place if she isn't.'

'I'm on my way to see her.' I hesitate. 'Amy, have you thought any more about—'

My sister's voice sounds raw, as if she's been crying, but her tone is final: 'We don't want him to come with us.'

This area, once so rundown with abandoned factories and the remnants of the boat-building industry, is going through a resurgence. Though I guess not for the boat yards. There's a new tapas bar on the opposite side of the Avon that looks like it should be in San Francisco; blocks of flats have sprung up: with their white walls and jaunty-coloured window ledges, they're reminiscent of cruise liners; the old gasworks has been converted into luxury penthouses, all steel and sepia-tinted glass. The flat my father used to live in during the week, when he was working at Bristol University, is perched up on the hill behind – he's letting me stay there for now. Bethany, after she left home, had a better offer and went to stay with one of Dad's friends – some prof with a posh house in Clifton – instead. Now she's renting one of those apartments nearby that were swanky about a decade ago. It's off Caledonian Road and is so close to the studio, we could hang out, if she liked me more than she does.

When I call my sister, she answers on the first ring, with a

'Haaaaay', like I'm her favourite person. 'It's Mr Nick Flowers.' She sounds far too chipper for this hour in the morning – and for a conversation with her brother, when we haven't actually spoken much for months.

'Do you want a coffee? I'm passing – on my way to work.'

Only a small lie, as I'm walking in the opposite direction, but I don't expect Bethany will stop long enough to figure it out.

'I'm with Joe,' she says, like I should know who that is.

Her boyfriend? That was fast; she hasn't been in Bristol long. I can hear a man's voice in the background.

She laughs. 'Chill. It's my brother.'

A jealous boyfriend?

'We're about to do HIITs on the towpath. Joe thinks you'll distract me. So yeah, get us an espresso from that caff past Wapping Wharf. Make that two – Joe wants one. Apparently caffeine blitzes fat.'

I duck down Gas Ferry Road, alongside Aardman Animation and Tamsyn's studio, and come out by the place Bethany's talking about, which is basically a shed on the waterfront. As I reach the river, a girl with a swishy blonde ponytail in a kayak speeds past. Bethany and Joe are doing short sprints and then pausing. Joe is holding a phone that beeps when the intervals start and stop; I figure he must be her personal trainer. He's wearing baggy black shorts and nothing else: he's completely ripped. I hate him already. Bethany is in Lycra and a baseball cap and shades, as if she really is famous and might be papped at any second. I sit on a stone bench with the espressos and wait for them. When they stop for a few seconds in between their shuttle runs, Bethany drapes an arm around Joe's shoulders and takes a photo of the two of them. He's glistening with sweat, she's all cleavage popping out of her sports bra, the sun sparking off the edge of her Oakleys. Joe pulls away and counts more loudly to the next interval, as if he's annoyed with her for not taking this seriously.

When they're done, they jog over, breathing heavily.

'Hi, I'm Joe,' he says, putting out his hand to shake mine. 'Thanks for the coffee. Can I give you some cash?'

Bethany waves this away on my behalf. So he's polite as well as good-looking; he has brown, curly shoulder-length hair, large dark eyes that slope down at the corners, designer stubble and a massive grin. He looks like a puppy and it's impossible to dislike him, especially as he pulls a T-shirt out of his back pocket and puts it on, so that I don't have to stare at his abs. I can't remember ever actually seeing mine, even when I was a kid.

'We've got another half an hour to go,' says Bethany, taking a sip of coffee. 'Got to get my money's worth,' she adds, elbowing Joe. She finishes sending the photo to Instagram and shows us the picture. The likes are already flooding in. She has one of those blue ticks next to her name, so you know she's the real Bethany Flowers, and she's got more than 100K followers.

'It's not like you to be sociable at this hour.' She looks at me pointedly, as if to say, *Or after all this time.* 'It's the anniversary, isn't it? It's coming up soon.'

I nod, my throat suddenly dry. I tell her about our plan, to go away together to Italy.

'Frankly, I'd rather hack off my own arm with a blunt penknife, but I get why she doesn't want to be here. I'm not going, Nick. I've only just started this new job at the BBC and I can't ask for time off already.'

'Italy?' says Joe, sounding childishly excited. 'Whereabouts?'

Bethany rolls her eyes.

'An island off an island. It sounds pretty cool. Remote, rural. The "real" Italy.' I do air quote marks. 'Beautiful sandy beaches. Pizza every day. Beer; no, hang on, what do you drink? Prosecco on tap.'

Joe does a thumbs up at me behind Bethany's back. I think back to last week. It was the first time I'd been to Amy's house for, well, ages; it was the first time she'd asked me to babysit for over a year, and I'd shown up late. It reminded me of what I've been missing: my family. I might find it hard to be with them some of the time, but I can't manage another year like this one.

'I'll tell her you won't speak to your new boss about taking a week off so that you can be with your family for the anniversary of the death of your three-year-old niece,' I say.

'You shit.'

'Whoa,' says Joe. 'Bee, you've got to be there! Family is the most important thing there is,' he adds, his expression earnest.

That was too much. I change tack. 'Anyway, aren't you freelance? And the star of the show? It's good for your image if you aren't always available.' She narrows her eyes, trying to assess whether I'm taking the piss. It might still be regional telly, but the new show she's presenting has almost a million viewers. 'With your powers of persuasion you'll have your new telly chief wrapped around your little finger in no time.'

'Stuart Linfield is the exec, and there's no way. Quit now, before you come up with any more crap.'

'I don't want to be there on my own?' I make it into a question, as if I'm trying out the line for size.

'Ah,' she says, punching me on the shoulder, 'that's the real reason.'

'Come on, where's your sense of adventure? At the very least, you'll get a tan.'

'Sense of self-preservation more like.' She pauses. 'Is Dad going?'

I shake my head and for a moment there's silence while we both look at our feet. If our father hadn't been looking after Ruby-May, our niece would still be alive, an almost-four-year-old, believing in unicorns and dreaming of being an astronaut. I don't say it because, well, it wouldn't help, but I think about it all the time; and I guess Bethany probably does too.

She avoids my eyes. 'Probably for the best.' She suddenly swings round. 'Hey, Joe, why don't you come with us?' He looks floored and glances at me, but Bethany carries on talking. 'I'll need to keep training. And we could do those photos you were talking about for the book. Nick's a photographer. He'll take them. Joe wants to write a book,' she tells me, speeding up, her words scrambling out of her. 'He's got to write a synopsis and add some photos, to pitch it to a publisher. We could shoot them on the beach. I'm going to write the introduction.'

'It doesn't seem appropriate,' says Joe, pushing his hair off his face.

I notice he's wearing an Alice band, like Lotte's, but it's not particularly girly on him, in spite of his long hair.

'You don't need to be there for the… for the anniversary. Just come for a few days. Two or three. Think of it like a working holiday. We'll come up with the pitch. We'll do our workout in the mornings and you can chill in the afternoons.'

'What do you think?' Joe asks me.

'Don't talk to him! He knows nothing.' Bethany glances at her watch, which is one of those bands that measures your heartbeat and the number of calories you've burned. 'I'll let you know if my boss okays it. We need to finish up at Joe's studio. See you around.' She slaps me on the back and jogs off. Joe, a small line deepening between his eyebrows, shakes my hand.

'Nice to meet you, Nick,' he says, and sprints after my sister.

My sister. Always hustling. I sit back down on the stone bench and finish my espresso. Joe seems like a nice guy and it might make Bethany less intense if he's there for a couple of days. Bethany has puppy-like traits, not because she's adorable – she certainly isn't – but because if she doesn't have regular exercise she's insufferable. A bit weird, though. If Joe comes, there'll be two people there who aren't part of our family – him and Luca. Two and a half, if you count Chloe. I text Amy to tell her that Bethany is thinking about it and wants to bring a friend for a couple of days. I'll let them work out the room arrangements.

A couple of swans float past and I get transfixed by the patterns on the water, coloured lozenges reflecting the Haribo-bright terraced houses on the hill opposite, broken by slashes of black and splinters of bright-blue sky. The sun is warm on the back of my neck, but I feel a chill seeping through me from the granite block I'm sitting on. It's such a cliché, but I can't believe I'll never see Ruby-May again. It's like she's with me, at the periphery of my vision. Sometimes I have imaginary conversations with her, or I worry she might get too close to the river. Which is really fucked up.

ONE YEAR AGO, SOMERSET

4

NICK

When I finally walked up the driveway that afternoon, swinging my purple unicorn and whistling, I saw the lights first. Blue-and-red, silently flickering against the white walls of The Pines. It took me a moment to realize what they were, because I couldn't see the police car; but my body knew before my mind caught up, my stomach immediately cramping into a knot. It was hot and so silent, I thought at first the place was deserted. I remember standing there for a second, panting in the heat, sweat trickling down my back, and then I started running.

Bethany told me later that when she couldn't see Ruby-May, she tried to wake Dad. As she bent over him, she smelt the alcohol on his breath. There was a glass of Merlot on the table next to him, and the almost-empty bottle, hot from the sun, was at his feet. He barely stirred.

She started looking for Ruby-May. It's a big garden. I think I said that already. She walked right round it. She looked in the house or, at least, downstairs. She walked back out and through the orchard. She checked the Wendy house, she peered into the treehouse, although Ruby-May wouldn't have been able to climb up to it. She searched the ruins of the cottage, tearing her shins on brambles, pushing her head into the hearth and the remains of the old bread oven. She scrambled over the stone wall and ran across the field at the bottom of the garden, frightening the black calves. She tore through the edge of the woods and splashed down the stream, burning her arms on the giant hemlock that Dad never got round to eradicating.

The place was eerily quiet. Chloe and Luca were still inside; Amy, Matt, Theo and Lotte were still in Clarks Village, trying on shoes, and I was still on the train, drawing nearer to The Pines. All of us were completely unaware of Bethany's growing fear.

It was as if Ruby-May had never even been there.

PART II

10 AUGUST, ITALY

5

AMY

They'd set off this morning, at 5 a.m., Bristol damp and shrouded in fog, and flew into blazing sunlight, ice-white clouds and brilliant blue skies. The children were tired and whiny on the plane, but after croissants and muffins at the train station in Pisa and slices of pizza by the harbour in Grosseto, they'd grown increasingly excited, shrieking as they were sprayed by sea water on the boat, screaming at a flock of seagulls that tailed them. Chloe had ignored everyone, keeping her headphones clamped over her ears for the entire journey. Amy, although she'd been irritated with her, remembered all too well what it was like being a teenager and wanting to distance yourself from your younger, annoying siblings. Nick had said some last-minute work had come through and he'd booked a later flight: he was due to arrive the following day.

It was mid-afternoon by the time they arrived on the tiny Tuscan island: *Isola del Piccolo Giglio* – Little Lily Island. Carlo Donati, a dark blond-haired teenager whose family owned the holiday house, collected them from the port in a pickup. He slung their luggage into the back with ease. Theo begged to ride in the front, and Luca went with him; Matt drove the rest of them over in the people-carrier they'd hired. Amy tried not to worry about the lack of booster seats for the children – at six and eight years old, they still needed them.

Now they pass a vineyard with a terrace cafe and then they drive between two sandstone pillars onto a rough track, veering quickly down another one and through an olive grove.

'*Maregiglio,*' says Carlo, grinning at them as he jumps out of the truck. 'Mean "Sea Lily".'

It's perfect, Amy thinks.

Her first thought is that Ruby-May would have loved it and she bites down on the inside of her cheek and swallows hard to get rid of the lump in her throat. She stands on the rough green grass of the olive grove in front of the house and looks out towards the sea. It's so blue, the sky and the water seem to have merged. There's the gentlest of breezes and the leaves of the olives turn like a shoal of silver fish. She can smell salt and oregano, baked by the heat.

She'd been anxious since she booked it. She'd found the house through an online company that lets people rent out their own properties via the website. She'd been worried it was too risky, or that it wouldn't match the description, which had been written in terrible English, or that the travel arrangements would fall through. But it had all gone to plan, and in the warmth and sunlight her tiredness and her spirits lift a little.

Carlo reverts back to Italian and speaks to Luca, who translates. He tells them that the house has been converted from farm buildings – his family live over the brow of the hill. *Maregiglio* is built from faded strawberry-pink stone and honey-coloured cement. There's no garden, only a water trough planted with bright-red geraniums next to a mounting block at the front; they're surrounded by the olive trees.

Carlo gestures for them to follow him. The house runs along two sides of a square bisected by a stone archway. They troop through it to a patio and a swimming pool; on the opposite side of the pool is what had once been another, smaller barn and is now a studio apartment. When Amy had looked at the details of the property online, she'd thought Joe could have it.

'It's gorgeous,' says Bethany, flinging out her arms and inhaling deeply. 'You're amazing, Amy!' She doesn't give her a hug, though, like she once would have done. She sticks her hand in the pool to test the temperature.

'It's stunning. Thanks so much for having me along,' says Joe. 'Where's the beach?'

Luca says, '*Il cavalluccio marino*. The name of the beach mean the seahorse. It is down there,' he adds, pointing through the olives, and Amy notices a thin, sandy path snaking between the wizened trunks. 'But it is steep. Carlo say it is not safe; we must not take any of the paths down the cliff. We only follow the road.'

Carlo and his friend start unloading their luggage, and Luca, Joe and Matt join in.

'Which room is mine?' asks Chloe.

Amy scrutinizes her, not sure if she's being difficult or simply direct. Chloe was four when Amy got together with Matt, and as Amy was only twenty-five herself, she's never felt like the girl's stepmother. Sara, her real mother, is too much of a force of nature for her even to attempt to compete with. Amy loops her arm through Chloe's.

'Let's go and choose our rooms together,' she says.

Chloe had been the same age then as Ruby-May would have been now, she thinks. She finds it hard to avoid these thoughts; they constantly snag at her, a running commentary about Ruby-May and what stage she'd be at in her life. Amy wonders if she'll carry on doing this every day until Ruby-May would have turned eighteen, twenty-three, thirty-six, fifty-five.

'You and Dad should have this one – it's the biggest,' says Chloe, as they look in one of the bedrooms.

'Too late, I've bagsied it,' says Bethany, pushing past them and dropping her case on the floor.

'Auntie Bee!' says Chloe.

'It's okay,' Amy says. 'Matt and I can go at the other end, next to Lotte and Theo. You can have the other room here or the one upstairs.' She's aware she's skirting round the real issue: that she's hardly seen or spoken to her sister for almost a year.

'This one! I'll be neighbours with my wicked step-aunt,' says Chloe.

Bethany flings open the window and takes a photograph of herself with the pool in the background.

'Come on, girls, let's get in,' she says, pulling her top over her head and exposing a flat, toned stomach and a lacy magenta bra.

Chloe giggles and disappears into her room. If Chloe and Bethany are in the downstairs bedrooms, next to the pool, that means Nick and Luca can have the two smaller rooms upstairs. She and Matt and the children can go in the two bedrooms above the sitting room in the other wing of the house. But how typical of Bethany to choose the best room. She doesn't want to fight with her sister, though – she still isn't sure she even wants her to be here – so she heads back out to tell Luca where he'll be staying.

Luca is with Carlo in the kitchen. Just as the pictures showed, it runs the length of one side of the house and opens up into a sitting room; colourful rugs are spread over the sofas, and the side tables look as if they've just been bolted together from newly planed wood. It's clean and everything feels new; but it's rustic and basic, from the uneven raw floorboards to the plastic Mira shower fittings. Which is good: they can't afford luxury, and Amy doesn't think she could deal with it – it would feel wrong. Luca and Carlo are talking rapidly in Italian. Luca would tower over the shorter, stockier teenager, if he didn't slouch. He turns to her.

'Carlo has explain me how everything works in the house. I tell to you later.'

'Thanks, Luca,' she says.

Carlo says, 'Ansonaco. Made by *mia famiglia Donati*.' He presents her with a bottle of white wine, holding it in both of his hands as if it's precious.

'How kind of you,' she says, taking it from him. The wine is cool in her hands and she slides it into the empty fridge.

He grins at her, his teeth white in his tanned face. Amy finds she's smiling back, as if her body is going through the motions of being somebody who is happy to be on holiday, delighted to have been given a bottle of wine.

'What a beautiful house,' she says, to cover her fading smile, as her mind catches up and she remembers how pointless it all is.

He nods and says something to Luca, then turns back to her. 'You tell to me if you need anything. Goodbye.' He shakes her hand.

As he's leaving, Amy notices that he looks around, maybe to check everything is as it should be, although there's something about his gaze that seems almost proprietorial. He steps out of the kitchen into the darkened archway, just as her stepdaughter and her sister emerge from the other side and stroll past him in their bikinis. Carlo pauses momentarily and gives them a quick salute, but she notices how his eyes skim their bodies.

'Anyone want to come for a quick run down to the beach?' says Joe, bouncing in, pushing his sunglasses back on his head.

Luca glances at her.

'You're on holiday, Luca.'

He smiles. 'I am happy to help.'

'Thanks. It'll be nice to have a break now and again,' she says, 'but please, feel free to go to the beach if you want to.'

He nods at Joe.

'I take my trainers.'

'Okay, see you out the front in five,' says Joe, and she catches sight of him a moment later, doing windmill stretches and jumping jacks in the driveway. She marvels at how quickly men can get ready, although it's a lot easier for them: no sports bra; not having to make sure they're suitably covered up and not exposing too many dimples or bulges; no decisions about whose turn it is to look after the kids or cook dinner; no discussions about how long you're allowed to be away for.

She and Matt unpack and sort out the children, slathering them in suncream and wrestling them into swimsuits and rash vests, though neither of them seems that keen on going in the pool. Lotte is anxious about Pearl, Ruby-May's doll, which she's brought with her. Amy puts Pearl on one of the sun-loungers and Lotte becomes a little less fretful.

'Pearl hasn't got a swimming costume,' she says.

Amy fills a jug of water and chops up the watermelon she bought before they caught the ferry. When she carries everything back out to the pool, Matt is setting up the sun parasols. Someone has put Lotte's bikini bottoms on Pearl, hooking the pant legs over the doll's shoulders to keep them on. Chloe and Bethany are stretched out on the sun-loungers, and she's struck by how similar they look. They're both tall and lean, although Chloe still has the skinniness of a teenager and Bethany is solid, with more muscle definition. They have long, straight dark hair, brown eyes and pale-gold skin. Chloe's mother, Sara, is half-Chinese, and you can see a hint of her ethnicity in the set of Chloe's eyes, but if you only glanced at the two of them, you'd think they were sisters.

She's jealous. There's no way anyone would mistake Chloe for her sister: she looks old enough to be the girl's mother; her own skin is so white there's a bluish sheen to her limbs. When she was a child she had blonde hair, but it darkened as she grew older and she used to dye it back to the original colour. It's now in a hacked-off bob, with four inches of roots showing and a yellow dip-dye effect at the straggly ends. Her high cheekbones and pointed chin gave her a pixie look when she was younger, but now they only heighten the gauntness of her features.

'Have you got the Wi-Fi code? I meant to ask that kid for it.'

Amy wants to tell Bethany to chill out. 'How's the new job going? What days does your programme go out?'

'It's a daily show,' Bethany says, giving her an icy glare. She should know this already.

'It must have been hard to take the time off?'

'That would the understatement of the century.'

Amy bites her tongue. If Bethany did lose her job on *The Show* to Tiffany, she's bound to be feeling insecure. On the other hand, Amy no longer thinks a career is important. She can barely summon up the enthusiasm for her own job, and she's sure her boss only keeps her on because he's too much of a wimp to sack a mother who's lost her child, when the charity she works for specializes in helping dying children to receive hospice care.

'Carlo gave the Wi-Fi code to someone. I need it too,' says Chloe, seizing her iPad.

'I'll get it for you, love,' Amy says.

Luca had pinned it up on the noticeboard, but she remains in the kitchen for a moment, gathering herself. Her family is grouped around the pool: Bethany, Matt, Chloe, Theo and Lotte; even though Nick hasn't arrived yet, she knows he'll be here soon. It makes her twin loss much more acute – the absence of her dad and her youngest daughter. And although part of her hates him, she misses him, and the children miss their grandfather. She doesn't know how to talk about him to them, and she can't bring herself to discuss her dad with Matt; she can tell her husband's barely managing to suppress his rage.

She wipes her eyes. *Right! Time to act like we're on holiday.* She sets her mouth in a rictus of a smile and goes back outside.

ONE YEAR AGO, SOMERSET

6
NICK

I still have nightmares about it. In my dream I'm running as hard as I can, but the driveway to our house grows steeper and steeper, and I'm not getting any nearer to the garden, where I know, even without seeing them, that the paramedics are crouching in the grass, laying a tiny body onto a stretcher. She was wearing a white dress with sequins that caught the sunlight; for a moment I thought she was moving. I expected her to sit up, push the sheet off her face and shout, *Boo!* But it was only the rocking of the stretcher as the ambulance crew lifted it, which gave the illusion she was still alive. They stood for a moment, their heads bowed, as if we had fast-forwarded to the funeral already.

I'm not sure what prompted Bethany to search the pond, because she'd already seen that the gate was still locked. She told me she'd looked everywhere else, but as she was heading towards the house to phone Amy on the landline, she decided to double-check. She climbed over the fence and that's when she saw her. Ruby-May was floating face-down in the water. One of her shoes was missing.

Bethany thinks Ruby-May got tangled in the water weed, and that was what held her below the surface. She tried to resuscitate our niece, but she knew it was too late. I think of her sometimes – my sister is strong and muscular, from all those press-ups she does every day – I think of those toned arms pressing down on that small chest. She kept trying. I know she'd never have given up if there had been even the slimmest chance.

In the post-mortem they said Bethany had broken one of Ruby-May's ribs.

I imagine strands of weed wrapped around Ruby-May's pudgy little wrists, and how she would smell of the water lilies that had rotted at the bottom of the pond. She must have spotted a newt swimming near the bottom, or wanted to pick some of those purple flowers that grow in the marshy bits round the edge.

No one knows how Ruby-May got into the area around the pond. The gate and the fence, though low enough not to obstruct our mother's precious view, are too high for her to have climbed over. Dad claims he has no memory of being asked to look after Ruby-May that afternoon. He'd drunk the best part of a bottle of red, Bethany said. It wasn't just that, though. She says he'd been growing increasingly forgetful, but no one had thought to investigate those memory lapses, or even raise them with him.

So it wasn't his fault. It's hard to remember that though, especially as he refuses – is still refusing – to accept responsibility. I do understand, I really do, why Amy can't bring herself to speak to him; and she's barely managing to talk to Bethany, since she was the one who asked Dad to look after Ruby-May. But Dad needs help. *We* need to help him. Or something in all of us will remain broken.

The verdict was accidental death.

10 AUGUST, ITALY

7
AMY

'Where are you taking us?' Matt says. He doesn't like being in the passenger seat.

'I told you, it's a surprise,' Bethany says. She flashes them a grin over her shoulder, her teeth glinting in the semi-darkness. Amy remembers when Bee had them whitened two years ago and only drank almond milk and ate bananas for two days while the bleach set. She feels her stomach lurch. The road is narrow and twisty, and she wishes her sister would focus on driving.

The people-carrier veers round a hairpin bend, the cliff dropping away to their left.

'Steady,' Matt says, his jaw clenched.

'Relax – I have to drive behemoths for work. This contraption is a tiddler.'

The car, loaded with the three children, Matt, Amy and Bethany, is struggling with the steepness of the hill, the engine over-revving.

'Here we go.' She slams the car down a dirt track that opens into a gravel car park and grinds to a halt.

'Where the hell are we?'

Bee jumps out and releases the kids and Amy from the back.

'This way, my darlinks,' she says in a faux Russian accent, sweeping her arm wide. Lotte giggles and rubs her eyes. Bethany's louder than normal, and Amy suddenly remembers how her sister would turn everything into a performance when she was a child; she was the only one who was aware that the bolder and brighter

Bee was, the more nervous her sister was feeling. She wonders why she's anxious. They crunch over the car park after her. Bethany is wearing iridescent snakeskin-patterned sandals and a white tunic; she flickers moth-like through the dusk. Lights, set low to the ground, illuminate a path that winds through a hedge. Lotte curls her hand into Amy's. The air is soft and warm and smells of rosemary and geraniums as they brush past the foliage. It's a world away from their grey, early-morning start.

'Ta-da!' Bethany wheels round, grinning with triumph.

They're standing on a terrace that runs along the top of the cliff. Next to them is an old, white farmhouse; the front has been turned into a cube of glass that blazes with light. Fairy lights have been strung across the glass balustrade and intertwined through palms in large pots, and all the tables are bathed in a warm glow from candles that gust in the warm breeze.

'Our table, I believe,' Bee says, striding over to the biggest, which has a reservation sign on it, with 'Flowers' written in chalk and a hand-drawn daisy; there's a bottle of wine already in an ice bucket.

They walk to the edge of the terrace and look down. The view is stunning. Below them, the sea whispers against the sand, leaving trails of foam. As far as they can see, there is only sea and sky, a rich indigo and dark plum, bleeding towards a horizon of tangerine and hot pink where the sun is setting.

'Wow!' says Theo.

'Is that Grosseto?' Matt nods towards the distant shoreline, sparkling with lights from the nearest town. It seems a million miles away and makes Amy feel small, as she realizes how remote the island is. The first star is shining.

'My treat,' Bethany says as she pours them a glass of chilled rosé.

'What's this in honour of?' asks Matt. He's sounding less grumpy now; she can tell he's impressed by the restaurant, and the children are happily tearing into home-made garlic bread, the waiters fussing round them, chucking them under the chin and bringing them extra lemonade. He hadn't wanted them to go out on their first night; the children are tired and it's been a long day. Bethany had breezily brushed away their concerns.

'I asked Luca and Joe to stay at the villa – thought this should be family only,' she says now, her voice scratchy. 'We haven't seen much of each other over the last few months – I've been wrapped up in work, transferring to Bristol and the new job, blah, blah, blah.' She takes a breath and a slug of wine.

Amy finds herself mirroring her sister, the wine loosening her muscles. She spears an olive and the taste seems to explode in her mouth: grass-green oil, thyme and salty lemon. The food tastes so much better here. She thinks of the bland supermarket tomatoes they get back home, as she takes slices of burrata layered with glossy green basil leaves.

'I wanted to say thank you for inviting me...' Bethany pauses again as the children shriek when they see the size of their pizza, the crusts floury, oozing with molten mozzarella. A waiter slides a plate of grilled fish in front of them, charred bulbs of garlic bursting in the juices; another of baby courgettes, their yellow flowers twisted into floral parcels stuffed with goat's cheese; flame-roasted red peppers, and tomatoes still on the vine, their skins bubbling and crisped. Amy's stomach rumbles.

'We couldn't not invite you,' she says, stretching out her hand and clasping her sister's.

Bee shakes her head. 'I know how awful this last year has been for you. And you must both have hated me for asking Dad to look after Ruby-May. You probably still do.' She looks down at her white plate. 'There isn't a day I don't regret—' She presses her napkin against her eyes and turns to Amy, grasping her hand in both of hers. 'I can't lose you, Ames. I've missed you.'

Amy opens her arms and Bethany almost falls into them. Her sister hugs her so tightly she feels her bones creak.

'I'm sorry. I can never make it up to you. And I miss her. I miss Ruby-May.' Bethany's tears are hot and slide down Amy's neck. She can't remember the last time she saw her sister cry. She was always the strong one.

Matt gets to his feet and puts an arm round Bethany, pats her on the back. She can see the effort it takes, but he manages finally, gruffly, to say, 'Not your fault.'

Bethany pulls away from them, smiling, her eyes wet and glittering, and gives the children and Chloe a hug and a kiss too, before she sits back down. Lotte and Theo are absorbed in their pizza and are arguing about what they're going to watch on the iPad when they get back to the villa, but Chloe is watching the three of them, nervously twisting her napkin, as if she wishes she was somewhere else. *Teenagers*, Amy thinks. *Can't bear any emotion on display.* Or does Chloe simply wish she was at home with her real mother?

'I'm famished,' Bee says, sliding a piece of fish onto her plate and raising a glass to toast Matt and Amy. She sniffs, then winks at Chloe and taps her glass against her step-niece's lemonade bottle.

'Yeah,' says Matt, stealing a piece of pizza from Lotte and leaning back in his chair, 'I could just about manage to live here. A nice little villa on the coast.'

Amy takes another sip of her wine, a perfect bone-dry rosé with a hint of strawberries, and smiles at her sister, who raises her eyebrows at her and grins indulgently at Matt. The air smells of ozone and oleander blossom, and it's as if something missing has clicked back into place and she remembers how the two of them used to be when they were children – roaming through the Somerset countryside whilst their mother was painting, practically inseparable from one another.

It's going to be okay.

11 AUGUST, ITALY

8
AMY

'When's Uncle Nick coming?' Lotte asks for the fifth time. 'He's ten minutes closer than he was ten minutes ago,' says Matt.

'What? That doesn't make any sense,' Theo says.

Amy checks the clock in the kitchen. It's early evening. Nick really should be here any minute, she thinks, but doesn't say it out loud, in case his taxi is late and the children badger them even more. She lays the table. There's fresh bread from Carlo's family's farm – Chloe went to buy it from them this morning. She's put pizza on trays ready to go in the oven (surely they've got to be better than shop-bought ones from home?) and has made a salad out of tomatoes, basil, mozzarella and olive oil. She's laid out butter, extra Parmesan, already grated, a plate of cheese and prosciutto, a jug with sliced lemon and cold water. It's not what she'd call cooking, but it makes her feel slightly calmer: she's managed to put together a meal without walking out or throwing it in the bin halfway through. It's progress of sorts. She pops the cork on a bottle of Prosecco and pours herself a glass.

'Would you like one?' she asks, as Bethany drifts in from the pool.

'I can't believe you've started without me!'

Amy hasn't even taken a sip of her own drink, but she sets her glass down and picks up a champagne flute for her sister. In spite of last night, she's still nervous around Bethany; she's afraid she'll remember what happened and will lash out at Bee when her guard is down. But then Bee chinks her glass against hers, making a high-pitched ting, and she realizes her sister wasn't being serious.

'Cheers!' Bethany says and squeezes Amy's shoulder, smiling at her. 'Thank God I'm on holiday and can have a glass or two of wine without Joe ticking me off. By the way, he won't eat that. Sorry, should have warned you.'

'I won't eat what?' asks Joe.

He's entered the kitchen almost soundlessly. He's wearing flip-flops, shorts and a vest and already has a warm glow from the sun on his shoulders and cheekbones. Amy hasn't got the energy for this conversation. She's been worrying about money. They haven't got enough to pay for the holiday, even sharing the cost of the house and the food and the hire car, but Matt had agreed to it because, well, what else could he do? Anywhere in the UK would have been as expensive and would have reminded them too much of Somerset. Not to commemorate the day in some way would also have been unthinkable. And if they'd gone on as they were, then Nick's right: it's quite likely they'd never have spoken to one another again.

She's not really listening as Joe, who's spotted the pizza, is telling her how he doesn't eat refined carbs, when they hear the crunch of tyres in the gravel.

The children scream and run to the front door, shouting, 'Uncle Nick! Uncle Nick!'

'How many Toblerones do you think he'll have bought them in Duty Free?' says Bethany, as she strolls after the children.

Theo and Lotte fight over who gets to open the door. Theo lets Lotte win, and the children tumble out. Amy takes a long draught of her drink and bangs on the kitchen window. Chloe, who's been lying on a sun-lounger by the pool, takes off her headphones.

'Is Nick here?'

Amy nods, and Chloe follows her outside. She shields her eyes from the sun's blaze as she steps into the heat. The sea and the sky have melded into one hazy blue line; a solitary cloud hangs in the sky. The driver is already popping the boot of the dusty car, as Nick shoulders his satchel and holds out his arms. His T-shirt is rumpled and sweat-stained and he looks awkward and embarrassed. She's not sure why, although maybe it's because he's hot, tired and late again. Nick crushes the children together in a giant hug and lifts Lotte over his head. She screams and kicks her legs.

He puts her down and says, 'Surprise!'

Her father steps out of the car.

Amy reels back as if she's been physically punched in the chest. Nick tries to walk towards her, but the children cling to him. She puts her hand out and grips Matt's arm. He's damp with sweat and her fingers slide down his tensed muscles. She doesn't know whether she's holding onto her husband for support or she's holding him back, the way you might restrain a dog that's pulling at the leash. The throb of the cicadas is an angry buzz in her ears. She's dimly aware of Luca and Joe hovering behind them. They are all still, for what feels like a long moment.

'Jesus, Nick,' says Bethany and folds her arms across her chest.

The driver heaves her dad's case out and looks puzzled. He shrugs, as if he always knew Brits were odd, standing around instead of embracing. He closes the car doors and reverses at speed back down the track until he has enough room to turn, stones spitting from the wheels.

'What the hell—' Matt starts, but the children suddenly realize who it is.

They interrupt, both yelling, 'Granddad!', and fling themselves at him. He hugs them awkwardly and rubs their hair. Nick pulls a bumper pack of Skittles out of his bag and rattles it.

'I could do with a cold beer,' he says, patting his father on the shoulders.

'It's wonderful,' her dad says, taking in the olive groves, the sweep of the sea, the curve of the cliff edge below them. 'Thank you for inviting me.'

Matt grinds his teeth together. 'You have a bl... a nerve, bringing him here.'

'What's a nerve?' asks Lotte.

'Let's get Dad out of the heat,' Nick says.

The children pull their grandfather into the holiday house, talking excitedly. Once they're inside, Lotte snatches the Skittles from Theo and rips the bag open. The plastic tears and hundreds of coloured sweets cascade across the floor.

'Lotte!'

'Oops-a-daisy,' Amy's dad says and ineffectually tries to pick up a few of them, wincing as he bends his knees.

'He's not staying.' Skittles skitter beneath Matt's flip-flops and he almost slips.

Amy feels as if she can't breathe. She holds onto the table to stop herself from folding in two. Bethany pours them both Prosecco and takes a long drink. She regards her father coldly.

'Dad, why are you here?'

He looks perplexed. 'I thought we were all gathered together for Ruby-May's anniversary.'

'That's why *we're* here,' Bethany says. 'I asked why *you* are here.'

Amy, in spite of how she feels about her father, winces. His face sags, as he realizes. He turns to Nick. 'I thought you said I was invited?'

Nick looks at the toes of his Converse.

Her father braces himself against the back of a chair and pulls himself straighter. 'I wanted to see you. I've missed you. My children. My grandchildren. I love you. And I would like to be here, with you all, for Ruby-May's anniversary.'

Amy can't bear the sound of her daughter's name on her father's lips. She sees Chloe, almost hiding behind Bethany, biting her nails as she looks from her grandfather to Amy and Matt.

'You need to leave right now,' Matt says.

'He's only just got here,' Theo says. 'Where are you going to sleep, Granddad?'

Luca gets out a brush and pan and starts sweeping up the Skittles, and Lotte and Theo chase the coloured balls round the floor on their hands and knees, scooping handfuls into their mouths.

'Okay, that is enough,' Luca tells them, and tips the sweets into the bin. 'David can have my room. I will share the apartment with Joe.'

'No, you won't,' Amy says, finally managing to speak. 'Dad, I don't know what you were thinking, coming here. You're not welcome. You ought to have known that. I'd like you to leave. Nick should never have invited you.'

'Amy, my darling—' her father says.

'Don't call me that!'

'Hey, kids, want to go and kick a ball about?' Joe asks.

He ushers the children outside.

'Chloe, why don't you go with them?' Amy says.

Chloe makes a face at being lumped in with the children, but she looks relieved. She slouches out, conspicuously pulling her headphones back over her ears. Luca slides a tray of pizza into the oven for Lotte and Theo and follows them, shutting the door quietly behind him.

'What were you thinking, Nick?' Amy rounds on her little brother.

He opens his mouth to speak, but her father says, 'Why can I not celebrate my granddaughter's anniversary with my family?'

'Do I have to spell it out?' Matt says, through gritted teeth. 'It's your fucking fault she's dead!'

There's a moment of silence and they can hear the children shouting with delight. Joe yells, 'Goal!'

'No one asked me to look after her. If I'd known...' There's a tremor in his voice and his eyes are damp.

'I asked you! *I* asked you to! And you still won't accept responsibility, after all this time,' Bethany says. She puts an arm round Amy's shoulder and pulls her sister in tightly against her.

'Look, it wasn't his fault,' Nick says. 'It was an accident! He can't remember—'

'He was drunk! While he was meant to be looking after our daughter,' shouts Matt.

Her dad holds his hands up and says with quiet dignity, 'If that's how you feel, I'll go.'

Luca reappears. They wait for him to slide the pizza onto a chopping board and head back outside, before speaking.

Nick says, 'You can't turn him away! There isn't another flight to Bristol today.'

'I don't care,' Matt says.

'Dad, if you simply accepted that you were drunk and your mind is no longer what it was, and you apologized—'

Their father shakes his head. 'I *am* sorry. Of course I am sorry. But, Bethany, I have no recollection of you asking me to look after Ruby-May that afternoon.'

'Christ! See what I mean?' Bethany looks at Amy. 'Your call. I'll drive him to the ferry myself, if you want him to leave.'

She can't do it. They're on a remote island off the coast of a larger island, miles from mainland Italy. She can't turn her seventy-two-year-old father out into the heat, this far from home. Nick's right, there won't be another ferry, or another flight. It would be cruel.

'There's pizza,' she says, and Matt glares at her.

Nick swiftly slides the trays into the oven, as if she might change her mind, and gets two beers out of the fridge. He hands one to Matt, who hesitates fractionally and then takes it. Bethany, rather pointedly, pours their father a glass of water. As Amy sits down, she sees Luca quietly heading up the stairs and hears the creak of his footsteps on the old floorboards. A few minutes later he reappears with his duffel bag slung over his shoulder and walks past the pool to Joe's apartment. *How can she make Dad leave now?* She thinks of what the children will do if she sends him home in the morning. They haven't been able to understand why they couldn't see their granddad for the past year, and she hasn't been able to explain. She looks down at her empty white plate.

There is no going back. Her father is here to stay.

9
AMY

'I couldn't do it,' Amy says again.

She's sitting on the edge of the bed, sliding her rings off and rubbing cream from a tube of Body Shop hemp hand-protector into the dry skin of her knuckles. The smell reminds her of the linseed oil in her mother's studio.

Matt is lying on the bed, reading a magazine about fishing. It's a new hobby. He used to coach five-a-side football, and she can't square the image she has of her husband – a man who spent his weekends running up and down the side of a pitch, shouting until he was hoarse – with the person he's become: a man whose Sundays are silent and solitary, communing with non-existent fish. It's still early and they can hear faint voices carried up from the beach on the wind, a reminder that other people are enjoying themselves, that other people have not yet been sapped of the will to live. It's not that long since they've got the children into bed, Pearl tucked next to Lotte. Her father has gone to his room. Nick, Bethany, Chloe, Joe and Luca are watching a movie on TV downstairs. A ripple of gunshots reverberates through the floorboards.

Matt sighs and rests the magazine on his thighs, removes his glasses. His earlier anger has slipped into something harder, sadder. 'I don't want him here, Amy. You shouldn't have let him stay.'

'You still don't think he has dementia?'

Matt looks towards the window but he's not really focusing on what's outside. The window is small and faces the pool, and they haven't closed the curtains yet. There's the sound of a muffled scream, followed by a splash. Amy looks out. Chloe has jumped in and there's a dark shape on the far side of the pool. She can't see who it is. The film must have finished or else Chloe has grown bored. Amy wants to tell Matt to make the girl go to bed, but he acts as if he hasn't noticed.

'David's always been arrogant and selfish,' Matt says finally. 'He never thought about you when you were children, and I haven't noticed a change. As far as I can see, he's still as sharp as a pin. He was reading some tome after dinner – a trawl through British politics from Thatcher to Brexit.'

His voice is pinched, final. Matt replaces his glasses and picks up the magazine again. There's a picture of an enormous trout on the front cover, bursting from murky depths, its mouth agape, gasping for air, the shadow of a man in the background.

Is something really wrong with her father? Bethany had taken him for a private check-up after the accident. Her sister said he showed early signs of dementia – and who knows, he could have got worse over the past few months.

But if Matt's right, and there's nothing really wrong with her dad, then that is much, much worse. Because it means that it was her father's fault their youngest daughter died, through sheer negligence, drunkenness and self-centredness, and not because he's in the grip of a disease that is rotting his brain, neurone by neurone.

She stands at the foot of the bed and notices the weary sag in her husband's shoulders, the smattering of hairs on his chest that have turned white, and the effort he's making to contain his anger.

Where will it stop? If Matt won't forgive her father, then he won't forgive Bethany for asking their dad to look after Ruby-May; he won't forgive Nick for not being there; he won't forgive *her*. He won't ever forgive any of them. They were all responsible.

Below her, Chloe is floating on her back in the water. Her hair is fanned out, straight as seaweed, and her white bikini glows in the moonlight.

'You should tell Chloe to go to bed,' she says.

'Don't take it out on my daughter!'

A muscle at his jaw twitches and he snaps the magazine back to the page he was reading.

There are so many stars in the sky: seventy thousand million million million; by their faint light, she thinks she can still see the dark shape in the shadows by the edge of the pool, watching her stepdaughter. Bethany? Or is it Joe?

10
AMY

She's sleeping in the bowels of a boat. Her bunk bed is rocking slightly. She gets up and the ground tilts beneath her feet. She's filled with a dreadful certainty that something is wrong. She climbs the narrow stairs up to the deck, holding tightly to the rail. It's a clear night. There's a smudged half-moon that's broken into fragments on the sharp-edged black waves. She looks around, but she's alone. The wind sings through the slack sails and the wooden hull creaks. They're drifting slowly: the sails are at half-mast and there's no wind. She turns towards to the tiller and sees there's no one at the helm of the ship. *Nobody is steering.* She chokes back a sob and makes for the ship's wheel, when she hears a splash and a gasp. She can't tell where it's coming from.

She looks over one side and then hears a desperate, 'Mummy!'

She runs to the other side, shouting, 'Coming, sweetheart, I'm coming!'

Ruby-May is in the sea, choking and sinking, splashing at the surface with the flat of her hands, sobbing and swallowing water. She's wearing a white dress and it billows around her in the black water, twisting about her feet. She's panicking.

'I'm coming!'

She can't see a life-ring. In desperation she climbs over the rail, ready to jump in. Ruby-May sinks below the surface and Amy screams.

She wakes, drenched in sweat and rigid with terror. Next to her, Matt mutters and turns away. Her heart is pounding so hard it hurts. There's a moment, while the adrenaline is coursing through her, when she still feels as if she's there, the salt spray on her lips, the cold breath of the sea on her skin, her daughter drowning. As her pulse slows, it seeps into her like some awful poison – the knowledge that Ruby-May is dead. She wraps her arms around herself. It's as if some essential part of her has been hacked off: a hand, a foot, her leg; and, like a phantom limb, she still feels the pain, although there is nothing left except the bleeding stump.

She takes a breath, preparing to get up and make herself a cup of tea, when she realizes that there is someone else in the room. She holds herself still and stares hard, as if through sheer willpower she'll be able to make out who it is. *I must be imagining it.* It's probably nothing – a towel hanging over the back of the door, one of the children sleep-talking, the old barn shifting as the timbers contract, now it's grown chillier. *I'm disoriented by the nightmare.* She moves to the edge of the bed, her toes touching the rough mat.

A floorboard creaks, just a few feet away from her. Whoever it is, they're right there. She can hear them breathing.

'Theo?' She doesn't think it's her son. They're much bigger. *A man.*

'Amy, darling.'

The tension leaves her in a rush and she stands abruptly, seizes a shawl and wraps it round herself.

'Dad? What are you doing here?'

Matt sighs and mumbles something, and then sits bolt upright.

'What the fuck?'

She takes her father's elbow and tries to steer him out of the room.

'What's he doing here?'

Matt snaps on the bedside light and she blinks. Her father's hair is uncombed and he looks grizzled; there are watery pouches beneath his eyes.

'There was someone in my room,' he says. 'I woke up – I'd forgotten to write in my journal – and I realized there was someone there.'

'Who the hell would be in your room?'

'He was standing at the bottom of my bed, watching me. I waited and then he left. I heard him walk down the stairs.'

'You must be imagining it, David. How do you even know it was a man? It was probably one of the kids looking for the bathroom,' Matt says.

'It was definitely a man. We should see if the children are okay,' her father says.

She feels her heart clench. Could there really be someone be in the house? Matt shoulders his way past her dad, pulling on his T-shirt. A moment later he returns.

'They're fine. I'll check on Chloe.'

'Shall we have a look in your bedroom?'

'I told you – he left. He went downstairs,' her dad says. He insists on going first, though, and she follows him along the landing.

'What's going on?' asks Nick, opening the door of his room and running his hand through his hair, making it stand on end.

'Dad thinks there was someone in his room.'

Nick frowns and pushes their father's bedroom door open. 'It's empty.' He even flings open the wardrobe for good measure. 'Must have been a nightmare.'

Matt reappears, with Bethany behind him.

'What's all the commotion?' she asks.

'There's no one else here,' Matt says, 'and I can't see anyone outside or by the pool. The front and back doors are locked.' He looks pointedly at Amy.

'Maybe you just thought you saw someone?' she says. 'Or, like Nick says, you had a bad dream.'

'I know what I saw!' Their father takes a couple of steps into his room. His tone is fretful: 'I can't find my journal. It was here. I left it right here, on the dressing table.' He points with one tremulous finger. 'He must have stolen it.'

Matt shakes his head. 'I'm going back to bed.'

'You probably didn't take it out of your suitcase, Dad,' Nick says. 'I never get round to unpacking.'

'I do! I put it there because I always write in it at night.'

Amy can't help noticing that Bethany is wearing a silk negligee over a pair of tiny shorts; a scrap of broderie anglaise covers her chest; her legs are toned and hard and laced with muscle. She must have had a boob job at some point. You couldn't be thirty-four, exercise every day and have breasts that pert. She pulls her shawl more tightly around herself.

'Dad, the travelling must have disoriented you. Why don't you get some sleep? There's no one here, and no one could have got into the house. I'm sure your journal will turn up in the morning.'

'I'll give him one of my sleeping tablets,' says Bethany. 'That'll stop him wandering about.' She puts her hand on Amy's shoulder and says quietly, 'I told you, didn't I? He's not himself.'

Amy feels the salt of tears burning the back of her throat and can't bring herself to reply.

12 AUGUST, ITALY

11

NICK

When I wake up, I'm wet with sweat, the sheet wrapped round my torso, my heart stuttering in my chest. For a moment I think I'm back in The Pines, in my room beneath the eaves, but then I remember. I'm in a small bedroom in a converted barn called *Maregiglio* on the *Isola del Piccolo Giglio* off the Tuscan coast. I brought my father here last night, even though my sister had expressly forbidden it, and now everyone hates me. It's three more days until Ruby-May's anniversary. I've got three days to get everyone to forgive him. And me.

The curtain moves very slightly; there's a thin draught of air coming through the sill, or maybe it's from the gap under the door where the floorboards are uneven. They squeak between my toes as I flex them. I stretch, letting my spine pop. I look in Dad's room. He's not there, but his journal is on the dressing table. He must have found it after all. It's navy-blue with elegant gold writing on the front. It's a two-year diary; he always used to complain that one-year planners never spanned the academic year properly, since it stretches from September through to the following May. He's always had a two-year planner for as long as I can remember; he wrote appointments in it and made notes about the meetings he attended, the lectures he gave. I guess he must have kept the habit, even after he retired.

I pad down the corridor, wondering where the kids are. There's the sound of someone talking coming from Theo and Lotte's room; I tiptoe in, getting ready to shout 'Boo!' at them.

Matt's sitting on Theo's bed, the iPad on his knee, smiling at whoever he's speaking to. He looks up in surprise. I hold up my hand in apology and retreat. Why is he hiding in here to make a FaceTime call? And what's with the guilty expression? Maybe he told Amy he wouldn't work over the holidays. He doesn't resume his conversation while I'm in earshot, though.

The children are in the sitting room, playing Snakes and Ladders with Luca.

'Hey, how are you doing?'

'Theo has gone down a giant snake all the way to the bottom. I'm winning!' Lotte yells.

'That's my girl,' I say, holding up my hand for a high five.

'Pearl is playing too,' she tells me, tucking Ruby-May's doll next to her.

'Luca is going to teach me chess,' says Theo. 'Snakes and Ladders is for kids.'

An ear-splitting noise, as if a builder with a drill has just moved in, makes me jump.

'Sorry!' shouts Joe, when it stops.

He's with my father in the kitchen, and they're both peering at a NutriBullet full of pond-scum.

'I'm making your dad a gritty smoothie,' Joe says cheerfully, taking the contraption apart.

'Don't you mean green?' asks my father.

Joe shakes his head, his curls bouncing against his chiselled jaw like some kind of men's aftershave ad. I find myself automatically sucking my stomach in, sticking my chest out; I'm glad I put my T-shirt on.

'Definitely gritty, David.' He takes a slurp. 'Gorgeous!' he shouts. He screws a grey plastic rim onto the cup part of the blender and turns it, so that the handle is facing my dad. 'There you go, get a load of that.'

'Hmm,' says my dad, inspecting it. He takes a tentative sip and then another. 'Not bad.'

'It looks disgusting. What's in it?' I ask, curious about why Joe would be making a gritty drink for my father.

Joe counts off the ingredients on his fingers: 'Coconut water, spinach, avocado, banana, ice, protein powder, flaxseeds, a handful of mixed nuts, squeeze of lime juice – oh, and an apple. Good for your brain,' he says and taps his temple. 'Have one of those every day, you'll be right as rain.' He slaps my father across the back and heads outside towards the pool.

I wonder if this is just something personal trainers do or has he somehow discerned Dad's forgetfulness – or maybe Bethany told Joe about our father wandering about last night, claiming there was someone in his room and that his journal had been stolen.

'You okay, Dad?' I ask. 'I see you found your journal – it was on your dressing table.'

My father frowns at me.

'Appearing, as if my magic,' Bethany says, her voice heavy with sarcasm, switching the kettle on. 'Coffee?'

'Thanks.'

'Why does no one ever listen to me?' Bethany asks, after Dad has gone to sit outside and drink his pond-scum by the pool. 'When I took him for those tests last year, he scored twenty-one on the Mini-Mental State Exam, had mild depression and his brain scan showed a slight shrinkage of his frontal and temporal lobes – all indications of the onset of dementia. I made a whole bloody programme about it, I know what I'm talking about. Not that any of you bothered to watch it.'

'He *seems* fine,' I say.

'Just a bit forgetful?' Bethany says. 'No shit, Sherlock.'

Matt thunders down the stairs. When he sees me, he clears

his throat and glances at Bethany. She's busy banging around the kitchen, getting out the cafetière and looking for the coffee.

'Sara,' he says in a low voice. 'She worries about Chloe, you know. I try and remember to call her. Let her know everything is okay.'

'Right,' I say, setting out mugs. Not a conference call for work, then.

'Best not to say anything to Amy,' he says. 'They don't get on. She'd think I should send a text and be done with it. But you know what women are like. Need chapter and verse.' He gives a dry laugh.

I have a queasy feeling, as if I'm betraying my sister by listening to her husband's bullshit. At least Matt's guilt has stopped him chucking me out of this house this morning, for bringing Dad here. I look up. Amy is stretched out on a sun-lounger next to our father, an untouched croissant on a plate at her elbow. She has her eyes shut, but she's frowning, the lines between her eyebrows deepening. It's unbearable witnessing her pain, especially when she doesn't even realize we're watching her. Matt follows the direction of my gaze and shakes his head.

'Do you think there really is something wrong with David?' he asks.

I shrug. 'At the end of the day, does it matter? I mean, he's our dad, Matt. Ruby-May's grandfather. A diagnosis isn't going to bring her back.'

'If he'd only say he was fucking sorry.'

I pat him on the shoulder. 'I know, mate. But for what it's worth, he's never apologized to me once, in his entire life. It doesn't mean he isn't heartbroken.'

'He has a hell of a lot to apologize for,' Bethany says, handing me a coffee.

12
NICK

We head to the beach after breakfast. It's only a few minutes' walk from the villa, although it takes for ever to get there, marshalling Lotte, Theo and Chloe, carrying reams of stuff like we're bearers for Tutankhamun. Lotte's swimsuit, her armbands and her bucket and spade are all varying shades of purple. Purple was Ruby-May's favourite colour. I try not to think about the unicorn that's still in my sitting room.

The beach is a perfect scoop of plain sand, with a Portaloo and a wooden shack where you can rent loungers or buy espressos, ice cream and beer. On either side there are flat, dark rocks pockmarked with barnacles, and cliffs rising sharply up to the olive groves and *Maregiglio*, which I can't see from this angle. It feels surreal, being here, the sun hot on my back at ten in the morning, a bruising light slicing from the surface of the sea, when only yesterday Dad and I were driving through damp fog to reach the airport. I can feel the tension in my shoulders start to ease.

I do a double-take when I see Chloe. Yesterday she'd been wearing one of those floaty things women wear on holiday, but now she's in a bikini. Her legs are long, smooth and a pale gold. She's sitting on a sun-lounger, rubbing oil down her shins. Her dark hair has fallen forward over her shoulder and she looks like a young woman. How did this happen? It doesn't seem two minutes since she was Ruby-May's age.

I never saw her as often as Lotte and Theo – I know they're only six and eight, but I'm not as clued up about Chloe, so when I did see her, I'd make those ridiculous comments adults always make about children: *Wow, you've lost your baby teeth; God, you've grown; What, you're at secondary school? You're fourteen?* She's still frozen in my mind aged ten, with braces and bony knees and her hair in plaits, and it was kind of okay because of being her step-uncle and not a proper relative, as I wasn't expected to remember her birthday or anything useful. And now she's almost sixteen.

I glance at Luca to see if he's noticed Chloe's practical nudity, ready to be belligerent on my niece's behalf if he so much as glances at her toes, but he's completely absorbed in playing with Lotte and Theo. Not that the other men on the beach have any such qualms. It's packed with Italians as brown as hazelnuts. I watch the men as their eyes drift lazily over Chloe, assessing her, and as if their skulls are as transparent as fish tanks, I can see the flicker of their thoughts shoaling through those shallow depths. I know what they want to do to her. Bad enough being the kid's uncle; Matt must constantly be contemplating murder.

I pull a sun-lounger over to the side of our group and drop a towel over it. It's from the holiday house. We're not supposed to take them to the beach, but I don't own such a thing as a beach towel. I keep my T-shirt on and roll my shorts up. I'm nearly blinded by the glare from my white legs. I glance at Chloe again. She's got her headphones clamped over her ears, a pink iPad and her phone peeking out of her bag. She doesn't look particularly happy. I wonder if it's a teenage phase, or boyfriend trouble, or that she really doesn't want to be on holiday with a bunch of grown-ups and two small kids. Not that I blame her. Amy and Matt don't seem to have noticed or, if they have, they're ignoring her mood.

My sister is emaciated; her skin is grey and she looks as if she's an outpatient from a cancer hospital. I try not to stare at her ribcage, the bars of bones in her chest. Matt also appears exhausted, his flesh slack, apart from the puffiness of his belly. Bethany and Joe have come with us, but instead of sunbathing like normal people, they're doing some insane workout, watched with amusement by the Italians. It involves sprints across the hard sand and bunny hops over the waves, and it could be fun if it didn't look utterly gruelling. Matt is watching them too.

Bethany is doing press-ups now, trying to keep pace with Joe. He jumps up and pokes her in the middle of her back to get her to dip lower. I'm thinking simultaneously that Bee's triceps are pretty impressive, and that Joe is being quite annoying. I lie back and try and relax. The sun is so warm, I could fall asleep right this second. Yeah, I could get used to this; certainly beats Photoshopping in Tamsyn's studio, or hanging out on my own in Dad's flat.

Matt suddenly murmurs in my ear, 'I can't stand it.'

'What?' I ask, surprised. Is he as jealous as I am of Joe's physique? I never had Matt down as the type to feel threatened by some kid with a six-pack, but maybe he's feeling insecure, now he's given up five-a-side. I sit up again.

Matt glances at Amy to make sure she's not listening and then goes back to staring at Bee. 'I can't stand seeing her working out.'

I'm still not sure what he means. Doesn't he like ladies being muscly? Or does he think women shouldn't have to leap through hoops to look good on telly, when no one gives a shit what the male reporters look like? Neither seems the kind of thing Matt would give a stuff about. I must be looking puzzled, because he says, 'She's so strong – for a woman, I mean. But every time I see her, like that,' he nods at her biceps, glistening with sun oil, 'I remember how she cracked Ruby-May's rib.'

I look up at the sky and the sun burns my retinas. Anything not to have to think about my sister pressing down on my dead niece's chest with those highly toned arms. I have no idea what to say to my brother-in-law. We sit in miserable silence.

After a few minutes Bethany and Joe run past us. They give us a cheery wave and jog up the hill and into the olive grove. There's no way I can doze off now.

My father is bolt upright in a deckchair, a couple of feet away, reading the paper, a sunhat shielding his face. He clears his throat and addresses us as if he's giving one of his lectures in politics to two hundred first-year students.

'I realize now that I was not welcome here, but I'm grateful that you didn't send me home.'

'We want you here, Granddad!' says Lotte.

I'm grateful the Italians can't understand us.

'Dad, shall we discuss this later?' Amy says, pushing her sunglasses into her hair.

Our father holds up one hand. 'I simply wanted to acknowledge your kindness and to say that I will pay for the holiday house.'

'You think you can *buy* us?' Matt's rage is so close to the surface he's gone from nought to sixty in seconds.

'It must be expensive, such a large house for all of you and those two young men. I am happy to pay for it, so that we may all come together for the anniversary.'

I know *I* can't afford this trip, and I'm pretty certain that money is tight for Amy and Matt right now – Amy has hardly worked this past year, and Matt's been on career autopilot.

'We're not taking your bloody money,' Matt says. 'And if I had my way—'

I butt in. 'Thanks, Dad, it's a really kind offer. Why don't we talk about it over lunch, when Bethany gets back from her fartlek?'

'Her what?' my father says.

Matt mutters under his breath, but he subsides back onto his sun-lounger.

'Did you just say "fart"?' asks Theo.

'Fart, fart, fart. Want to find some rockpools?' I ask him.

He shakes his head without looking at me.

I go on my own: the stone is already hot beneath the soles of my feet. The tide is almost fully in, but I bet, when it's out, you'd be able to walk round the headland to the next beach. There are dark crevices, cracks in the rock, that race towards the sea, the insides pulpy with anemones the colour of blood clots; the edges are jagged and sharp. Behind me an Italian couple unfurl raffia mats and giant beach towels. I sit on the end of one outcrop and lower myself in – I'm not sure how deep it is. The bottom is sandy. My toes feel the odd stone, smoothed by the waves; and the water, surprisingly cold at first, is invigorating. I thrash about, doing an ungainly butterfly stroke and a front crawl. I dive down and touch the bottom. I imagine Ruby-May with me, her blue eyes bright with sea water, the lashes stuck together in spikes, her little body solid between the palms of my hand as I balance her on the surface. She'd be wearing armbands and a swimsuit with a frill like a tennis player, splashing me with enthusiasm. I suddenly have no desire to carry on swimming.

I run up the beach towards my family, shaking the water from me like a dog. Luca is crouching on the ground, constructing something out of sand with Theo.

'We're making a sand-ship,' says Theo. 'We're going to fly to the Moon and then Jupiter.'

He's pressing small stones and shells into the base of the rocket. I guess they're meant to be the flames.

'Can I help?'

'Yeah, we need more water, Lieutenant Uncle Nick.'

'Roger that, Captain Theo.' I pick up the bucket. 'Hang on a minute, where's Lotte?'

'She is with your father,' Luca says.

I look around and spot them at the edge of the sea. Dad's hopping over the waves like an ungainly heron and it looks as if he's tugging her, trying to pull Lotte towards him, but her arm is at full stretch as if she's hanging back, away from the surf. I frown. Is it a game?

'Did you know that Earth can fit into Jupiter one thousand times over?' says Theo, as he pats down the nose of the spaceship.

'Do you think that makes the Earth very small or is it that Jupiter is very large?' Luca asks him.

Lotte screams shrilly. I start walking towards them, carrying the purple bucket that Theo has given me. Dad picks her up in his arms and begins wading into the sea. Lotte shrieks. I can't tell if she's having fun or not – the way she'll scream blue-murder if I tickle her, but then beg for more if I stop. She's kicking her legs and Dad is staggering, waves slapping against them. I look behind me, but no one else from our family has noticed. Lotte's yells go really high-pitched and I pick up my pace. Dad sinks into the sea, still holding her, Lotte thrashing in his arms. It doesn't look as if she's enjoying herself. Suddenly she stops yelling and goes limp. I drop the bucket and sprint towards them as Dad shouts, 'Lotte!'

He is struggling to stand, and Lotte's head lolls loosely over his arm, dipping into the sea. Her hair fanning out in the water and I feel sick.

'Nick! What's wrong with her?'

I put my hand under her head, pulling her out. Her eyes are shut and she looks lifeless.

'She didn't want to go in! I wanted to persuade her it would be fun. I thought I was helping – and then...'

I lift Lotte out of the sea. I'm wheezing with the effort of running down the beach. She seems heavier than she normally does. Her legs dangle, her heels clipping my thighs.

'What's the matter with her, Nick? Is she breathing?'

My heart is squeezing tighter and tighter. I'm trying not to think of Ruby-May. I wade through the waves back onto the beach, my father stumbling behind me. Thank God Luca has noticed. It only takes him a few strides to reach me and he lifts Lotte effortlessly. I follow him. He sets Lotte on a sun-lounger and I wrap a towel round her. The rest of the family crowd around us. Lotte's lips are blue and she's shaking.

Amy is hysterical. 'What happened? What's the matter? Is she okay?'

Theo is standing frozen by his sand-rocket, his face white, his eyes large.

Matt is desperately trying to get a signal on his phone. 'Someone call a fucking ambulance!' It doesn't look as if the Italians can understand him or even realize what's happened.

Luca doesn't respond, but remains focused on Lotte. I drop down on the sand next to her, breathing heavily, and take her small hand in mine. Her eyes flicker.

Luca is saying over and over, 'Look at me. Breathe. Breathe. You are okay. Breathe. You are okay. Breathe.'

Chloe gently squeezes one of Lotte's sandy feet. Lotte opens her eyes. Luca mimes breathing. She shudders and then her chest rises and falls. Her cheeks flush, although her lips are still purple. My heart is jack-hammering in my chest. Amy scoops Lotte up and sits with her cradled on her knee.

'What happened?' she asks, more quietly now, staring at me and then at our father, who collapses onto the end of Lotte's sun-lounger, his face ashen.

'I took her to the edge of the waves. We were playing. I was holding her the entire time!' he says. 'And then she – I don't know what's wrong.'

Luca says, 'It is the panic attack. They are still afraid of the water. It is not a surprise, no?' He cups Lotte's head in one large hand, then gets to his feet and starts pulling on his T-shirt.

Amy and Matt exchange a look. Chloe drops a kiss on Lotte's

damp cheek and replaces her headphones as she returns to her sun-lounger.

Dad strokes Lotte's knee. 'There, there, Lotte. All right now?'

'Don't touch her!' Amy spits at him.

Lotte burrows into her mother's neck.

'She did say she didn't want to go swimming,' says Theo, in his quiet, precise little voice, and pushes his bright-blond hair out of his eyes with one finger, scattering sand across his face.

Matt crouches down by Lotte. 'Sweetheart, there's nothing to be frightened of here. Mummy and I wouldn't let anything bad happen to you.'

He doesn't look at our father. His arms and shoulders are rigid with tension, and I'm acutely aware of what is left unsaid – that our father, yet again, is to blame; and the rest of us, the Flowers family, are culpable as well. Not one of us intervened in time. Not one of us is to be trusted.

Luca is damp but dressed, his cloth satchel slung across his chest. He holds out his arms and Lotte elbows her way out of her mother's embrace. He scoops her up and puts her on his shoulders. Theo grabs his sandals where they've been half-buried in the sand and stands next to Luca.

'I take them back to the house.'

'I'll come with you,' says Amy.

Luca shakes his head. 'It is okay. I think she have some quiet time. Is too hot here.'

'I don't want to leave her.' Amy's voice is shrill.

'I'm okay, Mummy,' says Lotte. 'I don't need you.'

I look away so that I don't have to see Amy's hurt expression. The plastic bucket is still lying where I dropped it by the water's edge.

'We'll pack up and follow you back to the house,' Matt says. 'Chloe! Take those headphones off and get your things together. No, you can't stay here on your own,' he adds as she begins to protest.

'Well, maybe,' Chloe says, standing up and sweeping her towel off her sun-lounger and showering us all with sand, 'you should have thought about it before you booked a holiday house with a swimming pool, right next to the sea!'

I think Matt is going to slap her, but he turns on Amy. 'We need to talk,' he says.

I don't look at my father, either, so that I don't have to witness his pain. I watch Luca instead as he walks up the hill, Lotte perched on his shoulders, Theo's face turned up to him, like a small pale moon.

I can still hear Lotte's screams echoing in my ears.

13
AMY

She pulls her shirt on and puts her suncream back in her bag. Thank God Luca's here and has such a calming effect on the kids – but she feels terrible for not realizing that the children might be scared of water. She and Matt have pretty much given up taking Lotte and Theo to any of their normal after-school clubs; they haven't had the energy or the will. But Theo has had swimming lessons at school once a fortnight. He's never said anything, but she feels a ripple of sadness and shame shiver through her when she thinks of him standing, thin and frail, at the edge of the municipal swimming pool, the rest of his class noisy and rambunctious, fighting his fear by himself.

She heads back up the hill towards the holiday house with Matt and Chloe, Nick and their father following behind. She'd been so tired she must have fallen asleep, and she'd only woken up when she'd heard Nick shouting and seen Luca running up the beach with her limp daughter in his arms. But even if she'd been awake, she wouldn't have stopped him. It seemed harmless enough, jumping over small waves on a sandy beach; he is their grandfather after all. Her mouth is dry and her stomach is tight with nerves. She can feel the heat radiating from Matt, his skin slick with sweat. He's an alarming shade of puce. He's going to insist their dad leaves, and she doesn't know if she should stand up to him or not, or whether Bethany will support her or Nick.

When they reach the house, the front door is ajar. It's quiet, too silent for a house with two children. She stops just inside the sitting room, letting her eyes adjust to the comparative gloom after the brilliance of the sunshine outside.

'Where the hell is everyone?' Matt asks.

She feels the first stirrings of fear. Chloe slides past them and disappears into her room.

'Hello?' Amy calls out, her voice cracking.

There's no reply. She takes a couple of steps towards the kitchen; a sliver of ice wedges itself at the base of her spine.

'Anyone here?' Matt says, dumping the children's buckets and spades in a sandy heap by the door.

'Mummy!' Lotte's voice is shrill, high-pitched with fright.

'I'm coming! Where are you?'

Her daughter thunders down the stairs and hurls herself at her mother, sobbing.

'What is it? What's the matter?'

She hugs Lotte and then holds her slightly away from her, to try and work out what's wrong with her. There's a thin bead of blood running down her chin.

'Lotte! What's happened?' Matt grips her arm. 'Where's Luca?'

'My wobbly tooth came out!'

'Oh!' Amy almost collapses with relief. She wipes Lotte's face with a tissue and crouches down in front of her. 'Let's see.'

Lotte pulls her lower lip down. The socket in her gum where her canine had been is filled with blood and Amy winces, although she knows it's completely normal. Lotte shows her the tooth, like a misshapen pearl, cupped in the palm of her hand. She sobs harder. Amy hugs her tightly.

'Does it hurt, sweetheart?'

Lotte shakes her head so vigorously that one of her tears splashes against Amy's cheek.

'The tooth fairy won't be able to find me in Italy!'

'Ah, I see. Well, maybe there are Italian tooth fairies,' she says.

'Oh!' Lotte brightens. 'Do you think so? Will she give me my money in euros?'

'Course she will, sweetheart,' says Matt, chucking her under the chin. 'Why don't you put your tooth somewhere safe and then we can leave it under your pillow tonight?'

Lotte's eyes well up again. 'If she speaks Italian, she won't understand my note!'

'You're mixing her up with Father Christmas,' says Matt. 'You don't need to write her a letter.'

'What do the fairies do with all the teeth?'

Amy pauses. It's grim when you think about it. She imagines a fairy palace made out of tiny human teeth, each one stolen from a child.

'Where's Theo?'

Lotte points at the window. She and Matt look out and see their son floating in the pool. He's still and silent, his eyes are closed and his arms are spread out, his white-blond hair haloing his face as if he's an angel. Luca is next to him, supporting him in the middle of his back with the palm of one hand. Sensing their presence, Luca looks up and smiles at them. The back of Matt's hand brushes Amy, and for a fleeting moment they hold hands and watch their son, lying suspended in the midst of that rectangle of perfect blue.

'Hey!' says Bethany, bursting in on them. She's lithe and glowing, her limbs slick with suntan oil and sweat. 'We've just been on the most amazing run! Right up the hill through the olives and then back along that clifftop path above the beach.'

Joe is with her, and Nick and their father have just reached the front door.

'Lotte, go and join your brother and Luca outside.'

Matt ushers her towards the pool and shuts the back door. He swings towards them and folds his arms.

'What's up with you all?' asks Bethany, looking from Matt and Amy to Nick and their dad. 'You look as if you've got heatstroke.'

'I'm going for a shower,' Joe says and backs out of the house.

'He can't stay. And you shouldn't have brought him, Nick.' Matt rounds on her brother.

'Can someone tell me what you're so—'

'Dad was playing with Lotte and she had a panic attack,' Amy says.

'He pulled her into the sea, even though she clearly didn't want to go in, and then he ducked her – actually ducked her underwater,' Matt says.

'I did no such thing. I was attempting to entertain my granddaughter. I had no idea she was so frightened of water.'

'I want you to leave, right now. I don't want you near my family again,' Matt says, addressing David directly, for almost the first time in a year.

'Matt!' Bethany says. 'It doesn't sound like it was his fault.'

'Like the time he allowed my daughter to die?'

Their father stumbles slightly as if Matt has physically pushed him. He walks out of the sitting room and they can hear his heavy tread on the creaky floorboards as he goes into his bedroom upstairs.

'You can't say that to him!' Bethany says. 'He's not himself. You know I took him for that dementia test last year. And you can see how forgetful he's being. I'm sure he meant well this morning. He's just a little insensitive and confused right now. Did you even know the kids were scared of water? Because if you did—'

'Shut up, it's none of your business.'

'Matt's right,' Amy says, turning on her brother. 'I asked you not to bring him, Nick. It wasn't fair to him or to us. I can't tell whether Dad has dementia or he's forgetful because he's getting on, or he's his old, arrogant self, thinking he knows best, but whatever it is, he can't be round our children right now. It's not safe. We can't have him with us.'

Nick opens his mouth to protest, and then closes it again and runs a hand through his hair. Bethany gets herself a glass of water and downs it in one. Her clothes and hair are dark with sweat. She swallows and wipes her forehead.

'Well, it's up to you, Amy,' she says. 'We're all here for you. Nick, you should start looking into flights home for Dad. Maybe take him back to your flat; no, wait, *his* flat, since you like hanging out with him so much.'

'There's no need to be nasty,' Nick says. 'Just because you didn't want to stay there when you left home.'

Bethany inhales sharply, but before she can reply, their father comes back down the stairs, banging his case on each step. He holds his sunhat in one hand.

'I can see I'm not welcome,' he says and walks stiffly past them and out into the blaze of sunlight. They're all silent for a moment, listening to the crunch as the gravel on the driveway snags beneath the wheels of their father's suitcase.

'Thank God!' says Matt, sinking into one of the dining-room chairs and resting his head in his hands.

Bethany gives her a hug and Amy leans into her sister. She's missed Bee so much over this past year.

Nick looks at the three of them, horrified. 'Guys, you can't let him leave! How's he going to get to Bristol from here?'

'He shouldn't have come.' Matt's voice is muffled.

'He's in his seventies. It's thirty degrees out there! He can't speak a word of Italian and we're on a remote island!'

'He managed to get to the Zhoushan archipelago by himself,' Bethany says, resting her chin on Amy's head.

Amy flushes. Tears prick her eyes. She's regretting siding with Matt already: it feels unspeakably cruel. And Bethany seems to think she agrees with her about his dementia, when Amy has no idea if what happened last year can be blamed on memory loss, alcohol or old age – or themselves, because they haven't cared for their father as they should have done.

'It's years since he went to China. He was much younger and fitter,' she says. 'Maybe...'

'For God's sake!' Nick throws up his hands. 'What is wrong with you? He's our dad!'

He runs out, slamming the front door behind him, and Amy feels sick, her stomach churning with a toxic combination of guilt, remorse and revulsion, at herself and at her father.

14
NICK

The keys to the hire car are on the table by the door, and I grab them on my way out. I don't have a plan in mind, but I don't suppose Dad will have got far. He hasn't. He's almost reached the road that leads from the beach and up through the olive grove to the main highway. He's red with exertion and damp with sweat. It's midday and the heat is intense; it feels like a lead weight pressing down on me. I pull over next to him.

'Go back, Nick.'

'Get in,' I say, leaning over and popping the door open. He hesitates and then heaves his suitcase into the boot and climbs in the front. He's panting slightly and he sits, his hands knotted in his lap, fingers trembling. As we reach the road, I wind both windows down to get a breeze through the car. I head away from the port, although I don't think Dad will notice, following signposts with a picture of a castle that looks like a chess piece.

From the air, when I checked on Google Earth before we came, the island is shaped like an embryo, curled around the scoop of an inlet, its backbone a reptilian hump, *Maregiglio* tucked on the inside of its tail. We're driving along its spine: the land is dusky green and scrubby, with none of the features that would normally say Italy to me – no sunflowers or olive groves, Tuscan villas or vineyards – only the sea, glittering as sharp as flint, on either side of the island. When we finally see the town, it looks like an ice-cream cone, a swirl of houses in apricot and peach, with the castle, the colour of drying sand, at its peak. There's a harbour and a spit of beach, packed with plastic sun-loungers and parasols, a wide sweep of promenade edged with date palms.

I'm not sure I can take the people-carrier up these narrow, corkscrew twists of road; I'd probably prang it. I pull in at a car park next to a supermarket opposite the harbour.

'What are we doing here? This is not the ferry,' my father says.

'I thought we could go for a beer.'

'I don't drink,' he says stiffly.

'A coffee then. Come on.'

He sits in the car, staring straight ahead, stubbornly refusing to look at me. 'I'd like you to take me to the ferry.'

'Yeah, sure, but let's have a coffee first.'

'It's lunchtime,' Dad says, sounding grouchy, as he steps stiffly out.

We follow the road through dark alleyways that are bisected by slices of light: houses the colour of marmalade, a burst of salmon-pink flowers, an azure triangle of sky, until we come to a small square with giant chess pieces laid out on a chequerboard of marble and granite and a sluggish fountain. A dog is lapping the water and a toddler is splashing in and out of the spray, his nappy sodden. Two old men, dressed in black, are playing chess; or at least sitting next to the board and contemplating the pieces over the rim of thimble-sized espresso cups. There are three cafes round the edge; their interiors are dark. Flags snap in the stiff breeze. I wish I'd brought my camera with me. I'd deliberately stopped carrying it everywhere, so I could have a proper break from work and the angst I get sometimes when I feel my life ticking by and I still haven't made a name for myself as a photographer.

Dad sits outside and I order him a *caffè latte*, focaccia for both of us and a Stella for me. He takes a bite of the bread and stirs his coffee monotonously, watching the sugar dissolve.

'Why did you bring me?' he says. 'It's clear they don't wish me to be here.'

'I hoped they'd have forgiven you,' I say, taking a long swig of my beer. 'It wasn't your fault.'

'Of course it wasn't my fault,' he says. 'Bethany was meant to be looking after Ruby-May.'

'She asked you to,' I say, putting my bread down and wiping the grease from my fingers.

'I have no recollection of her doing so,' he says with spirit.

'Look, Dad, they just want you to say you're sorry. We're all sorry. How hard can it be?'

It'll be the anniversary of Ruby-May's death in three days. I have a churning sensation in my stomach. If they don't forgive Dad, if we don't knit back together as a family by then, I don't think we ever will. It's bad enough watching your mum walk out on you, followed by both your sisters, whilst your father drinks himself stupid, but we were still a family. I don't want to lose that. It's pretty fucking lonely, as it is. My girlfriend left me on New Year's Eve too. *Thanks, Maddison.* Although, to be fair, I hadn't paid her any attention for months. Not since 15 August, to be precise.

'It's monstrous that Ruby-May is no longer with us. Obviously I am sorry. But it was not my fault,' Dad says. 'Why should I be held responsible for that poor child's death?'

There's something monstrous about Dad's statement and I don't feel like I can even process it right now. One of the old men gets up and shuffles a black pawn over to a white square and then sits back down. The two chess players contemplate the pieces.

'We should tell Luca to come here,' I say, trying not to think about Ruby-May. 'He told me he goes to one of the cafes off Queen's Square in Bristol. He plays chess with a group of old men who are there every day. It reminds him of home, but he says he misses the giant sets like this one.' The other man now gets up and pushes a rook across the stone slabs. 'Luca says you think about chess differently when the pieces are so large; it's as if your brain is wired to respond like it's real and no longer a game.'

My father ignores me. 'She even says I was drunk.'

I don't say anything. Dad spent much of my childhood in an alcoholic stupor, as far as I can remember. Although he wasn't there for more than half the time – he stayed in his flat in Bristol during the week, instead of coming home to us. It's probably why Mum walked out.

He looks at me from beneath his thick, wiry eyebrows. 'I know what you're thinking, Son, but I stopped a couple of years ago when the doctor put me on Warfarin. You can't drink when you're on blood-thinning medication. I thought he was being a scaremonger, and I had a pint in the pub and passed out. Cracked my head on the hearth.'

'But Amy told me—'

'I know what she said,' he mutters. He pushes his focaccia aside, his appetite gone.

I think back to that day when I'd arrived so catastrophically late. Dad had been groggy, spaced out, and I'd believed them when Bethany and Amy had told me that he'd had more than half a bottle of red that afternoon, leaving Ruby-May on her own in the garden. Maybe he didn't even remember drinking. He has been confused and forgetful since we arrived in Italy, and yet, in everyday conversations like this, he seems his old self: razor-sharp and acerbic.

He puts down his empty coffee cup and stares at me. His eyes are paler than they used to be, but clear, unclouded.

'I know you're angry with me, Son, and you may very well not have forgiven me. I am sorry for how I behaved to you and your mother. I should have said so many years ago, and I'm sorry about that too. But there is nothing wrong with my mind.'

I drink my beer and look up into the clear, blue sky. There are two parallel white lines marring its perfect clarity: the past trajectories of planes, or the trajectories of past planes?

I wonder if it's possible that someone else is lying to me about what really happened that day, almost a year ago.

EIGHTEEN YEARS AGO, SOMERSET

15
NICK

I waited for a bit, because sometimes she came to get me and sometimes she didn't. She disliked being pinned down, or being made to let go of the moment.

When you're painting, she said, *it's like chasing a butterfly, you have to follow it wherever it takes you.*

She'd traced a dreamy line in the air and I knew what she meant: the speckled brown butterflies we found on the bridleways near our house alighted on a flower for a fleeting instant, before spiralling into the sky or darting over one of the pines, their flight a crazy zigzag before they disappeared towards the heath. But I didn't understand how pursuing butterflies was like painting, and why that meant she couldn't pick me up from school.

It was a long walk home, although it was shorter if you cut across the fields. I was twelve years old. It was May, or maybe June. I frightened the cows and got home smelling of horse manure and fresh mud. I thought she might look up and smile and tell me the butterfly had landed on her fingertip, before giving me an ice-cold glass of milk and a chocolate-chip cookie. But I'm mixing her up with someone else's mother. I poured myself some orange juice and ate one of the last apples from the previous year, wrapped in newsprint, the skin waxy and puckered.

I didn't disturb her – she didn't like that – but eventually, maybe a couple of hours later, I went upstairs and peeked in the doorway of her studio. She wasn't there. It was strangely tidy: her paints had gone. A bee buzzed around, banging against the windows until I let it out. I looked in all the other rooms, but they seemed exactly the same as they had been that morning. The crusts from my plate of toast, left over from breakfast, were still on the kitchen table. I ate them absent-mindedly and wandered round the garden, hoping to come across her trying to capture the elusive dart of a dragonfly or the exact shade of the shadows as the evening drew in. There was no sign of her. I ate most of a packet of stale digestives, some Cheddar that had gone hard and cracked and half a bar of cooking chocolate. I was watching TV, up way past my bedtime, and feeling distinctly weird, hungry and sick, all at the same time, when Dad arrived.

He whistled as he walked up the path through the velvet darkness, his keys clinking in his palm, his breath sweet with brandy when he leaned over the sofa to tousle my hair.

'Where's your mum?' he said.

I shrugged and he did a kind of slow double-take, as if he was a deep-sea diver.

'Eleanor!' he called. 'Eleanor?'

I don't remember what happened after that. I know there was some shouting when he phoned her mobile – I'm not sure he even spoke to her that night; he may just have left several ranting messages. But he was in a grim fury when he bundled me off to my room, without checking that I'd wiped the chocolate off my face or brushed my teeth, and I lay rigid in bed, staring up at the shadow-pattern of leaves on the ceiling, with this cold, tight pain in my chest. Somehow I knew that she wasn't coming back. I wasn't angry with my mother, not then; I was furious with my sister, because Bethany, the month before, when she'd turned sixteen, had left home and left me behind, as if I was just another one of her possessions that she could carelessly shrug off. And now, without my mother or my sisters, I would be alone with my father.

16
AMY

It's late afternoon. They're all outside on the terrace. Lotte, thanks to Luca's patience, has got in the pool. She's wearing armbands and will only go in the water if she can sit on the blow-up unicorn, but it's progress. Luca has a textbook on child psychology next to him, but he's reading a well-worn copy of *The Divine Comedy*; and Matt dozes with his fishing magazine on his stomach. Amy lies opposite Bethany and Chloe, but she can't stay still.

Her stepdaughter and her sister are leaning conspiratorially over Chloe's neon-pink iPad, whispering and giggling. She wishes Chloe would play with her younger half-siblings, instead of spending all her time looking at Instagram and trying on Bethany's make-up. As for her sister, why can't she act like an adult and help out, instead of pretending to be Chloe's friend? She suspects it's about Bethany's ego: she loves Chloe looking up to her. She sighs. Is she overreacting? She's probably jealous: envious of their smooth, honey-brown skin, their thick, gleaming hair, their obvious closeness. Bethany, only two years younger than her, is in a white halterneck bikini and a filmy kaftan; her breasts are firm, her stomach flat and taut. She can see the sinewy movement of Bethany's biceps, the way her thigh muscles glide beneath her oiled and bronzed skin.

She doesn't even own a kaftan, so she's thrown a large white shirt over the top of her swimsuit and has wrapped a sarong around her waist. It's an all-in-one costume, so she doesn't have to reveal the loose grey skin she's left with, after her sudden weight loss last year, and she knows she'll end up with vicious tan lines. The whole outfit is too hot and she envies Chloe's spare body, the way she can sling on a spaghetti-strap vest without any lumps or sags or stretchmarks showing.

She keeps thinking of her father, struggling down the track with his suitcase. The children haven't yet asked where he is, but they will. She sighs. She wishes Nick hadn't brought him, but at least he went after him. He'll make sure David gets home safely. But then, of course, how could Dad get back, unless Nick goes with him? It's a ferry ride, a taxi, a train journey even to reach the airport. Her father couldn't do it on his own.

She's not surprised when she hears the car pull up outside the house. She goes and stands at the corner, in a pool of shade, and watches her brother helping their father out of the people-carrier. She waits for Nick to carry David's suitcase up to his room and then come back down the stairs.

'Hey,' he says. 'I couldn't...'

'I know. Let's go for a walk,' she says.

They go round the far side of the apartment where Luca and Joe are staying, through scrubby grass, stiff with seedheads and vetch pods, and past row after row of olive trees and shrubby juniper bushes, the land rising steeply and sharply, the earth dusty and red-gold. She half-imagines she can see the scalloped roof of Carlo's farmhouse, but she knows it isn't possible from this angle.

'There weren't any flights,' Nick says.

'You didn't try, did you?'

'He couldn't get home by himself.'

Standing behind the converted barn, she sees how crude it is – the rough attempts to plaster the walls, blue plastic tubing erupting from the ground. There's coiled black hose beneath the olives, cigarette butts and shotgun casings, the occasional glint of a glass bottle; detritus left by farm boys who must have been standing right by the holiday house. They walk round the back of *Maregiglio*.

'Matt's going to kill me,' Nick adds.

'Or Dad.'

'Or both of us.'

She's not sure what's worse: Matt's rage or his emotional absence. She rubs her eyes. There's a half-open shed a little way from the house, screened by some stunted cypress trees. In the cool darkness at the back, there are large plastic containers with chemicals for cleaning the pool, a rusting rake and a brush. Drifts of desiccated olive leaves crunch beneath her feet. For a moment they pause. From here, in between the trees, she can see bright slivers of the pool, of her family, sprawled out on their loungers. In fact from this angle they can see directly into Bethany's and Chloe's bedrooms. She imagines her sister padding about, naked; Chloe in her bra and pants admiring herself in the mirror or, more likely, obsessing about how she looks, trying on different outfits. Amy shivers in spite of the heat. She should tell them to keep the curtains closed.

'If he'd only apologize—'

'He says he wasn't drunk,' Nick interrupts. 'He can't drink, because he's on some medication.'

'Warfarin. It hasn't stopped him. He isn't drinking wine any more, but he still has shots of that cider brandy his neighbour Tony brews.'

Nick frowns. 'You said he'd had half a bottle of red.'

She shakes her head. 'You must have misremembered. You weren't even there. It was definitely brandy. That stuff Tony makes is lethal. Dad probably isn't even aware of how much he's drinking. What does it matter anyway? The point is, he was drunk.'

The wings of cricket-like creatures brush drily against her calves and she walks on. Nick follows. They turn the corner and face the sea. Gulls wheel on the thermals like pterosaurs, and shouts and laughter drift up from the beach hidden below.

'It's just an excuse,' she says, suddenly angry – with her father, for his stubbornness; and with her brother, for making her face the anniversary of her daughter's death with the person responsible. 'You do know he used to bring them to the flat, the one you live in now.'

'Who? What are you talking about?'

She wants to hurt him for bringing their father here. 'The women. All the women.'

'What women?' he asks.

'Nick, you must have known.' She's impatient with him now. 'That's why Dad didn't come home during the week. It's not like Bristol is that far away. He lived with them in his flat, and then he came back to Somerset at the weekends.'

'What? Dad did that?'

She wants to shake him. 'All through our childhood. Why do you think Mum left?' She wonders if Nick still blames himself for their mother leaving; kids often do, don't they?

'I didn't...' He presses his fingers against his temples. After a few moments he says, 'She should never have left. Us, I mean. What kind of a woman does that? Even if—'

'She didn't want to be a mother,' Amy says. 'She wanted to be an artist. He didn't let her. And then he betrayed her. Again and again and again.' She thinks of Eleanor, now living in a commune in Santa Fe, painting spare landscapes: bones and blistered wood, seedpods and paintbrush trees. They email now and again, but as far as she knows, Bethany and Nick refused to keep in touch with her.

'It wasn't his drinking, then?'

'It didn't help – he was a heavy drinker, but he wasn't an alcoholic. He was absent, whether he was with us or not.'

She looks out at the impossible blue of the sea and feels as if her mother is right there, like a mirage, shimmering in the desert, sand swirling round her long tunic, holding a paintbrush in her hand. *What would she say now?*

Nick looks upset. 'Did Bethany know? Is that why she went and lived with one of Dad's friends, instead of moving into his flat?'

Amy feels bad now, but it's not up to her to tell him Bethany's secrets. 'I don't know, Nick,' she says, the guilt fuelling her anger.

Well,' he says, 'people change. He's our dad. He needs our help. Please, Amy.'

She folds her arms. 'I can't forgive him. And I don't know why you have. But I won't turn him out on the street.'

'Or into an olive grove? Thanks, Sis.' He hesitates and then gives her a hug.

13 AUGUST, ITALY

17
NICK

Dad doesn't appear at breakfast, and Amy must have spoken to Matt because he doesn't have a go at me. I'm sitting in miserable silence, hunched over my toast, wishing the Italians made marmalade and doing my best not to think about what Amy told me yesterday. I keep imagining Dad in my – or, rather, his – flat. The grief and sadness I felt when I was twelve years old, after our mum left, threatens to overwhelm me all over again. I'm also not sure what to make of his assurances that he wasn't drinking – that he doesn't drink any more – and of Amy telling me he has shots of cider brandy when he thinks no one is watching.

Bethany and Joe bounce in, like a fake couple in a sportswear catalogue.

'Joe's found this amazing beach. We should go. Come on guys, you'll love it!'

Bethany's enthusiasm is legendary, as is her ability to get her own way. She bulldozes through our inertia and, in a little over an hour, which I'm beginning to realize is fast when small people and a teenager are involved, we're en route. We can just about fit all of us in the people-carrier by squashing Lotte and Theo on our knees, in spite of Amy's protests.

'Well, love, we never had any child seats to start with,' Matt had said.

I stare out of the window at the olive groves as we drive past, the leaves rippling silver in the sunshine, the twisted trunks a glazed pewter, and feel bad about Dad. No one suggested that he come with us, but maybe it's for the best; my siblings might have calmed down, after a day at the beach, and be a little more willing to forgive him.

I shout at Matt, who's driving, to wind the window down and hang my head out in the breeze. Even the dust smells Italian. The kids start shrieking as gusts of air pummel them and make their hair stand on end. Matt closes all the windows and blasts us with air con. I lean my hot forehead against the glass; Lotte's bony knee is digging into my ribs, and Chloe, whose lap she's sitting on, is wriggling, lip-syncing to Selena Gomez, her headphones catching my ear, and it reminds me of all those other car journeys I've been on with Bethany and Amy as kids; shoehorned in the back, me in the middle, my sisters elbowing me, singing, smiling and squabbling.

We head in the opposite direction from the town, skirting round the tail end of the island and down a tortuously steep track between burnt sandstone-coloured cliffs.

'Hey, doesn't this remind you of Watchet?'

It's a beach in Somerset that our parents used to take us to sometimes. It's famous for fossils, not that any of us had the patience to look for them – too busy chucking sand at each other and skimming stones.

'Er, no,' Bethany says, laughing at me. 'Did we ever go to Watchet when there was blazing sunshine?'

'Of course we did!'

'Do you remember that time Dad insisted we had a picnic on the beach and it was snowing?' Amy says. 'Mum was desperate to have a bit of time to herself to finish her painting, and he made us those terrible cheese sandwiches, doorstops of stale bread and wedges of butter, and forced us to get out of the car and eat them in a howling gale?'

'It wasn't actually snowing,' I say.

'There were drifts at the bottom of the cliffs, and sleet coming in from the Bristol Channel,' Bethany says. 'I remember crunching ice crystals in my sandwiches.'

'You always bloody exaggerate.'

'Oi,' shouts Matt at me. 'No swearing in front of minors.'

'We're here,' says Joe, and we all pile out. 'You won't need your bucket and spade.'

I take a deep breath, half-expecting my lungs to burn with a rush of cold air, the smell of salt and vinegar and deep-fried chips, but the wind is warm, with a seaweed tang. In front of us, flat rocks stretch straight out into the water and, perhaps because there's no sand, the place is practically deserted.

'This isn't a beach,' says Lotte.

'It's better,' says Bethany, scooping her arm around her shoulder. 'There's rockpools.'

'I don't like it.' Lotte flaps a jelly-shoe at us, to get rid of pieces of grit trapped between her toes, and her face contorts.

'I'll buy an ice cream for the first person to find something exciting in a rockpool,' I say.

'That'll be me!' Bethany says, sticking both hands in the air. She pretends to push in front of Lotte and leaps across the rocks to the water's edge. I'm not sure how much of a pretence it is, but my uber-competitive sister's antics stem our niece's tears.

Amy covers the hot, jagged stones with towels, so that we can sit without burning our bums, and dips one toe gingerly into the water. She leans forward and, within minutes, she and the children are entranced. I have a flashback to seeing my sister crouching on a rocky outcrop, cautiously lifting flaps of bladderwrack, her pale skin bluish from the cold, strands of blonde hair whipping in the stiff coastal breeze. And then Bethany running over to join her, small, dark, skinny legs like a boy's, boldly pushing apart the strands of seaweed, hoicking out crabs and chasing them into a bucket for Amy.

On this beach the lines of rock stretching into the sea have created warm, shallow pools that are protected from the sea's waves; perfect for the children to wade through. In the dazzlingly clear water there are shoals of small, translucent fish and pale-pink and green anemones. Chloe stretches out on her beach towel, firmly away from the shrieking kids, and puts her headphones on. I don't blame her: there's only so many fish I can look at. Plus I'm too hot with my T-shirt on.

Matt and I wander back up the road to a shack we'd spotted on the way here, and buy espressos that we neck then and there, bracing ourselves against the bitterness and caffeine kick. We get cold beers, cans of San Pellegrino and fat sandwiches, the bread oozing oil, bursting with tomatoes and cheese.

'Blimey, not like a ham-and-cheese Warburtons,' Matt says with relish, watching the barman wrap them in greaseproof paper. 'Hey, mate, one of those.' He taps the side of a jar of pickled *giardiniera*. 'I'll give them to Joe for his lunch,' he adds, with a guffaw.

'Yeah, not much here for Mr I-Love-My-Abs,' I laugh, but then feel a bit bad. Can't be easy living on spinach and an almond. I buy Joe some rotisserie chicken and, with much miming and head-shaking, manage to persuade the barman not to give us extra focaccia.

'Got any plans for the big 3-0?' Matt asks as we head back towards the beach with our greasy paper bags.

I shake my head and make a face.

'In denial?' he says, but I don't have to say anything about my looming birthday because he's off on one, telling me how he wishes he was thirty again, whole life ahead of him, the choices he'd make... 'Don't give up your freedom,' he says. I'm not the only one in denial.

'Thanks, mate, you're the man!' Joe says, clapping me enthusiastically on the back when we return. He doesn't say anything about the Tupperware container that I now see sticking out of his bag, full of what looks like chopped kale.

'You're a rock star,' Bethany says, taking one of the hot, greasy packets. Through a mouthful of bread and cheese she says, 'Do you remember that time we went to Uphill beach?' *A tenner she only eats half of it.*

'What time? We went, like, every weekend in summer...'

'Autumn, winter, spring,' Amy joins in.

Lotte and Theo have lined up all their buckets and are arguing over who's caught the most fish.

'That beach in Weston-super-Mare?' asks Matt.

Bethany starts talking at fifty miles an hour about how incredible Uphill is – how perfect that stretch of sand was; the time we tried to dam the river; the day Amy fell in with all her clothes on.

I nod and say to Matt, 'Far end of Weston. Uphill's a village – you know, past the golf course?' The Flowers, when they get going, have a tendency to leave other people out. Amy joins in.

'Do you remember that time you "borrowed" a dinghy? You just untied it and rowed out to sea!'

'Dad didn't notice, he was so busy marking student papers, sitting on a bench by the car park.'

They're right: it was pretty amazing – the River Axe running down one side, the quaint little village behind, the long, rabbit-bitten length of hyper-green grass of the golf course flanking it, and those great, empty skies Somerset is so famous for. It had felt safe. It had been safe. In my memory, every time we went there the sun had shone, and we'd spent hours playing with balls and Frisbees, building sandcastles, stealing people's boats and screaming at how cold the water was. The three of us kids together. Usually it was only Dad looking after us, because Mum was at home painting, but it still felt like we were on a family outing because, back then, we knew where she was, and if her painting had gone well, she'd be pleased to see us. Dad would buy us a Chelsea bun from Banwell Bakery, and chips to eat in the car on the way home.

Yeah, I think, *we were happy then*.

18
NICK

We exhaust the possibilities of the rocky beach, and as the sun becomes searingly hot, we return to the villa. Dad is waiting for us in the sitting room. I feel my skin prickle with guilt: I wonder if he's going to accuse us of abandoning him. Or maybe, just maybe, he's going to admit he was responsible for Ruby-May's accident and we can all move on. He clears his throat and I find myself leaning towards him, desperately hoping it's going to be okay.

'Has anyone seen my picture of your mother?'

Bethany and Amy exchange a glance. Matt goes outside with the bags and starts shaking the sand out of the towels, banging the buckets and spades over-loudly against the stone steps, his back to us. He's one of those men who likes to lead – coach football squads, manage men at work, be the head of a family – but this particular team derailed in August last year and now he's lost. I'm the sort of guy who'd be looking for the hot-dog stand next to the football pitch, so I'm no stranger to the feeling.

'What picture?' Bethany asks.

'It's in a little silver frame.'

'Why would you have a photo of Eleanor here?' Bethany shakes her head. 'You must be mixed up. It's probably back in Somerset. You do know we're in Italy, don't you?'

'I'm aware of that, Bethany. It's a small, silver heart-shaped frame. I have it on my bedside table at home, but I bring it with me when I travel.'

I look at him in astonishment. 'I gave you that.'

'You did. It was a Father's Day present.'

'That was years ago. I was, what, ten?'

I'm vaguely aware of Luca and the children heading out the back door, clutching coloured chalks like an amulet against our swimming pool.

'And it's gone missing?' Amy asks him.

Chloe arches her perfectly manicured eyebrows. It looks as if she's mimicking Bethany. Maybe she overheard that we found Dad's journal, after he'd claimed it had been stolen by a stranger standing in his bedroom.

'Who would have thought you'd be so sentimental?' Bethany says under her breath.

'Someone's taken it,' Dad says, sounding plaintive. 'It was by my bedside table. I remember unpacking it last night before I went to sleep.'

'Want me to take a look?' I ask.

'If you would,' he says. He sounds distressed, which is not like my father.

I check the open-plan living room and kitchen first, then go into his room. He follows me, getting in the way. It's definitely not here, nor is it in any of his drawers or the wardrobe. He hasn't left it in his suitcase, and it's not in the passport holder he used when he was travelling. I check his wallet and his wash bag and pat the pockets of his jackets.

'Amy says you were drinking,' I say, looking under the bed. 'Cider brandy.'

He sits down heavily, as if all the fight has left him. I give his hand a squeeze. I was going to ask him whether he's sure he brought it, but then I wonder if that's simply cruel. It seems as if Bethany is right, and he is slowly losing his mind. I keep looking under the bed, to hide how upset I feel. It's one thing having a dad I remember to be angry with, now and again; it's quite another to have a father who is slowly losing the person he once was.

I cough. 'I'll go and check in the other rooms.'

From my window I can see Lotte and Theo scribbling a crazy green-and-purple galaxy across the stone flags by the pool, and I bang on the window and wave at them and pull a face. They grimace grotesquely back. I look in the bathroom, and in Matt and Amy's bedroom, and I'm just about to go into the kids' rooms when I hear Matt's voice. I hover outside the door. Yup, he's talking to Sara again. He's even laughing. *Christ! I should tell Amy.* I would, if I wasn't such a wimp.

I join Luca and the children. Luca has got out a pile of textbooks, but he's flicking through a book called *The Divine Comedy*, although it doesn't look remotely funny.

'Tell us a story,' says Lotte, as she draws googly-eyes on a lopsided dog.

'Who? Me?' I say.

I glance over at Luca, feeling self-conscious. I mean, he's a child psychologist, a man who's been part of these kids' lives, literally for years; a guy who's studying for a master's at one of the top universities in the country in his second language, whilst I haven't even managed to go to college.

'Once upon a time,' I begin. *Fuck knows what comes next.* I look at the amorphous collection of space-ponies and alien anthropoids they've scrawled over the terrace next to the perfect blue of the pool, but find no inspiration there. I consider telling them the plot of *Blade Runner*, but that might be a step too far; Luca could dob me in, for unsuitable tale-telling.

'I'm going to make the coffee,' says Luca, stretching.

I make a thumbs-up sign to him. Either he really is a caffeine junkie or he can read my insecurities like a book.

'Well, when I was twenty-five-and-three-quarters, your little sister, Ruby-May, was born...' I say, once Luca's in the kitchen.

'So she was zero?' asks Lotte.

'Literally zero. She'd just come out of your mum's tum.'

'Mum's tum. Hey, that rhymes,' Theo says.

I can't think of what to say next, and Lotte admonishes me: 'Uncle Nick, you're not very good at telling stories.'

'I've got a better one,' says Theo, putting down the lurid green chalk he's been using to colour in the aliens. 'One day we all had a bath together – me, Lotte and Ruby-May. And I got out, because I didn't want to be in the bath with two girls, and then Ruby-May did a poo. In the bath!' He collapses with laughter. 'And it floated!'

Lotte starts giggling too. 'It floated right past me. Daddy said it was like a tugboat.'

'A poo!' says Theo and clutches his stomach, doubling over.

Abruptly they both stop.

'She's dead now,' says Lotte.

'Er, yeah,' I say, taken aback at how matter-of-fact she is.

'Will she come back?' asks Lotte.

I cough. I'm not sure what Amy has told them. I brace myself for questions about God and heaven. *Where's the bloody child psychologist when you need him?*

'No.'

'She must be far away,' says Lotte.

Christ! Luca is walking towards us, carrying a tray with two mugs and drinks, and snacks for the kids.

'I'm going to make a parcel of things for Ruby-May,' Lotte says. 'She'll need stuff, if she can't come home. And you can post it to her, Uncle Nick.'

Right. That'll be an interesting address.

She gets up and runs inside, and Theo races after her.

'You must have told them a good story,' Luca says, raising his thick eyebrows at me and passing me a cup of coffee. He waits until the children have gone and then he says, 'Can I ask something to you?'

'Yeah, sure,' I say, surprised at his politeness, but I guess it's something to do with being foreign and not knowing how to speak English, even if he can write a dissertation.

He folds himself into the sun-lounger, pulling the back upright, and crosses his legs. He takes a sip of his espresso.

'It is the difficult thing to say.'

I fidget with the hem of my shorts. I'm not good at emotional disclosures and I'm starting to worry what he's going to reveal. Maddison was pretty frustrated by my inability to tell her how I felt, or to somehow guess what she was thinking. Like I was some kind of futuristic mind-reading droid.

'So. Is about your father. I do not want to cause offence, but I find it hard to be here with him. Why do you bring him back?'

I sigh. 'He's our dad. I couldn't let him try and get home on his own. He should be here, with us.'

'Why?' He takes another sip of his coffee, which is thick and oily, it's so strong. 'I love Ruby-May. I *love* that little child. I feel like I lose a part of my heart when she die.' He bangs his chest with one fist.

Bloody hell. I haven't even talked like this with my family.

'I know Dad was meant to be looking after her—'

'He should keep her safe! She is the tiny child, no?'

'Yes, but the thing is, he's having problems with his memory. We didn't know at the time. We thought he was being a bit forgetful – you know, getting older, nothing to worry about. But afterwards, after what happened, we took him for some tests and it looked like he was starting to suffer from dementia.' It all sounds so straightforward when I say it like that. I don't even mention the wine, or the cider brandy, or whatever it was he was drinking. Or not drinking. 'So it's our fault, you know? We ought to have realized and done something about it sooner. He shouldn't have been left to look after Ruby-May on his own.'

'You were not there,' he says.

I glance over at him, and Luca pushes his hair out of his eyes. I can't work out if he's absolving me or accusing me. *If I hadn't been so fucking late.*

'It was such a short amount of time... And the gate to the pond was locked... No one could have known... It was an accident. An accident,' I say more firmly, and I feel my guts twist. I'm disgusted with myself for blaming my father. But I still do. I can't help it. I stand up. *I should have been there.*

'I have made you sad. I am sorry.' He holds out one hand to me. I take it and we shake. I want to laugh, it's so formal.

'So, he has the dementia. Maybe.'

'Yeah,' I say.

'I am sorry,' he says again. 'Must be difficult, no?'

'Oh, it's tough all right,' I say. *Nothing about being with my dad has ever been easy.*

♜

I wake suddenly, jumping back into my body as if I've been somewhere else. There's a trail of drool down my cheek and my shoulders are stiff. I'd lain down on one of the sun-loungers and I must have fallen asleep. I wipe my mouth surreptitiously, hoping no one saw. I think I'm on my own – all I can hear is the drowsy hum of cicadas – and then I start. Lotte and Theo are a few feet away from me. They have their backs to me and they're standing shoulder-to-shoulder, rigid and silent. I can almost imagine Ruby-May is in this line-up, her head level with Lotte's collarbone, her long blonde hair in a knotted straggle that reaches to her bottom. There's no one else here. The children are staring at something inside.

'Hey, kids', I say, trying to sound cheerful and not as if I'm perturbed by their unnatural behaviour.

'Good afternoon, Uncle Nick,' says Theo formally.

Neither of them looks at me as I lumber over. I crouch down next to Lotte and feel a shiver, as if I've trodden in Ruby-May's damp footsteps, the wet spots her pudgy toes and chubby heels would have made. Pearl is dangling from one of Lotte's hands; the doll's foot scrapes on the tiles. Inside, Amy is dipping a teabag in her cup and I'm just about to ask them what's so fascinating about their mother when I realize, and something grips my heart as if a child has clenched it in their cold little fist.

Amy continues to dunk her teabag, in and out, in and out, staring at a spot a foot or so in front of her. She's still, apart from the small, mechanical movement of her wrist. The two pale children, fixated on their whey-faced mother, with her hacked-off blonde hair and her dead eyes, standing motionless in the dark kitchen, are like a scene from *The Others*.

'Death of a loved one can lead people to do the strangest things.'

'Yeah, she often does that,' says Theo. 'You know, like that robot beetle I built at school? And it got stuck in this feedback loop, and it kept going two steps forward and then two backwards? Over and over, and over and over. She's like that.'

'Oh,' I say. *She's thinking about Ruby-May.* I hope I didn't say that out loud too.

'Look,' says Lotte, 'there's that man again.'

What man? And then I see him – a dark shape at the back of the sitting room, too short and muscular to be Luca, Joe or my dad. The hairs on the back of my neck prickle and my heart speeds up. *Amy is in danger and she's not even aware of it. What should I do? Go in? Call the police? Hide the kids?*

'You know, the blond one?' says Theo. 'We've seen him before.'

'Carlo?' I say, with relief. 'Course you have. His family owns the house.'

Carlo must have come to check everything is okay, and the children would have met him when they arrived. But why didn't he knock first? He shouldn't just walk in! Then again, he might have done, and Amy wouldn't have responded. I get to my feet, shaking out the stiffness in my legs, and that's when I realize that Carlo was coming into the sitting room not as if he'd entered through the front door, but as if he'd just walked down the stairs. He steps into the light and says something and Amy screams and whirls round, and I flinch; there's a crack as her mug hits the kitchen floor and shatters. *What the hell is he doing?*

'That happens quite often too,' says Theo, matter-of-factly. 'Can we play Minecraft, Uncle Nick?'

'Yeah,' I say. I have an uneasy feeling. 'I'll just go and see if your mum needs any help.'

The pool of tea, so stewed it's almost black, slides across the tiles.

19
AMY

'No, I do it,' he says and holds up his hands. 'You, back. No shoes.' Carlo points to their bare feet. She's surrounded by a slick of tea and smashed china; Nick is hovering ineffectually behind her. The boy knows where everything is, naturally. He sweeps up the bits of broken cup with one of those long-handled dustpans and brushes, and then mops up the spill.

'I'll pay for the mug,' Amy says.

'No. My fault.' He points one finger at his chest. 'I make you...' He mimes jumping.

'I saw,' says Nick. 'What were you doing?'

Lotte and Theo sneak in quietly behind them and get out the iPad.

'I come to see if you are okay. Need anything. I knock.'

'I'm sorry, I didn't hear,' she says.

He smiles at her, his teeth white in his tanned face. He's handsome, but with an arrogant air that she thinks a particular type of young, good-looking man can have. He's in a muscle vest and his shoulders are broad, his biceps defined; no doubt from working on the farm and renovating this house.

'We don't. Need anything,' Nick says. He's looking aggressively at Carlo, but she doesn't know why.

'A cup of tea,' Amy says, trying for a feeble joke.

'I'll make it.' Nick doesn't offer one to Carlo. 'Where is everyone?' he asks, his brow furrowing, as he fills the kettle.

'Luca is in his room writing his dissertation. Dad went for a short walk by himself. Everyone else is at the beach. They didn't want to wake you. I was going to try and encourage Lotte and Theo to go in the pool again, without the whole family standing around watching them.'

Amy falters. That's what she had intended to do, but instead they're inside playing a computer game and she hasn't even managed to make a cup of tea. She's not quite sure how this has happened.

'It is a nice pool,' says Carlo.

Nick glowers at him.

'Yes, it's lovely. Thanks, Carlo. We're fine. We'll come to the house and find you, if we need anything,' she says.

Carlo picks up a glass vase that's sitting on the worktop. She'd put a spray of the blood-red geraniums in it. He turns it in his hands and nods. She can't tell if he's being proprietorial – it's *his* vase, and he's making sure they know it – or if he approves of her picking the flowers. He smiles at Nick and then carefully replaces the vase.

'Goodbye,' he says formally.

Nick hands her the tea. 'I couldn't find Dad's picture frame.'

'I doubt he brought it.' She sighs and wipes her eyes. 'I guess Bethany's right. It must be the beginning of dementia. All that stuff he said to you yesterday about not drinking. I thought he was lying, but he must genuinely not remember.'

Nick glances at the children. They're still absorbed in the iPad.

'What the hell was that kid doing?'

She shrugs. 'Seeing if we're okay.'

'*Are* you okay?' he asks, keeping his voice low.

She wants to say, *Are you insane? I will never be okay, not for the rest of my life. I wake up in the morning and, for a few seconds, I feel vaguely like the woman I used to be and then I remember, and it's as if every one of my vital organs has been cut from my chest using a kitchen knife without an anaesthetic.*

'I was thinking about Ruby-May's anniversary. What we should do.'

'Oh.' Nick looks unhappy. He puts his hands in the pockets of his shorts and says, 'It would have been her birthday, so why don't we have a sort of party tea and cake – the kind she would have liked?'

'What, and pass-the-parcel? Musical chairs?'

'If that's what you want,' he says. His hair flops in his eyes and he brushes it away. 'I'm going to make some coffee. Shall I do some for Luca?'

'He never says no to coffee,' she says, sorry that she snapped at him. 'No speeches then? Poetry on the beach? A eulogy at dusk.'

'Amy,' he says, setting the cafetière back down, 'I wanted us all to get together. That's why I suggested we all go on holiday in the first place. It's kind of now or never for our family. And it's a minor miracle: everyone is in one house, and some of us are speaking to each other. We're all here for you. Even Dad, no matter what you think. We'll do whatever you want us to.'

She nods and feels tears fill her eyes. What does she want? *Ruby-May. Ruby-May, alive and well. Nothing else.* She can see why someone could be tempted to make a pact with the devil – why you would sell your soul, if that is what it would take to bring your child back to life.

'Ah, my timing is perfect, no?' says Luca, stepping into the kitchen. 'I smell the coffee from over the swimming pool.' He pats Nick on the shoulder and crosses to the sofa, where Lotte and Theo are curled up together. 'Look!' He opens a slim black box.

Nick watches curiously as he measures out the ground coffee. She knows what's inside already. Luca carries it everywhere with him. It's a travelling chess set. She imagines when he's struggling with a thorny problem in his dissertation, he takes it out: the tiny pieces, the rigid rules, the endless combinations of moves and the infinite possibilities must ease him and jolt the other problem into his subconscious, so that he can crack it later.

Nick goes to a set of tall shelves at the back of the room filled with tatty paperbacks. The bottom of the bookcase is stacked with games. He pulls out a full-size chess set and hands it to Luca.

'Ah, your clever uncle,' he says, pocketing the minuscule set. 'Much better for the small fingers and the clumsy big ones,' Luca murmurs, as he starts to lay out the pieces.

20
NICK

It's early evening and, thankfully, slightly cooler. With my pasty-white skin, I'm not cut out for this weather and I'm beginning to get a prickly-heat rash. Since our morning at the rocky beach, Bethany and Matt have retreated into a stony silence – with me, at any rate – and Amy is practically monosyllabic. She passes me things to set on the table: beers dripping with condensation, a carafe of Primitivo, a jug of water, baguettes and a bottle of bright-green olive oil, fist-sized tomatoes and spiky cucumbers, all from Carlo's farm. There's cheese, bizarre white peaches and prosciutto. It's an odd mixture, not quite a meal, but apparently Joe is doing his special roast chicken later. I'll need to fill up on bread. Lotte and Theo are sitting by the edge of the pool, dangling their toes in, but not venturing any further, and Chloe is hunched over her iPad, watching something; in the dusk, the colours of the screen flicker across her face. A bat swoops over the terrace, dipping into the water, and the children shriek. Luca is reading *The Divine Comedy*, absent-mindedly dunking chunks of bread into a puddle of balsamic vinegar.

The rest of my family drift over to the table.

'Chicken's marinating and the veggies are roasting,' Joe says, clinking his protein-shake against Bethany's wine glass and smiling at Amy.

'This is the life,' Matt says, turning a Peroni in his hand, as if he's trying out cheerfulness like it's an old coat he's rediscovered.

Dad isn't here, and no one has thought to tell him it's time to eat. Or maybe they've deliberately not said anything. I sigh and go inside to look for him. When I find him in his room, he's reading some thesis about British politics. He carefully slides his bookmark in, to hold his place.

'I still can't find that photo of your mother,' he says.

'It'll turn up,' I tell him, taking his elbow and helping him up out of the armchair. I don't bother reminding him that he's left it at home.

'Wait a moment, Son.' He turns back at the door and retrieves his jacket from the arm of the chair. I suppose he feels the cold more than the rest of us, and even a balmy evening might seem a touch chilly to him.

Everyone falls silent as we walk out onto the terrace. The scrape of Dad's chair against the tiles is loud.

'A veritable feast,' Dad says. 'Thank you, Amy.' He raises his glass of water.

'Joe's cooking tonight.'

'Ah. No end to your young man's skills,' Dad says, and Bethany splutters.

'That's about the size of it,' Joe says. 'Cooking and running about like a nutter. Didn't make it to university, Prof.'

'You're not the only one,' Bethany says, nodding at Nick.

'Thanks for the reminder, Bee,' I say. Dad went on about it for ages when I dropped out of my journalism course. Not that Bee went to uni, either. The two of us: an endless disappointment to our highbrow father.

'Ah, well, there's still time.'

Bethany rolls her eyes.

I feel slightly bad that my sister has lured Joe here under false pretences. She told him I'd take photos of the two of them for the book proposal he's putting together, and what with all the drama going on – Dad not being welcome – I haven't managed to shoot any.

'Hey, you know what, Joe, you could have a social-media campaign with a hashtag: #FitInFive.'

'#FitInFive?'

'Yeah, and then you could do loads of tips that only take five minutes – five-minute workouts, five-minute stretches, a five-minute meal plan.'

'That is genius, mate. Thank you. You are the man. I owe you one.' He high-fives me.

I grin and feel slightly better about myself.

Dad mutters something about it being chilly in the evenings. He pauses for a moment with his jacket half on, crumpled across his shoulders.

'You all right, Dad?' I ask.

He pulls something out of his pocket and places it on the table with a tiny chink. It's a heart-shaped silver frame, with a photo of my mother and father. It was taken nearly twenty years ago: my father is handsome, his hair thick and brown; my mother's is long and blonde with a slight wave. They're both smiling. I get a lump in my throat as I remember they're smiling at my ten-year-old self. The photo is at a rakish angle because I'd cropped it badly, so part of Dad's head is missing and there's a big green space next to Mum. I'd taken it in the garden with Bethany's camera. At ten, I still thought everything would work out.

'Where was it?' Bethany asks.

'In my pocket.'

As if she's speaking to a child, she says, 'Do you think it was there all along?'

'I could have sworn... I looked everywhere.'

'So did I,' I say, puzzled. I'm sure I checked his pockets, but maybe I hadn't looked in that jacket.

Matt, who has been studiously ignoring my father, now pours a large measure of red wine and pushes the glass over to him.

'Maybe this will jog your memory.'

Amy inhales sharply, and I bang my beer down, nearly choking on a mouthful. I've never thought of Matt as a cruel man, but I guess grief can warp a person. Joe and Luca look stunned. They both leave the table at the same time: Luca heads over to the children, who are playing with the chess pieces on the other side of the pool, and Joe goes into the kitchen. Presumably he's going to pretend to look at the chicken.

No one says anything, and then Dad starts to sob. I can't remember ever seeing my father cry before; not even when Ruby-May died, not even when our mother left. It's horrible, as if each tear has to be forcefully and painfully dredged up from some deep recess in his body. Amy reaches across me and takes my father's hand. He holds hers tightly, enclosing it in both of his, just as he did when she was a child. He lets go and fumbles for a handkerchief, which is where he always keeps one: in his breast pocket. He rubs his eyes and blows his nose.

'My mind... No one likes to think they're losing their mind.' He bows his head and his whole body shakes. 'I'm sorry,' he says. 'I'm so sorry.'

Matt wipes a tear away with the back of his hand and sniffs. 'Nothing will ever bring her back, but it's all we wanted you to say.' He strokes Amy's shoulder. 'Any help you need – medication, lift to the clinic – we're here for you.'

A whisper of the old Matt, I think. My sister nods and reaches for her husband. They cling to each other.

I move the wine glass away from my father, and Bethany, her eyes swimming with tears, takes it from me and tips the contents onto the parched earth.

Maybe, I think, looking round at my siblings, *we can start to heal; maybe our family is going to be okay.*

21
NICK

That night I dream I'm falling, dark shapes crush me and I can't breathe. I wake, wet with sweat, the sheets tangled round my knees, clutching at the empty air. I lie still for a moment, waiting for my heart to stop racing, telling myself it was only the dream – the recurring one I've had ever since the day Bethany nearly killed me.

As my heart rate returns to normal, I remember what has been troubling me all evening: Matt and Bethany said Dad had drunk most of a bottle of red wine; Amy insisted it was cider brandy. I suppose they would tell me not to get hung up on details – the point is, they'd say, if I asked them, that he was drunk when he was meant to be looking after their child. And if I pressed her, Amy would tell me to stop going on about it, because Dad has admitted he was in the wrong and that he has dementia, and that's why he couldn't remember he wasn't meant to be drinking. Old habits are hard to break. I sit up and the hairs on the back of my neck prickle.

Something has woken me or, rather, *someone*.

There is someone here.

I stare into the darkness. The room resolves into shades of shale and slate. I let my breath out slowly. I can't see anyone here, hiding in the shadows.

I left the window open, and a shallow breeze stirs the curtains. I'm not sure, but I think the sound I heard is coming from outside. It's faint and then it's gone. I lean on the windowsill to look down at the swimming pool, and something sharp digs into my palm.

I wince; embedded in the heel of my hand is a human tooth. It's so tiny it can't be an adult's: sharply pointed, it's a dull ivory, with a hollow where it once grew in a child's jaw. A canine. I shudder. Whose is it and why is it on my bedroom windowsill? It must be Lotte's or Theo's – but even I know how much a tooth is worth to a child. Neither of them would have left it here.

I look out again. I can only see the dark expanse of water below me; the outline of the hill and the roof of the farmhouse where Carlo and his family live. I quietly pull on my jeans and T-shirt, slide my feet into flip-flops. I put the tooth in my pocket; it seems wrong to throw it in the bin. I listen at my father's door, but he's snoring. Bethany probably dosed him up with sleeping pills again. The wooden floorboards creak beneath my feet as I walk along the landing and squeak down the stairs.

The living room is empty. I open the back door – somebody has left it unlocked – and step outside. There's the dull thrum of insects from the brush, but I can't hear anything else and I wonder if I imagined it. Although the moon isn't visible, there are so many stars it's possible to make out the shape of the sun-loungers and the tables grouped around the pool; the water lapping at the stone sides, the Milky Way refracted on its surface. It's beautiful. The faint stir of the wind is refreshing. I walk a couple of paces towards the pool. I'm wide awake now, all my senses tingling and alive, adrenaline fizzing through my veins. I don't think there is anyone here, and I imagine the feel of that cool water against my skin. I'm about to peel off my jeans and dive into the inky depths when I notice something floating on the surface, gently bumping against the edge. I reach down and grab it. The water is colder than I expected. As I lift the object out, I realize it's one of Lotte's floats. In the starlight I can just about read the writing on the front. It says: **Warning: will not protect against drowning**. I shudder and drop it on a sun-lounger. I'm just about to go inside when I hear the noise again.

I start, my heart contracting. I bunch my hands into fists. I'm painfully aware that I'm in flip-flops, there's a fifteen-year-old girl, a couple of kids, two women and my elderly father inside – and I'm the only man who's awake.

I swing towards the sound. It's coming from the stand of cypresses at the far end of the property, before the land tails off into scrub. I walk slowly towards it. There's a half-open shed with cleaning products for the pool on the other side of the trees, and I'm certain whoever it is, they're inside. I pause, wondering whether it would be wiser to go back and wake Joe or Matt.

Or call the police.

It's grown harsher, more guttural.

I pat my pocket. I've left my mobile in the house. I only have a child's tooth with me.

It's louder, faster, nearer. I freeze.

And then I realize what it is.

It's a man's breathing, his breath coming quicker now, accompanied by a rhythmic creak, and someone else is with him, another person who is breathing heavily as well. *They're having sex.* Bethany has finally got what she wanted: Joe. I almost laugh out loud with relief.

As quietly as I can, I go back inside. When I was a kid and I couldn't get to sleep, my mother would recommend hot milk with a teaspoon of honey. Occasionally she'd even make it for me, if she was having a break from her painting. I heat a cup of milk in the microwave, swirl some honey in. I notice a small pile of Dad's things on the corner of the dining-room table: the book on politics that he's reading, his Sudoku collection, a pen, his glasses and his journal. He must have forgotten to take them up to his room: he usually reads before he goes to sleep.

I'm not the slightest bit interested in politics, to Dad's disappointment. I pick up his journal and flick through it. I feel a bit guilty, but I justify it to myself: I'm checking he's okay, not forgetting any appointments. It's tragically empty. Once he was so busy, giving lectures, attending conferences, supervising students, plus all the extracurricular activities I'm trying to avoid thinking about. There's hardly anything here: *Tea with Tony*, his neighbour who makes the apple cider brandy; a dentist's appointment; a note about mending the fence; a reminder to book an electrician. I flick further back in time, to 1 September last year. It simply says, *Funeral*, and the time and the church: *St Margaret and All the Angels*. It took two weeks before the coroner would release Ruby-May's body.

But the week before, there's another entry: *The Castle*. What the hell is that? I can't think of any castles near our house in Somerset. There's nothing about a Mini-Mental State Exam or a brain scan. I rifle through the whole of September, October, November. I skip back to 15 August. Nothing resembling a hospital appointment.

I carefully replace Dad's journal on top of his politics book and beneath the Sudoku. Either our father's memory is so bad that he didn't even remember to write down his appointment, or else my sisters are lying. But why would they lie about taking him to hospital?

14 AUGUST, ITALY

22
AMY

Matt grunts and rolls over. Once, he'd have begun the day by enveloping her in his arms, and they'd have eased into wakefulness together. He must have drunk the best part of a bottle of red last night and his snoring kept her awake. She grabs her dressing gown and staggers downstairs to make breakfast for Lotte and Theo. The curtains are still drawn and they're huddled together on the sofa, watching a DVD.

'Too loud,' she yawns at them, as another dragon annihilates its opponent with an ultra-violet fireball. 'You'll wake everyone up.'

She opens the kitchen door and feels vaguely surprised that it's been left unlocked overnight. The air is fresh and smells of dew-damp oregano: a thin mist floats between the silver olive trunks and the sky is the colour of a split peach. She steps outside and inhales deeply. As she does, she catches a tiny movement out of the corner of her eye. She walks round the edge of the pool, the tiles cold against her bare feet. The shadow of a tree in the wind, she thinks. But the day is still. She stands on the edge of the terrace and looks through the cypresses to the shed; the interior is dark and she can't see anyone or anything there. She tightens the sash of her gown around her waist. She must have imagined it. Or maybe it was a bird, or a cat.

She turns slowly in the opposite direction, so that the green-black trees are behind her. The shutters are tightly sealed in Joe and Luca's apartment, but in the wing of the house where Bethany, Chloe, Dad and Nick are sleeping, the downstairs windows are ajar, the curtains slightly open. Her stepdaughter is still in bed, the covers pushed down to her waist, one bare leg on top of the sheet, her hair spread across the pillow. Through the gap in Bethany's curtains, Amy can see her moving around, pulling on a top, stepping out of the shorts she was sleeping in. Amy drops her gaze, feeling embarrassed, as if she's been caught spying on her sister, and hurries back inside. She must remind them to keep their windows closed; but then she thinks, *I'm being alarmist: there is no one around.*

They're completely hidden, here in the midst of this olive grove.

She makes a coffee and starts putting out the children's cereal.

'I'm going to take the kids into town. Do some shopping,' she tells Matt later, over breakfast. *The anniversary is tomorrow and we'll need party food.*

Through the archway she sees Joe and Bethany. They're at the front of the house, just back from their training session. Even though it's early and the air is still cool, they're both drenched in sweat. Bethany is bent over, sucking in air. She's wearing a sports bra and Lycra leggings with a tropical print. Amy has seen the same pair in the window of Sweaty Betty's on her way to work. She feels a sharp stab of jealousy. Of course Bethany has the latest design, even though a pair costs more than Amy earns in a day.

When her sister's got her breath back, she takes a picture of herself, with Joe behind her, as if he's her own private gladiator: every muscle on his torso is defined, the veins running down his forearms stand out, a sea-breeze stirs his dark, curly hair. *How much younger than her is he? A decade?*

'I can look after Lotte and Theo,' her dad says. He looks eager, even hopeful.

'No,' she says, before she can help herself. 'I'm going to take them with me and buy them an ice cream as a treat.'

He can't be trusted with the children, she thinks, not when he's so forgetful. And she still hasn't forgiven him. It'll take time, she reminds herself.

'Oh. Well, they'll like that.'

'Is there anything you would like me to get you?' she asks more gently. She doesn't want to invite him to come with them, but she feels guilty for leaving him here.

'If you see an English newspaper. Or a magazine like *The New Statesman* or *The Economist*,' he says, but he looks crestfallen.

'Do you want any help?' asks Matt, pausing momentarily from stacking their cereal bowls in the dishwasher.

She's immediately irritated. Why has he assumed he's not coming with them? They're still a family, aren't they?

'You don't have to,' she says with some coolness.

'I don't think Chloe would be up for it. And she's still in bed.'

'You don't need to babysit her,' Amy says. 'She'll be fine here, if you do want to keep us company.'

'Okay,' he says, but he sounds reluctant.

'I'm not up for what?' asks Chloe, walking in.

She's wearing an extremely short nightshirt and her feet are bare. Her hair is tangled and falls over her face. She tosses it back and flops into a chair at the table, her eyes half-closed, as if she's just returned from working a night-shift. Amy frowns. Chloe looks so like Bethany: the same beautiful, thick chestnut hair, the pale gold of her skin. No wonder Joe is attracted to her sister.

'Do you want to come shopping with us and go to a cafe in town, sweetheart?' asks Matt.

'Nope,' says Chloe, shaking Cheerios into her bowl.

Luca strolls in at the same time as Bethany and Joe.

'We're thinking of going for a long old run,' says Joe. 'Into the hills and far away. Anyone up for it?'

'Thought you'd just done your workout?' Nick says. He's just come downstairs and he yawns and stretches.

'That was a baby one,' Joe tells him. 'Come on, before it gets too hot. You know you want to.'

'Can we have the breakfast first?' asks Luca.

'Espresso and a banana. That'll turn you into a fat-burning machine.'

'Okay, I will have that, and then I come with you,' says Luca and he grins at Joe.

'Amy.' Matt clears his throat. 'Would you mind if I—' he nods his head towards Joe – 'go for a run with the guys?'

She frowns again. 'If that's what you want. Come on – teeth, faces, clothes on,' she says to Lotte and Theo, who are still in their pyjamas and are playing Minecraft on Chloe's rhinestone-encrusted neon-pink iPad. Chloe notices and snatches it out of their hands. Matt doesn't say anything. *He's so lenient with her.*

'Nick. You up for it, mate? Get you Fit in Five,' says Joe.

Her brother hesitates. 'I'm pretty tired. Didn't sleep that well.'

'Should have had a sleeping pill,' says Bethany. 'I have no trouble getting a good night's kip, in spite of the snoring going on around here. Stopped Dad wandering around at night too,' she says, looking smug.

'Go on,' says Matt.

Her brother still seems reluctant. He's so out of shape, she can't imagine him being able to keep up with the others.

'Who'll look after Chloe?' Nick asks.

Chloe speaks through a mouthful of cereal. 'I don't need a bloody babysitter!'

'I shall be here,' David says, shaking his three-day-old paper and looking at his step-granddaughter over the top of it. 'Not that you need looking after, my darling. Shall we go for our usual stroll up to the farmhouse and buy some bread from that young man?'

Amy's taken aback. She hadn't noticed that Chloe has been walking up to the farmhouse with her father. Perhaps she hasn't taken sides against him, like the adults have. After all, she's still a child – one who misses her grandfather. Chloe, her cheeks bulging with Cheerios, gives her granddad a thumbs up. Amy glances at Matt to see how he's going to react, but he's joking with Joe and doesn't notice.

'Thanks, Dad,' Amy says, although she feels uneasy.

'Come on, mate, let's turn you into a lean, mean fighting machine,' says Joe, throwing a mock punch at Nick, who pushes him off. 'Don't think I've seen you take your top off this whole holiday,' he adds. 'How are you going to get a proper tan?'

Amy exchanges a glance with Bethany, but she doesn't say anything.

'No one should have to see this,' Nick says, patting his stomach.

'Nothing to be ashamed of,' Matt replies. 'I'm sure you worked hard to get it. All those ciders and burgers down the Grain Barn.'

She doesn't know if Matt has seen Nick without a T-shirt. It's not like they've been on a beach holiday as adults before. 'Lotte! Theo! Upstairs! I haven't got all day.' She wants the kids out of the way in case Nick does give in and takes off his top.

'Come on! Slap a bit of suntan lotion on and you're good to go. The ladies love a killer tan – and I can get you a six-pack in four weeks, I guarantee it.'

She looks at Bethany again, hoping she'll tell Joe to leave Nick alone, but her sister crosses her arms and stares resolutely out of the window at the sea.

'Go on! Go for it, mate!'

'Nick,' she says, at last, 'you don't have to.'

Nick stands up and grabs the edge of his T-shirt.

'Nick, really, you don't—'

'That's my lad,' says Joe, giving a whoop and clapping him on the back.

Nick pulls his T-shirt over his head. Amy can't bring herself to look. There's a moment of silence.

'Holy cow,' Joe says, under his breath.

'Are those real, Uncle Nick?' asks Theo in a hushed voice.

'Bona fide. I didn't tattoo them on, Scouts' honour,' Nick says.

'What's a Scout? We say "pinkie promise",' says Lotte.

'Theo, if you don't go and get dressed right now, I'm not buying you an ice cream,' Amy says.

Theo ignores her. 'Did a pirate slash you with his cutlass?'

'I got in a fight with an alien,' Nick says. 'In fact, it was a pirate alien.'

'Wow,' says Lotte, 'that's awesome!'

Joe claps his hands together. 'The ladies will go wild when they see those scars. You look like one tough mother. Grab your kickers and let's hit that hill.'

Matt hasn't stopped staring at her brother. 'Is that from—'

'Yep,' says Nick.

Bethany still has her back to them.

'They don't look quite as bad now, Son,' their father says.

Nick shrugs on his T-shirt and grins at Amy. 'Don't want to scare the natives,' he says, studiously avoiding looking at Bethany.

Amy doesn't respond; she can't bear him smiling at her when he still doesn't know the truth.

TWENTY-FIVE YEARS AGO, SOMERSET

23
NICK

I must have been about Lotte's age. It was probably late May, because it was coming up to my birthday. I can't remember if it was the end of term or a weekend – there was no school, but in other respects it was a usual day for us – Dad was at work and our mother was painting and didn't want to be disturbed. Bethany was supposed to be looking after me. To be in Bethany's charge meant that she would tell me what game we were playing and what I had to do, but there was nothing actually comforting or caring about it. We'd stolen some stale Jacobs crackers and the tail end of a packet of mixed dry fruit from one of the kitchen cupboards. I was picking all the bits of orange peel out of my share and moaning about the burnt taste of the raisins. I left a trail of crumbs and rind on the lawn and was followed by a robin, as if I was a juvenile Pied Piper.

It was definitely Bethany's idea to play in the ruin at the bottom of the garden. I would never have dared, because it was strictly forbidden by our father. Once the valley where we lived was well populated: there was some kind of industry here and there'd been a railway. Now all that was left was a flat length of track that had been turned into a cycle path for hobby bikers, and the tumbledown ruins of cottages, hovels, pigsties and kilns. We had one of the better-preserved cottages in our garden: two walls remained, one had a chimney and the remnants of a bread oven. The outline of the house was marked out in crumbling brick and the whole thing was festooned with ivy. Buddleia and brambles sprouted from cracks in the masonry, and sycamore saplings had invaded the living room.

'I bet you can't climb to the top!' Bethany said.

I was pretty sure I couldn't, but I didn't want her to know that. I felt the sparrow flutter of my heart; I knew she was going to call me a coward.

'Course I can,' I said.

'Go on, then. Prove it!'

'Don't want to,' I said, scuffing the toe of my trainer against the lintel and wishing we'd found some cooking chocolate, or even leftover dates rolled in sugar. But then our mother didn't bake, so it wasn't likely.

'You can't do it,' Bethany said.

I found myself climbing on top of the hearth, searching for handholds in the powdery cement and wrapping my fingers between the thick stems of ivy. Bethany stood below me and, now that she'd got her way, switched to cheering me on enthusiastically. I don't suppose I got very far, but it seemed as if I was really high up. I was level with the top of the sapling, looking down at Bethany's upturned face, the sun hot on my own, once I was no longer sheltered by the trees. I was too frightened to go any further. And that was when it happened.

I remember realizing that something was terribly wrong; I was no longer upright. I was falling backwards, still clinging to the ivy, the bright blue of the sky disappearing. There was a whoomp and my lungs were emptied of air. Something hot and wet against my face. Someone was screaming. The sky fell in on me like I was Chicken Little.

Amy told me afterwards that the ivy had come loose and the wall I was climbing had collapsed. In the ambulance the paramedics said I'd hit my head, splitting my skull open; I'd broken my forearm, smashed several ribs and fractured my collarbone. I'd have a few scars when I was all patched up, they said, like that would please me. One of them described how they'd dug me free from the fallen stones, as if the story would entertain me on the way to the hospital. I was lucky, the doctor said later, that I hadn't been buried alive. I was lucky, he added, that I hadn't died.

Since then, but only to myself, I've always rephrased his statement: *I'm lucky my sister didn't kill me.*

24
AMY

When she and the children reach the piazza below the fort, she's surprised to see it's bustling with activity. There's a marquee; men are setting up small fairground rides, and others are unfolding tables and weighing down awnings and buntings with sandbags.

'What's going on?' she asks the young woman in the cafe, as she orders ice cream and a coffee for herself.

'It is *Ferragosto*,' she says. 'Happen every year, a special holiday. Tomorrow evening everyone will be here. There is some food – all the specialities of the region, a festival to celebrate. Fireworks.' She looks bored by the prospect.

Amy drops a couple of euros in the ashtray for tips next to the cash register. She wonders how she feels about this strange coincidence, the summer fete and Ruby-May's anniversary occurring on the same day.

She's about to take the ice cream to the children, when she turns back to the waitress and, on impulse, orders a shot of Frangelico. She tips it into her coffee and hands the girl the glass.

The waitress grins at her and fills it up again.

'*Offerte della casa*,' she says, and then adds, 'Everything is closed tomorrow. Is a holiday. Nothing open, even the *stazione di polizia* is closed. I say you, in case no one remember to tell to you.'

'Thank you,' Amy says, grateful for her kindness.

'Look! Can we go on that?' asks Lotte, pointing towards a carousel with chairs dangling from it on long chains.

'It's not open until tomorrow evening, sweetheart,' she says.

'So can we come back? Please, please?' Lotte is bouncing up and down on her chair with excitement.

She takes a breath, wondering how best to explain about the anniversary party, when she notices the writing in large letters above the carousel: *Lasciate ogni speranza o voi che entrate.* There's a cartoonish skull and crossbones on either side of the phrase. She says it out loud, no doubt messing up the Italian pronunciation.

Amy bribes Lotte to be quiet with the promise of playing a game on her phone in a minute, and puts the phrase into Google translate. It comes up almost immediately. It's from Dante's *The Divine Comedy: Abandon all hope, you who enter here.*

'Can I play a game now?' asks Lotte, as soon as Amy puts her mobile down.

'Yes – when you've finished your ice cream and wiped your sticky fingers.'

How am I going to tell them about the anniversary? She tousles Theo's hair. *Will they understand? Will they be upset?* Perhaps she should leave it until tomorrow morning, so that they don't have time to worry or think too much about their little sister.

'I love ice cream,' says Lotte suddenly.

She smiles. 'I know.'

'It reminds me of Ruby-May,' she continues, as if her mother hadn't spoken.

'Yes, she loved ice cream too,' Amy says, thinking that perhaps this is the perfect opportunity to talk about the anniversary.

'That's not why,' says Lotte.

Theo shakes his head in agreement. 'No one made anything to eat after Ruby-May died, so we got ice cream out of the freezer by ourselves and ate it straight from the tub.'

'Chocolate...' Lotte says, widening her eyes with delight.

'And then vanilla...'

'And then strawberry...'

'Every day for a week!'

'A week?' Amy says. 'Surely—'

'Yes. A week! And then it was all gone.'

25
AMY

When they return to *Maregiglio*, her father's asleep in the shade, a new book on European politics on his lap, and Bethany is showing Chloe her Instagram feed and telling her which hashtags to use. Chloe is nodding and trying out her aunt's contour kit. Joe is doing something complicated with a spiky foam roller. Theo and Lotte quickly disappear up to their room. Amy had burst into tears after they'd told her about the ice cream, upsetting both the children, so she still hasn't managed to say anything to them about the anniversary party. There's no sign of anyone else.

'Where's Matt?' she asks. Her eyes are red, but Bethany doesn't notice.

'He overdid it,' she says, grinning.

'What do you mean?'

'It was hot and he pushed himself too much,' Joe answers. 'I tried to get him to stop and go back or just walk the route, but...'

Amy can see it now. Joe running ahead with his shirt off, the muscles in his back rippling, Luca lolloping easily along, Bethany grimly keeping up with the boys, and Matt, determined not to be shown up.

'Heatstroke,' Bethany interjects.

The shame and sadness Amy had felt this morning, when she realized she'd barely fed her surviving children for a week after Ruby-May's death, and the hazelnut liqueur, which has gone straight to her head, threaten to turn into hysteria.

'Heatstroke? He's collapsed? On a run where you're meant to be looking after everyone?'

'Amy, Joe's not Matt's personal trainer! It wasn't his responsibility!'

'He hasn't got heatstroke, more like heat exhaustion,' Joe says quickly, 'but he needs to have plenty of fluids.'

'Where is he? Or did you just leave him lying out on a hillside somewhere?'

'Amy! When did you turn into such a bitch?'

'Auntie Bee! Dad's having a lie-down upstairs,' Chloe says. 'He feels sick.'

'I'm going to check on him.'

'I'll do it,' Joe says, leaping up. 'Make sure that husband of yours has been drinking the coconut water I left out for him. Got to replace those electrolytes.'

He gives her a sympathetic smile. She puts her hand over her forehead. It feels as if the pain is chiselling into the centre of her skull. She'll go in a minute, after Joe's looked in on Matt. She stands at the sink and runs cold water over her wrists to cool herself down and pours a glass of lemonade. She's angry with Matt for being such an idiot, and with Bethany for bringing this young man into their midst. Nice as Joe is, it's not appropriate. She adds more ice and takes deep breaths, tries to let her heart rate slow. She crunches a cube and thinks miserably about tomorrow, the day of the anniversary.

Bethany and Chloe are taking turns to film each other on Bethany's iPhone, while her father sleeps on. Chloe is wearing even more make-up than usual; Matt really should talk to her. She has a sudden thought. Is Chloe getting made up like this for *Joe*? They'll have to watch her properly. She double-checks that neither of them is looking. She can hear the floorboards protesting above her head, as Joe jogs along the landing towards their bedroom. She pulls a bottle of vodka out of the freezer and pours a measure of the viscous liquid into her lemonade. She takes a large swallow of her drink. It courses through her, burning and freezing at the same time. The ice melts so fast it turns into tiny clear pebbles at the bottom of her glass. She wishes she had Bethany's iron willpower. Bee cut back on her drinking when she was trying to get into TV – although she's aware that her sister does go completely overboard now and again, when the pressure of being scrutinized on social media gets too much for her. She adds another slug of vodka and swills it around, then replaces the bottle before anyone notices.

Just as she's about to go and see if Matt is okay, there's a loud clattering and her husband bursts into the sitting room and flings open the back door.

'What the fuck are you doing?' he yells.

She's never heard him speak to Chloe like that, but then she realizes he isn't. He's shouting at her sister. Amy runs after him, the vodka swirling uneasily in her stomach.

'What's going on?'

Bethany gives an elaborate shrug and Chloe looks upset.

'I saw you from the window!' Matt says. 'You were filming her.'

'I was coaching her,' Bethany says, as if she's addressing an imbecile, and Chloe's shoulders relax a little. She looks defiant and crosses her arms.

'Coaching her to do what? To be a—'

Amy puts her hands on his arm. He's hot, sticky with sweat and glassy-eyed. He shrugs her off as if he can't bear her touch. Her dad sits up groggily and slides his glasses back on.

'I was giving her some lessons in how to be a presenter,' Bethany says, her hands on her hips, her tone aggressive.

'You were making her look like a porn star!'

'I was not! I was showing her how to stand so she won't look fat.'

'What's happening?' her father asks, looking from Matt to Bethany, both of whom ignore him.

'Fat! Fat? My daughter isn't even half the size you are!'

'I know she's not fat. The camera adds around ten pounds, so it's important to learn...'

'There's nothing my daughter could possibly learn from you.'

Bethany gapes at him.

'Dad! I *asked* her to help me,' Chloe says.

'She's fifteen. She's not going to be parading about on YouTube like some dumb b... bimbo. She's got a brain. She's got a future ahead of her.'

'Are you saying *I'm* stupid?'

'Why are you both shouting?' their father asks.

'Because your son-in-law is being a prize arse!'

'My daughter is going to get some qualifications and go to university. You didn't even make it to the end of secondary school.'

Amy glances up at the children's bedroom and sees two pale faces pressed against the glass.

'I've got a degree in Theatre Studies.'

'That's my point exactly! You could print your fucking diploma on a paper napkin.'

'Matt!' Amy says. 'Dad's right. Let's stop all this yelling. Shall we talk about this inside?' She starts to reach for him, but then she remembers how he pushed her off. 'I'm not sure what you're so worked up about...'

'You're not sure what I'm worked up about? My daughter is out here, covered in slap, while your sister is filming her in a bikini and uploading the footage to God-knows-where, and you were standing idly by, taking absolutely no notice. Probably drinking, knowing you. Chloe might only be your stepdaughter, but for Christ's sake, Amy, you could act like you give a damn about her.'

Chloe bursts into tears and marches past them into the house.

'Are you going to let him speak to me like that?' Bethany demands, and she too storms inside and a moment later slams her bedroom door.

Her father grips Amy's wrist. 'Why is everyone so angry?' he asks. He sounds shaken, upset.

'It's okay, Dad. I'm going to sort it out,' she says, her eyes filling with tears. She pulls away from him sharply.

Sometimes she does this – reacts instinctively, kindly towards him – and then she remembers, and it's as though she has a visceral response; she wants to push him away, never have to see him again, slide a knife between his ribs.

Chloe is hunched on the sofa, sobbing. Amy sits next to her and puts her arms round her shoulders. She's shaking, and Amy's own heart is hammering. She can feel the tremor in her fingers. She'll deal with Matt later, she thinks. She wonders if the almost-heatstroke has made him so hateful, or if something has happened between him and Bethany. *Or is it because he's been spending so much time talking to Sara?* Matt thinks she doesn't know about all the calls he's made. She passes Chloe a tissue. Perhaps this is payback for avoiding Sara over the years. She was so young when she and Matt got together, and she didn't feel confident enough to negotiate with his ex and establish some boundaries. She's always felt drab and self-conscious compared to Sara. Maybe Matt's wishing he'd never left her; maybe Sara has seen her chance and is wedging herself back into his life.

'I can't find my iPad. Bethany was taking photos of me, so I could post them on Instagram. It was here, I know I left it here.' Chloe hits the sofa with the flat of her hand. 'I bet Theo and Lotte have taken it.'

'They've been using our iPad, love.'

'They haven't!' Chloe is outraged. 'I saw them, this morning! They were playing Minecraft on it.' She blows her nose and wipes her eyes.

'I told them not to borrow it again. Shall we look for it together?'

'Look for what?' asks Matt, standing over them, his arms folded across his chest. There's a grey tinge to his skin.

'My iPad,' shrieks Chloe. 'Your bloody kids have stolen it!'

Matt sucks in his breath. 'That is not the way you speak about your brother and sister.'

'Matt, can you check if Theo and Lotte have Chloe's iPad?'

He ignores her. 'We've got more important things to discuss first.'

'Let's talk about it later, when it's cooler.'

No one has had any lunch yet, she thinks, so they're probably all suffering from a blood-sugar low, which isn't helping the anger levels, and she's finding it hard to think straight after downing that double vodka. Matt's about to argue, but turns on his heel and strides upstairs, shouting the children's names.

'It's not fair,' says Chloe. 'He never lets me do anything! And Auntie Bethany was only trying to help. He's so mean.'

'He's just worried, love. He doesn't want you to post anything online that you might regret later.'

'Why would I regret it? Anyway, Bee was really careful. She texted me the photos she took and then she deleted them from her phone. She knows more than you two do about social media and the "dangers" it poses.' Chloe air-quotes the word 'dangers' and blows her nose again.

'Why don't you look in your room for your iPad, and I'll see if it's here?'

How can you possibly lose a neon-pink, rhinestone-encrusted iPad? She searches the sitting room and the kitchen, tossing aside the cushions and crouching down to peer under the sofa. She sorts through the games on the bookshelves and checks it's not caught up in the tousled rugs and throws.

Chloe slouches back in. 'It's definitely not in my room or Auntie Bee's.'

'It's not in our bedroom, and Lotte and Theo haven't got it,' says Matt. He sounds more normal now, and he rubs his hair as if he's embarrassed. 'It's not likely anyone else here would have taken it.'

'It's not in my room or Dad's,' says Nick coming in. 'I overheard,' he adds. 'Hard not to.'

He's clearly been having a lie-down after the run; his cheek is creased from the sheets. Joe had tactfully joined Luca in their apartment when the argument started, but he reappears and says that he and Luca have searched their rooms too.

'It's been stolen!' Chloe says.

'Are you sure it's not by the pool? Did you take it to the beach?'

'No! I left it right here. It could easily have been pinched. None of you lock the house. There's people coming and going all the time – you never know who's here and who isn't. Anyone could walk in! This place is weird. I feel like there's someone watching me, at night, when I'm sleeping.' She bursts into tears again.

Amy has a vivid image of Chloe lying on a sun-lounger by the pool: a slice of her thigh, the white of her bikini bottoms, viewed from between the cypresses at the end of the garden by the shed; the blank space of Chloe's ground-floor bedroom window, which anyone could stare into from that side of the house. The person watching Chloe by the pool. She'd thought it had been Joe or Bethany.

'You're overreacting. It'll be here. No one could steal it,' Matt says. 'We're in an olive grove in the middle of nowhere!'

Matt's probably right, she thinks. They're safe here – it's a tiny island with a handful of Italians. And who locks the doors when they're on holiday? Or wears much, when they're wandering round a private pool.

'Maybe we should call the police,' Nick says. 'I mean, if you can't find the iPad, at least you've got the report, in case you need to make a claim on your insurance.'

What about all the photos on the iPad? Amy thinks. If someone gets hold of pictures of her stepdaughter and starts putting them on the Internet...

'There's a national holiday tomorrow – *Ferragosto*,' she says. 'The police station will be closed for some kind of fete in the town. We should phone now, if we're going to report it.'

'Bloody hell, you Flowers are daft!' says Matt. 'First of all, if there's a festival, the police will be there. They can't shut the police station! And second, you probably left it lying around somewhere, Chloe. You're so careless of your possessions. I've got a good mind to confiscate it when we do find it.'

'Matt!' Amy notices Lotte and Theo creeping down the stairs behind him. She hopes they didn't hear him swearing.

'What did I tell you? My iPad has been stolen and he doesn't even care,' Chloe shouts at Amy. 'He's a horrible father, and I wish he wasn't my dad.'

She strides into her bedroom, slamming the door behind her. Amy's headache has spread; it's a dull throbbing across the whole of her forehead.

'Anyone want a cup of tea?' asks her father.

'I was thinking of something stronger,' Amy says, as she pulls a bottle of cold white wine out of the fridge.

'I'm hungry,' Lotte says.

Matt starts assembling bread and cheese for their lunch. Lotte and Theo huddle together on the sofa and start playing something on their own iPad.

Joe pushes his hair behind his ears and looks suddenly awkward. 'Thank you for having me here. I know it's not the best time for you. And having a stranger with you must be—' He stops.

She flushes. How did he guess what she was thinking? Has she made it obvious? And how awful, if she has. This is not like her; at least, not how she used to be. A year ago she was a warm and caring person. *How fragile our sense of self is*, she thinks.

'We've liked having you,' she says, trying to dredge up something of the woman she once was.

'Yeah, so, er... I'm leaving early tomorrow morning. I thought I'd say thank you now, and I'll see you back in Bristol,' he adds, giving her a hug and shaking Matt's hand. 'Don't want to wake you when I leave.'

'Luca is going the day after tomorrow too,' Matt says. 'We won't know what to do with ourselves.' His sudden good cheer sounds false.

'Right, then.' Joe claps his hands together and bounces on his toes. 'Well, I'm not off just yet. David, you up for a superfood salad? Got to get some omega-threes in you.'

'A super-salad?' mutters her dad. 'I'm not sure I like salad. All that chewing. And it doesn't taste of anything.'

Amy takes a sip of her wine and feels as if she's floating a couple of inches above the floor, as the cold, crisp Pinot mingles with the spirits already in her bloodstream.

'Should we report the stolen iPad to the police? If we're going to, we have to do it today.'

'Kids!' Matt ignores her and puts two plates of bread and cheese and a bowl of cherry tomatoes on the table.

'In a minute,' says Theo. 'Just got to figure this out.'

She glances over and sees they're playing chess, but it doesn't look as if they're following any rules.

'I must say, you two are being remarkably nice to each other,' her dad says.

Amy hopes Theo and Lotte won't reply. They were never this close a year ago – they used to argue all the time – and now they cling to each other as if they have no one else to turn to.

Her father sits down in front of one of the plates of food and starts to eat the children's bread. Matt makes an exasperated noise at the back of his throat and gets another baguette out of the bread bin.

'Theo! Lotte!' I'm not telling you again.'

'Granddad's eaten my lunch,' wails Lotte.

'Oh, my dear, I'm so sorry,' her father says, offering Lotte a piece of cheese from her own plate.

Matt fetches plates and glasses, banging them on the table as he sets them down.

'It's not been stolen – it'll turn up,' he says, dodging round Joe, who is chopping up avocados and shaking a pan that he's dry-toasting nuts in at the same time. He glares at her. 'Can someone help me?'

Amy looks at what he's done so far: Lotte and Theo are sharing one plate of bread and cheese and, for some reason, are both trying to sit on the same chair, while her dad is eating the other child-sized portion. There's a basket of baguettes, a few tomatoes and a jar of olives on the table, as well as the wine bottle and Nick's beer. It's not much of a lunch.

Joe slides a large salad of crisp lettuce leaves and spinach strewn with pumpkin seeds, walnuts, feta and avocados into the middle of the table.

'Suuuper-greens coming up. There's enough for everyone.'

Nick makes a face and slaps a packet of salami next to the bowl of leaves.

'It's a shame you're going.' Amy smiles at Joe.

Matt's right, she thinks. She's worrying unnecessarily. *If someone had broken in, they'd have taken more than just an iPad.*

26
NICK

It's late afternoon by the time everyone has finished eating and arguing about Chloe's missing iPad. My step-niece's lovely face was all puffy and blotched and she barely spoke to anyone. When Bethany finally emerged from her room, she was in a foul temper. We all went to the beach, even though most of us weren't speaking to one another. What with Matt collapsing of heat exhaustion, losing it with Bethany and then Chloe's iPad going missing, I haven't had a chance to talk to Bethany on her own about Dad, and why there's no record of his hospital appointment, and what the hell The Castle is. I wonder if I'm making a fuss about nothing: if he forgot to write it down, it shows how bad his memory is, and we ought to get him a follow-up appointment.

I decide to come back by myself. I can't bear watching Joe leaping about with a Frisbee, flaunting his perfect abs, or take the tension crackling between Amy, Bethany and Matt. It's not like I can join in with Joe's game of Frisbee, either, as I can barely move after our run this morning. Luca doesn't look that sporty, but he can run faster than me and catch a Frisbee as if he grew up playing Ultimate. I'll speak to Bethany tonight, I decide.

As I'm leaving the beach, Matt jogs up the path after me. Four days in and he's still pale, except for a savage red slash of sunburn across the back of his shoulders from this morning's excursion into the hills.

'Wait up,' he says.

He winces and holds his side. He looks in as much pain as I feel, but I don't want him to know that. His calves bulge with blue-green varicose veins. *Christ, I hope I don't get old.* I also hope he's not going to tell me something I don't want to hear about Sara.

'I'm worried about Chloe,' he says when he's got his breath back. I'm expecting him to go on about the bloody iPad or how miserable she is, but he says, 'Have you seen the way she looks at Joe?'

'What? Joe?'

'Well, he is a good-looking boy, there's no two ways about it. And she's fifteen. You know what teenage girls are like.'

No, mate, I don't.

'Sixteen in a month. Thinks she knows everything.'

'Oh. Yeah,' I say, suddenly remembering Bethany at that age; well, before she walked out on us and went to stay with Dad's friend in his big, posh house.

'She's still a child, Nick. And Joe isn't that much older than her – he's twenty-four. I googled him.' He gives a gruff laugh. 'But he must seem grown-up to her.'

'I haven't noticed anything inappropriate,' I say, feeling foolish. And then I have a cold sensation that shivers down the nape of my neck as I recall the sounds coming from the shed in the garden. I'd assumed it was Joe and Bethany. *Could it have been Joe and Chloe?*

'Really?' he says, and his relief makes me feel like a complete tool.

'He's heading back home tomorrow.'

'Not a moment too soon,' Matt says, wiping the sweat off his brow. 'Not that he isn't a nice guy. But – look, could you do me a favour and keep an eye on Chloe? I'm going to be caught up helping Amy get everything ready for the... for the – you know...'

I nod, to put him out of his misery.

'And it'll be much easier if it's you. If I ask Chloe what she's doing or where she's going, or make the slightest comment on what she's wearing...' He mimes a grenade blowing up in his face.

I feel sorry for him. The embarrassing dad with the beautiful teenage daughter, who is having an affair with his ex-wife and can no longer ask Chloe's aunt to look out for her, because he's called her a thick bitch, so he's left with the kid brother of the family. But if ever I start feeling annoyed with my brother-in-law, I only have to remember the fishing trip.

It was about a month or so after Ruby-May had died. Matt texted me to ask if I wanted to go fishing with him. I've never fished in my life. It's not exactly top of my list of ways to spend my leisure time, and kind of weird for Matt, when he used to spend his weekends surrounded by kids in football kits doing drills and keepie-uppies. I said yes. Obviously.

We met at Tesco's and walked through the underpass beneath the M32. We passed some graffiti on the side of the motorway of a boy blowing a horn; out of the end fluttered a cloud of purple butterflies. It filled me with a dull rage that someone, somewhere, had such hope. We continued through Eastville Park to a large pond, and Matt led us down a muddy track to the far side. Opposite a wooded island he set out two canvas chairs, two rods and all the paraphernalia that goes with fishing. Flies. Hooks. An ice-cream tub of writhing maggots. He helped me cast and then we propped our rods up and sat in our khaki chairs. He handed me a can of cider. The pond was dark green and filmed with a layer of scum. Bedraggled swans, coots and geese ploughed up and down. Mallards, seagulls and pigeons fought over crusts passers-by scattered. The roar of traffic was an angry hum. It was a grey, cold day. We were overshadowed by the trees behind us; their dying leaves dripped water on us, in fat drops. There was a constant parade of people on the other side of the pond, with buggies and dogs and bikes; most of them in shredded jeans and Adidas hoodies. The smell of skunk mixed with the stench of decaying vegetation and the stink from the maggots. At some point that afternoon, maybe after two cans of Thatchers, I started to cry. I haven't cried since I was a child, but I sobbed until my ribs ached and my eyes burned.

We didn't catch anything and Matt didn't speak. Not even once.

'Of course,' I say to him now. 'Anything to help.'

'Thanks, mate.' He claps me on the arm. I can feel the heat radiating from his palm.

When I get back to the house, I lie in semi-darkness on the sofa, drinking a beer and watching my favourite *Star Wars* movie, *The Empire Strikes Back*, enjoying the peace and quiet. I can't concentrate, though, because I keep thinking about Chloe and Joe. Would he have sex with an underage girl? Would she have let him? Should I say anything to Matt? It's not like I know for certain. I've just got to the bit where Yoda is trying to persuade Luke Skywalker to go into this cave beneath a tree and he says, *A domain of evil it is. In you must go.* Luke doesn't want to, and he asks what's inside. Yoda replies, *Only what you take with you.*

'Only what you take with you.'

I say it at the same time, doing my best Yoda impersonation, but I'm not enjoying it like I normally do. I ought to talk to Chloe, but what the hell would I say? Plus Joe is about to leave, so maybe I don't need to say anything. *Coward!* I pause the film and get up to fetch another beer, and that's when I see it. A triangle of neon-pink. It's on a side table under a couple of books.

How did we all miss it? I feel stupid now for suggesting we should have called the police. I open Chloe's iPad to check it's okay. It turns on immediately and I swipe the home screen idly. There's no passcode. Chloe should be more careful. The device opens straight into Photos, as if that was the last app she was using, and I'm faced with a number of albums. One of them is labelled **Ruby-May**.

I click on it and see around fifty thumbnail-sized pictures of my niece, from when she was born until... I shouldn't be looking at Chloe's iPad, I know, but I'm caught between wanting to be reminded of Ruby-May and not wanting to think about her. I leave the album as it is, as I don't want to see any of the photos full-size. That would be too much. I can't get rid of the images of Ruby-May I have in my head: her little fat feet with their tiny, perfect toes, white and wrinkled and dotted with pond weed; or her lips, with their Cupid's bow, slightly parted and purple, the colour of the flowers she wanted to pick. As still as a doll, when she'd never been still in her life.

It's good to be reminded of what she looked like before. Some of the pictures are of Chloe and Ruby-May. Chloe's birthday is coming up soon; I could print one properly and frame it as a present. Without opening the images, I attach three to a text and I send it to myself, then delete the text from Chloe's iPad. I want it to be a surprise.

As I try to close the app, it reverts back to all her pictures. I shouldn't look, but I'm intrigued by what all the fuss was about. What kind of shots was Bethany taking of Chloe, to get Matt so worked up? I assume they'll be of my niece in her bikini and shades by the pool, prepping to be an Instagram star. The first ones I see are of her and Carlo, goofing about at his farm. No sign of Dad, so it must have been one of the times she went on her own. I scroll through them.

The last pictures on the iPad aren't what I was expecting.

They're dark, grainy and there's a certain beauty in the strips of light and shade between doorways and walls. Chloe is in all of them, but as a distant and indistinct shape. Sometimes she's a silhouette, and in others her bare skin is the only glimmer of brightness in a dreamy, underwater darkness. The second-to-last photograph takes me a while to decipher: it's all curved lines, pale gold and white, urban-grey and black. And then I realize. It's Chloe's back. She's naked to the waist, the sheets pushed down and draped around her hips. She's lying in bed and the picture has been taken from *outside* her bedroom window.

Who the hell took these photos? Bethany? Joe? Chloe herself? I've noticed her taking the occasional photo of herself using a selfie-stick and a timer. I swipe through to the last one. It's of her face; it's so close, though, she's out of focus and looks like an abstract painting. There's a trace of a smile on her lips. Did she know whoever took this picture – *all* these pictures – intimately? Or was she completely unaware that someone was stalking her?

I snap the iPad shut.

15 AUGUST, ITALY

27
NICK

Matt is hovering in the kitchen when I get up and he greets me like a long-lost friend. It's not like I'm up really late or anything, but I was woken shortly after I'd gone to bed by Bethany and Joe having an argument outside. Bethany isn't good at self-censorship, so she was pretty loud. I couldn't hear Joe's replies clearly. I put earplugs in, but I still couldn't get back to sleep. It's good in one way, though, because it probably means it must have been Bethany, and not Chloe, I overheard having sex with Joe earlier in the week. If my sister has started sleeping with him and now he's heading home – maybe back to his girlfriend – that would make her annoyed. You don't yell like that at a personal trainer you're paying by the hour. But I definitely should have taken Bethany up on her offer of sleeping pills. At least Dad's stopped wandering around at night since she's been giving them to him.

'Mate,' says Matt, pouring me a coffee, 'can I ask you a favour?'

'Um, yeah,' I say, rubbing the sleep from my eyes. I have a queasy feeling as I remember what day it is. I should tell him about those photos on Chloe's iPad. He'll go ballistic, though. Maybe I ought to have a word with her first...

'Joe's left – he's on his way back to Bristol.' Matt interrupts my train of thought. 'Bethany isn't up, not that she's speaking to me any more. Luca isn't here – no idea where he is.'

'Probably out for a run.'

I notice he hasn't mentioned my father, but that isn't surprising.

I don't think Matt will ever let Dad look after his children again. Dad is sitting outside, reading under the shade of a parasol. He looks lonely, but to be honest, I'm struggling a bit, not wanting to think about how frightening it must be for him, now that he's aware he's losing his memory, and at the same time my old anger is resurfacing, ever since Amy told me how he drove Mum away.

'I really need some time with Amy before... you know, before...' Matt runs his hand through his hair and it stands on end like a bristle-brush. He looks thoroughly miserable. 'I lost it yesterday. Said some things... Anyhow, I thought we could go into town for a coffee, just the two of us.'

'Good idea,' I say, pulling some bacon out of the fridge and then, as my stomach clenches, I change my mind and grab the jam instead.

'So you're okay looking after the kids?'

Ah! Nick Flowers, you can be so bloody dense.

'The bread's finished. Chloe's gone up to the farmhouse to buy more. She'll be back soon.'

'Right.' I take a sip of coffee. I wonder why she didn't go with Dad this morning. I must remember to nab her when she gets back, for a chat about the photos on her iPad.

'Yeah, if you could keep an eye on her, but basically she'll look after herself. Lotte and Theo are in their bedroom. Meant to be getting washed and dressed. We won't be long.'

I look at Matt properly. His thin face is ashen, in spite of a few days in the heat, and his stubble is grey. He's aged about twenty years in the last one.

'Happy to.'

Maybe this will get me back into everybody's good books, since they all think I'm such a waste of fucking space for bringing Dad here. And maybe, just maybe, after today everyone will start acting like a family again.

Matt jiggles his keys in his pocket. 'I once drove out of a multistorey car park with Ruby-May – you know the one at Cabot Circus that's a really tight corkscrew? And she said, "Careful, Daddy, don't break the car." I told her we'd be okay because I'm good at driving and she said, "Good boy. Well done!"'

He stares out towards the swimming pool. I try and make my mind blank. There's a long, awkward pause. I have no idea what to say.

Matt clears his throat. 'Anyway, thanks, mate. Suncream's there. Give them a snack at some point.'

I drink my coffee and stand in the sitting room, looking through the tips of the olive trees and out at the pure blue sky over the sea, and I think about this time, four years ago.

I don't remember either of the other two being born. I'd like to say I was too young, but obviously that would be bollocks. I was still with Maddison then, and she was ridiculously excited that I had a new niece. I went to the Bristol Royal Infirmary the day Ruby-May was born. Amy was in a ward on the fifth floor, her bed next to the window. She was as white as PVC, but had this sheen, like she was so happy... I swallow uncomfortably as I remember. Matt looked knackered, but ecstatic. He took the kids to the cafe, promising them juice and biscuits, leaving the three of us alone. Two babies were wailing, a woman was sobbing quietly, people were talking, the TV was on in the corner, nurses banged in and out with metal trolleys. I couldn't image how anyone slept there.

Ruby-May was in a Perspex box on wheels, next to Amy's bed. She was curled up on her front, with her bottom in the air and her fist in her mouth. I could imagine my father exclaiming: *She's bald as a coot.*

'You can hold her, if you want,' Amy said.

She looked improbably tiny. I was about to say, *Nah, you're all right*, and then I realized I did want to.

'I might drop her.'

'Don't be an idiot. Of course you won't,' said Amy, smiling at me. Her voice was like sandpaper, as if she'd been yelling at a football match. 'Just support her head. She can't hold it up by herself.'

I held Ruby-May against my chest. Her whole cranium fitted into the palm of my hand. She made little sucking noises against my collarbone. She smelt hot, earthy, like a sun-warmed mushroom. I stood at the window and looked out at Bristol spread below me: the office block with the bowler-hatted man graffitied five storeys high, the skyrise hotels, the glint of the river and the jostle of boats, serried rows of red-tiled roofs and, in the distance, the green fields and hills of Somerset. It suddenly struck me that this was what life was about; this was what life was for. Something surged through me, fizzed like electricity. Maybe it was love, love for Ruby-May. Four red balloons drifted across that perfect blue sky and I laughed out loud. For a moment it was like I held the secret of the universe in my hands. I felt both strangely energized and calm – like this baby was the key, and now I knew what the meaning of everything was and I just needed to rush home and tell Maddison, *Yeah, let's do it, let's have a family!* Maddison would probably have laughed at me; we hadn't been dating for long. And by the time she was ready and wanted us to move in together, that feeling had ebbed away, along with whatever it was I thought I'd felt for my girlfriend. Or my life in general.

Matt salutes me as he and Amy walk past the window of the holiday house. After they've driven off, I go upstairs and rap on the children's open bedroom door. They're both sitting on one of the beds, playing on the iPad.

Theo says, 'Did you know there are five hundred billion galaxies in the universe?'

'Wow, that's a lot.' I join them. 'How far away is Andromeda?'

'Two-and-a-half million light-years from Earth.'

'Well recalled, young Padawan.'

'Uncle Nick,' says Lotte, 'why is everyone being so strange today?'

I'm not sure what Lotte is wearing, but it makes my eyes hurt: everything clashes and is a riot of spots, stripes and flowers. She must have got dressed by herself.

'I guess it's because it's the anniversary.'

'The anniversary of what?'

Oh, shit!

'Well, this time last year is when your baby sister died. We're going to have a party later on.'

'Why would we have a party when she's dead?' asks Theo.

Good point.

'Like, with pass-the-parcel and musical chairs?' asks Lotte.

'Er, I don't think so, but I don't know what your mum's got planned.'

'Do you remember when Ruby-May wanted a baby?'

I shake my head.

Lotte says, 'For ages and ages she walked around with a toy dragon stuck up her jumper and said she was going to have a baby! She went to nursery with it. She cried every time the dragon fell out. She said when baby Cinders was born, she was going to grow up to be a human bean!'

'Do you remember the time she had to have those injections at the hospital?' Theo says. 'When we came home, she got a syringe out of her pretend doctor's kit and practised giving everyone a shot.'

'Yeah, and when it was your turn, she banged it right into your heart.'

'And made a bruise.'

'But she said it would make your heart big and strong and beautiful!'

I have no idea what to say. I don't know how Amy copes with this.

'I miss Ruby-May,' says Lotte. 'When will she come back?'

'Lotte, I'm really sorry, but she's never coming back. That's what happens when you die. You don't come back. Ever.'

'Yeah, but where did she go?'

Fuck, fuck! Why hasn't anyone talked to them about this?

Theo closes the iPad and they both look expectantly at me. Neither of them went to the funeral, so maybe they haven't – as my ex would say – had *closure*. Maddison's from New York and she's obsessed with Gyrotonics, green juice and emotional intelligence. Actually she'd get on really well with Joe. I must remember never to introduce them.

'Tell you what,' I say, and I explain the brilliant idea I've just had.

♖

The gratifying thing about children is their enthusiasm. They think my idea is brilliant too. And after I've helped them achieve 'closure', everyone will realize what a damn fine uncle I am and we'll all be one happy family again. Once we've assembled everything we need, we head down to the beach. I don't tell Dad we're going – he's fallen asleep anyway – and there's no sign of Chloe. I send her a text and she replies, saying she's still up at the farmhouse taking photos, but she'll be back soon with bread and cheese for lunch. *Pictures of Carlo*, I think. I assume Bethany's in bed sulking, but as we near the sea we spot her. She's sprinting up the road and jogging down. Over and over again. She's wearing shorts, a sports bra and a cap. Her hair is in a ponytail and her arms and legs glisten with suntan oil and sweat. Even though it's only mid-morning, the heat is intense. It makes me feel lethargic, and what Bee is doing looks punishing. I guess this is what it takes to be a star on regional telly.

She passes us, her eyes focused on something in the middle distance, but when she gets to whatever rock is her marker, she jogs back and kisses both children.

'Yuk,' says Lotte, wiping her cheek. 'You're all wet, Auntie Bee.'

'This is excruciating,' she says to me. 'I feel like I'm waiting to have my molars pulled out.'

I don't suppose she's talking about running.

'I've got some special presents for you,' she tells Lotte and Theo. 'I'll give them to you when you get back from the beach.'

They nod solemnly, accepting presents as their right, since we're going to have a party. Bethany is about to dart off again. I put out my hand to stop her.

'Listen, Bee, do you remember when you took Dad for that memory test?'

She frowns. 'Sometime last year.'

'But when?' I persist. 'Was it before or after the funeral?'

'I can't remember. After, I think. Amy was barely speaking to anyone. I thought it might help her understand what had happened. Why?'

She does a calf stretch and knots her hands behind her back; the muscles in her shoulders pop. She's wearing sunglasses, so I can't see her eyes.

I shrug. 'No reason. Just Dad couldn't remember when he went.' Only a small lie. I don't want to tell her I've read his diary.

'That's no surprise, is it?' she says.

I scuff the ground with my toe; the children, who've grown bored, start to drift down the hill towards the beach. That's true. Or it *might* be true.

'I was going to make a follow-up appointment. It's been a year. He could have got worse.'

'He probably has. I'll do it when I get home,' she says.

We both glance towards the kids, but they're fine – they've almost reached the sandy bay.

'I can go with him. I've got more time than you.'

'To be fair,' she says, swapping legs and stretching the other calf, 'I know a lot more about dementia than you, so it's best if I take him.'

'Okay. Where?'

'Back to the hospital, where I took him before,' she says, like I'm an idiot.

I nod and shout, 'Wait up!' before jogging to catch up with the children.

Am I being an idiot? Why would my sisters lie about what my father was drinking, or about Bee taking him for a check-up at the hospital? It's much more likely that my father really is suffering from dementia. After all, he has been forgetful since we got here.

And the only reason – absolutely the only reason for Bethany to lie – is unthinkable: that she didn't ask Dad to look after Ruby-May one year ago today. *Literally unthinkable.*

Lotte, Theo and I choose our spot carefully: at the far end of the beach, away from the Italian holidaymakers and just before the rocky outcrop. Using toy spades, the three of us dig a shallow grave.

'Do we say anything or do we just put her in?'

'Whatever you want.'

Lotte drops Ruby-May's doll, Pearl, into the hole. She lands with a soft thud. The doll is naked, apart from a purple ribbon around her neck, because Lotte didn't want to part with any of her clothes. Both children carefully arrange a collection of objects around her: a conch shell, an ice-cream wrapper, a pure white pebble, a chocolate coin, a twig of driftwood bleached to bone and an amethyst-coloured bead. I crouch on my haunches, the sun beating down on my shoulders. They're so serious and diligent. Pearl reminds me of an Egyptian mummy being sent into the hereafter with all that she – or, rather, Ruby-May – held dear.

As if the same thought had occurred to Theo, he says, 'When an important person died in Egypt, Anubis would cut out his heart and weigh it. If it weighed less than a feather, he would go to the afterlife. If he'd been bad, the god Ammut would eat his heart.'

'I don't think anyone will eat Ruby-May's heart!' Lotte says.

'We should put in a feather!' Theo says.

We find a seagull's and Theo threads it into Pearl's plastic fist. Some of the damp sand caves in as he leans over the doll.

'It's okay,' I tell him, before he can get upset. 'It's time to fill it in anyway.'

We shovel sand on top of Pearl and then pat the mound until it's smooth. Lotte places a scallop shell in the middle, and Theo lays a few stones round the edge. We picked all the geraniums from the trough at the front of the house on our way here, and the two children push the thick stems into the sand. Most of the flowers fall off in the process and our little patch of beach is bright with the blood-red petals.

'Do you want to say anything?' I ask. 'You know, like a poem or something Ruby-May might have liked?'

They stare at me as if I've gone mad.

'She liked Peppa Pig,' says Lotte, 'but I don't know any of the words.'

They both snort like pigs and fall about laughing.

'Bye-bye, Ruby-May,' says Theo, and then the two of them race back along the beach.

They leave me standing next to a baby-sized grave, feeling as if I've been flayed, and unable to get the thought out of my head that my sister, with her diploma in Drama Studies, is lying exceptionally convincingly to me.

28
NICK

Chloe has put fresh bread and new cheese on the table, along with those weird prickly cucumbers, ugly tomatoes, olive oil, balsamic vinegar, a bunch of basil and some Padrón peppers. *Christ, I could murder a burger.*

I suddenly remember one Saturday when Amy came round unexpectedly with the kids and I had nothing in the house that a child would possibly want to eat. Ruby-May had grabbed one of the red peppers Maddison had bought to make into a chilli that evening. She held it in both hands, took a big sniff and said, 'Hmmm, smells like money.'

It made me laugh at the time, but almost as soon as I start smiling at the memory, I stop. *This is shit. When will it end?*

'What's this – create your own lunch?' asks Matt, as he slides a couple of sharp knives into the middle, so we can peel the spines from the cucumbers.

'Looks perfect,' says Bethany, putting her arm round Chloe's shoulders.

'It's what they gave me at the farmhouse when I went up this morning,' she says. Her cheeks are slightly pink. 'Oh, and some eggs. They were still warm!'

'Because they'd just come out of a hen's bottom?' asks Lotte, her eyes wide with delight.

'I can make everyone omelettes,' says Dad.

There's a pause. No one looks at my father, until Amy says, 'That would be nice. Thanks, Dad.'

She and Matt seem a bit more at ease with each other, but I'm no expert. If Maddison had been here, she'd probably have rolled her eyes and told me that of course they still weren't getting on, and wasn't it obvious Matt hadn't apologized to her? I still haven't had a chance to talk to Chloe on her own about those photos of her, and it doesn't seem right to bring it up with Matt and Amy, today of all days.

'There's the big plan for tonight,' says Luca. 'I went into town with Joe before he left and saw all the stalls for the *Ferragosto* celebration. The speciality of the region is chilli! Lots of hot food, fairground rides, fireworks. We should go, no?'

'Oh yes!' says Chloe. 'I'm so bored. I would kill to do that. Carlo says some of his friends are going and I could hang out with them?'

Amy's mouth tightens into a thin line. She picks up a cucumber and starts skinning it.

'Yeah, fireworks!' Lotte jumps around and pretends to explode.

'Can we go, Dad? There's a really cool ride. It even says, "Abandon all hope, you who enter here" on the front,' says Theo.

'Do any of you even know what day it is?'

'Amy,' says Matt.

There's a crack as Dad drops an egg. The white oozes across the floor.

Amy takes a breath and says, 'We're going to have a little party for Ruby-May, who would have been four.'

'But the *festa* is in the evening! We could go afterwards,' says Chloe.

'Show some respect,' Matt says. 'And no, you're not hanging out with Carlo's friends. We have no idea who they are.'

'Why can't we see the fireworks? Ruby-May loves fireworks.'

'We'll be able to see them from here,' Amy says.

'But what about the rides?'

Dad breaks another egg. It slides into the bowl, along with some sharp shards of shell.

'Mum would let me go. I'm going to ask her.'

'My house, my rules,' Matt says.

'It's Carlo's house,' Chloe says. 'He invited me! It would be rude not to go.'

Amy starts chopping the cucumbers, faster and faster.

'It wouldn't kill you to go to the festival afterwards. Or I can take the children and Chloe, if you're not up for it,' Bethany says.

'No! I said *no*!'

'You're such a control freak.' Bethany grabs the bread knife and starts sawing chunks off the loaf. 'Dad, you're butchering that omelette.'

There's egg on the floor, yolk is smeared in shiny streaks across the work surface, and Dad's attempting to whisk the egg, including the bits of shell that have fallen in. Some of the beaten egg slops out of the top and spills across his shirt. He's also turned the pan on already and the kitchen is rapidly filling with black smoke. Amy spins round, the knife still in her hand, and I half-expect her to stab it into his back. She turns the heat off and opens the back door. No smoke alarms have gone off, which isn't a good sign.

Matt takes the bowl from their father.

'Oh dear, I haven't done a particularly good job of this. I used to make omelettes all the time. They were rather delicious, even if I say so myself. You enjoyed them, didn't you, Nick?'

'I don't remember you ever making me an omelette in my life,' I say.

'I wish Joe hadn't left,' says Bethany, sighing and tossing a piece of bread onto each of the children's plates.

I'd been thinking the same thing. Who'd have thought it: I'd give anything for a cheery person whizzing up a green smoothie right now. On second thoughts, I'd rather be back in Bristol, eating a bacon bap from Yummy's van by the army surplus. Why did I insist we all went on holiday together?

'My memory mightn't be what it once was, but I know I spent years caring for you after your mother left.'

'I want to go on the rides!' Theo says.

'*Caring* isn't how I'd have worded it,' I say.

'Anyway, we already buried Ruby-May this morning, so we don't need to have a party,' Lotte says.

Amy bangs the frying pan into the sink and turns the cold tap on. A cloud of steam rises into the air.

'Sweetheart, the funeral was a year ago, and you and Theo weren't there. Remember? Mummy and Daddy went on their own. Today is the anniversary. Dad, please sit down.' She picks up the knife again, wipes it on a cloth and starts hacking chunks off the cheese.

'No, we buried her this morning. Well, we buried Pearl, because Ruby-May has gone away, but we put all the things she likes in the grave.'

'Who has been buried?' asks Dad.

'What are you talking about?' Amy says, and I have a sinking feeling.

'It was Uncle Nick's idea,' says Theo. 'You know, so Ammut won't eat Ruby-May's heart?'

Shit, shit, shit!

'Er, that version is a little out of context,' I say, as Amy, her face drained of colour, stabs the knife at me.

'Are you telling me you *buried* Ruby-May's doll? You buried Pearl? And you got the children to *help* you?'

'It's not like it—'

'That is sick!' says Chloe. 'You really dug a grave and—'

'What were you thinking, Nick?' When I don't reply, Amy starts screaming, 'We asked you to do one thing. One thing! Is it too much for Matt and me to go out on the anniversary of our child's death, without you screwing up our other kids in the time it takes to have a cappuccino? What is wrong with you?'

'Don't be mean to Nick. He was only trying to help,' Bethany says, through a mouthful of lettuce leaves. 'I did tell you to take the kids to the funeral. You can't shield them from everything. They've got really strange ideas about death. And letting a trainee child psychologist practically raise them clearly isn't helping.'

'Stay the fuck out of this!'

I can't remember the last time I heard my eldest sister swear, but it was probably when she was a teenager. I glance at Luca, wondering if he'll back me up. Surely play-acting a funeral must be a good idea, according to some learned psychiatrist? Luca is staring at his plate, looking thoroughly despondent. I guess he's not going to stand up to Bethany. Matt folds his arms and glares at me. So far, no one has eaten any lunch, apart from my middle sister; Lotte and Theo are nibbling on dry bread. I wonder if Dad is angry with me too, since I reminded him what a dreadful father he was. He hasn't obeyed Amy's orders and he's now ambling towards the table, carrying something, and I close my eyes for a brief moment, because I know this day is going to get much worse.

'Dad,' I say, jumping to my feet, hoping to head him off.

It's too late.

'This is delicious,' he says, his mouth full, sputtering out crumbs.

Our father puts a large chocolate gateau in the middle of the table. It's covered in a thick layer of buttercream and decorated with Smarties; a piece has been chopped out.

There's a beat of silence, thick as treacle, and then Lotte says, 'Wow, look at that cake! Can I have some too?'

Amy drops onto a chair and covers her eyes with her hands.

Something inside me that's been coiled tightly all week snaps.

'What the hell is the matter with you, Dad? It's bad enough that you never cared about your own children, but do you have to fuck up Ruby-May's anniversary?'

The lines across Dad's forehead deepen and, as he stares at the cake, shame and guilt suffuse his features.

'Oh, darling,' he says to Amy, who is crying silently, 'I'm so sorry. It's Ruby-May's cake, isn't it?'

Chloe leans forward and says, 'Did you even remember that she died? It's not her birthday cake, you know.'

I'm stunned at Chloe's hurtfulness. Where the hell did she learn to speak to her grandfather like that?

'Shut up,' I shout. I bang on the table with my fist. 'Shut up, shut up!'

Amy looks as if she's about to faint. Luca takes Lotte and Theo's hands and leads them outside. Matt crouches by his wife and cradles her in his arms. Does Dad really not remember? Has his memory got that bad?

'Don't you understand?' I yell. 'She's dead. You killed her! You fucking killed her!'

And I watch as his face caves in on itself. For a moment I'm victorious. I've stood up to my father for the first time in my life. I'm glad he's suffering. Bethany strides over and slaps me across the face. My teeth clatter together and my head cracks back.

'How dare you speak to him like that! It was not his fault.'

Dad buckles at the knees and sinks into an armchair. If I let it, the pain that is waiting will cripple me. Of course it's not my father's fault. I know that. I'm mad with grief about Ruby-May, angry with my father for driving my mother away, furious with my sister for almost killing me and then, later, leaving me on my own with my emotionally absent, adulterous and semi-alcoholic father. I remember the hospital appointment she's fabricated.

'You're right,' I say. 'It's not his fault, is it? *You* asked him to look after Ruby-May. A two-year-old child. You left her in his care. It's *your* fault.'

'Nick,' she says quietly, 'none of us realized he was suffering from dementia.'

She's standing so close to me I can smell the pina colada of her suntan oil. I open my mouth to speak. I'm about to retort, *Is he really? Or did you lie from start to finish?* But before I can say anything, Bethany says, 'If you'd actually been on time for once in your life, you could have looked after Ruby-May. But no, as usual, you were late. Spectacularly late. Because,' and she pokes me in the chest with her finger, in time with her words, 'everything is always about you. You've never cared about us – about Amy and me.'

'Stop it!' shrieks Amy.

I feel as if my breath has been sucked from my body at the magnitude of my sister's unfairness.

I seize Bethany and shake her as hard as I can, and I shout in her face, 'I will never forgive you!'

When I finally release her, I expect her to hit me again, but she doesn't. She staggers, then steadies herself against a chair. When she's recovered, she marches over to the fridge, grabs a bottle of Prosecco and walks out of the front door, slamming it behind her.

Matt stands up. He's trembling. 'Get out. Get out now!'

I do. I go in the opposite direction to Bethany, through the kitchen and towards the pool. Luca is sitting outside with Lotte and Theo, his travel chess set on the table in front of them.

'Nick,' he says.

I ignore him and keep going.

'Nick,' he says again, more urgently. He stands up and comes over, reaching out an arm to detain me. 'I saw...'

I dodge him and break into a run. I'm so angry my heart is hammering in my throat and my hands are bunched into fists. I sprint through the stiff grass and into the olive grove, and keep going up the hill until I can't breathe and my throat feels raw, blood pounds in my ears and the cicadas throb like the dullest of aches.

29
NICK

I return as dusk is falling. The house is in darkness and there's no one by the pool. For one moment I think they've all left and gone back to Bristol, leaving me behind, and my breath catches. I walk silently through the empty sitting room; Chloe and Amy's iPads are on the table and the full-size chess set is laid out with a black king and a white queen facing each other in a silent stand-off. I go into the coolness of the archway connecting the two parts of the former barn and see my family in silhouette.

They've moved the tables and the chairs to the front of *Maregiglio* and they're sitting watching the sun set. Amy and Matt have opened a bottle of Prosecco and the children have glasses of lemonade. The sky is purple with layers of gold and pink folding into the sea; the sun is a blood-red ball. I slip in behind them and Amy silently pours me a glass of fizz.

Luca says quietly, '*There is no greater sorrow than to recall happiness in times of misery*' and raises his glass to me. 'Dante Alighieri,' he adds, when it's obvious the quotation has passed me by.

Amy lights four candles on the chocolate cake and they flicker in the twilight.

'All right, Son? You ready?' asks Matt.

Theo nods and unfolds a sheet of lined notepaper and reads:

I will lend you, for a little time,
A child of mine, he said.

For you to love while she lives,
And mourn for when she's dead.

He and Lotte blow out the candles and we all clap, and Amy and Dad wipe their eyes. Chloe leans over and kisses Theo on the cheek.

'I'm so sorry, darling, I'm so sorry, I can't—' Dad says.

Matt puts a hand on Dad's shoulder and he blows his nose into his handkerchief. Amy cuts the cake and passes him a slice. Fireworks whistle and boom; the sound reverberates in my chest. I can't see them, though, sheltered as we are by the slope of the hill, facing towards the ocean.

'Remember when Ruby-May had chocolate cake for her birthday? She put the pointy bit in her mouth, and then she put both hands on the other end and stuffed the whole piece in her mouth at once,' says Theo.

'You know that time when she heard Uncle Nick singing?' says Lotte. 'She put her hands over her ears and she kept shouting, "Stop, stop, you're going to break that song, Uncle Nick!"'

Luca clears his throat. 'Do you remember the time I say to her, "I love you"? And she reply, very satisfy with herself, "Yes, you love me!"'

Tears are running down Luca's cheeks. Chloe has her hands clasped tightly in her lap and she stares down at them. I can't see her face. I glance at Matt and Amy to see if this is going to break them. Amy tries hard to smile.

She says, 'Do you remember that time when I couldn't find my best bra? And then Ruby-May came back from the park with Daddy and she was wearing it!'

'Fastened at the front, with the boobs on her back,' says Theo, 'Daddy hadn't noticed she was wearing a lacy pink bra. On the swings!'

'I tried to take it off her and she got very annoyed. She said it was her—'

'Rucksack,' shouts Lotte. 'And when you tried to put in on, in the bit for your boobs, you found a Peppa Pig plaster, a gummy bear and a toy stethoscope!'

My skin itches with dried sweat; my hair is sticky with it. I haven't shaved for two days and my stubble prickles. I could do with a shower. And I'm not sure I can listen to one more story about my dead niece. I raise a glass to my sister, who is laughing and crying at the same time, and to her husband, and I force myself to sit down, to take a piece of cake. I feel a complete tool, now that the anger has drained from me as suddenly as it had sprung up. Christ, today of all days I had to be such a monumental wanker.

'I'm sorry,' I say, to no one and everyone.

Matt grunts.

'We forgive you,' says Lotte and grins at me, her smile gappy where she's lost a tooth.

I let my shoulders relax and perch on the corner of the chair Theo's in and he leans companionably against me. Without the candles, it seems even darker. I wonder if my father is still upset with me, and then I feel guilty for thinking that, even if he is, he'll have forgotten what I said to him soon. *Hopefully.*

Strike while the iron is hot, I think. Otherwise, with my shit memory, I'll probably forget. How ironic: forgetful son forgets to make dementia appointment for father. If Bethany wants, she can take him. I go inside and google 'private hospital', 'Bristol' and 'Memory Clinic'. The first hit I get is for a private facility on the outskirts of the city. It's called The Castle. I feel an overwhelming sense of relief. So Bethany had taken Dad, and he'd remembered enough to write it down in his journal. *Thank God.*

Perhaps because it's not NHS, the phone is answered immediately and within seconds I'm transferred to the Memory Clinic. A voice as warm and smooth as caramel assures me that my phone call is of the utmost importance and, although no one is in reception at the moment, if I leave a message, someone will get back to me as soon as possible. I'm an idiot; it's Saturday evening, of course there will be no one there. I leave a message requesting a follow-up appointment for my father. I give his full name and date of birth, and my mobile phone number.

'Bethany,' I say out loud, when I rejoin them. 'Did she go to the *festa* after all?'

Chloe looks at me and then away. Bethany's anger can be incandescent, but the good thing about her is that she never holds grudges and bounces back quickly.

'I haven't seen her since lunchtime,' Amy says. She sounds tired. 'I thought she was sulking in her room. Or drinking in that bar at the top of the road.'

'Wasn't she with you?' Matt asks me.

'You told me to get out, if you recall.'

'I meant, get out of the way for a few minutes, so we could calm down and clear up. I didn't mean for you to disappear all afternoon. Bee left the house when you did. With you,' he adds pointedly.

I jump up and snap on the outside light and we all blink in the glare. I go inside and knock on her bedroom door, then push it open. She's not there. I check every room, and the shed in the garden.

Lotte and Theo trail after me, calling in sing-song voices, 'Bethany, where are you?'

Luca looks inside his apartment and comes out, shaking his head.

'She's probably at the *festa*,' says Matt. 'I wouldn't worry about it. Right, you two monkeys, it's time to have a big, bubbly bath and hit the hay.'

'But we haven't had any tea! Or lunch,' protests Theo.

'You've had cake,' says Matt.

'And many, many snacks,' adds Luca.

I don't look at him. It's bad enough acting like an utter tosser in front of your family, without a stranger witnessing it too.

Chloe shrugs. 'Can I go to the *festa* too?'

Matt shakes his head. Chloe slouches off to her room, but she knows him well enough not to push him. I guess she's annoyed Matt wouldn't let her hang out with Carlo and his friends and watch the fireworks.

'The last time I saw her today was at lunch,' I say, echoing Amy.

I can't remember whether Bethany left before I did, because all that I can dredge up is my rage and shame, and the incessant chop of the knife that Amy had been wielding.

My sister calls Bethany, but it goes to voicemail.

'Nick? What's going on?' asks my father.

He's sitting at the table, his hands resting on the wooden surface. His wrist bones, jutting from his shirt cuffs, are bony, and his hands are flecked with age spots. He looks forlorn and I think how lonely old age is; even in the midst of family, even surrounded by others, he is isolated, as powerless as a child, but without the vitality. He is no longer the leviathan he once seemed to me.

'We don't know where Bethany is.'

'She's probably in her room. Or out. She always was a party girl,' he says.

Not any more, I think. Her towering ambition and rigid self-discipline put an end to that.

I go back and stand in the doorway of her bedroom, as if I believe him. It smells sweet, of her breezy, floral perfume. Her clothes are strewn across the floor, workout bras drying on the back of a chair. And then I see her phone lying on top of the bed. The hairs on the back of my neck stand on end. I can't imagine Bethany ever leaving her mobile on purpose. Usually she's surgically attached to it.

Amy is in the sitting room, looking forlorn.

'Where is Bethany?' she says. She sounds fretful. 'She should be here. She would be, if you hadn't shouted at her. I know she can be self-absorbed, but really this isn't like her. Not when it's Ruby-May's—'

'Matt's right. Bee's probably at the *festa*. She said she wanted to go. Or at that bar at the vineyard up the road, like you said, and she's lost track of time. You remember when she was Chloe's age? Dad wouldn't let her go to a party at James Mason's farm. His parties were legendary. All that cider. You'd left home already. Bee propped a ladder against the wall and climbed out of her bedroom window. Came home for breakfast. Dad hadn't even realized she'd gone.'

'Yes, I remember,' Amy says, smiling. 'I guess she wouldn't hear her phone at the *festa*.'

'She didn't take it with her. It's in her room.'

She stares at me.

'That's really not like her,' Amy says slowly.

'No. And she doesn't drink much these days,' I add.

'She does have blowouts now and again, when it all gets too much for her – you know, the endless push-ups and early starts. Perhaps today was the day.'

'Maybe.'

The most likely explanation is that Bee accidentally forgot her phone and is nursing one glass of wine and a tall soda in some cafe. I tell Amy I'm going to go and see if I can find her. It's a tiny place. How hard can it be? I check the bar in the vineyard. Carlo is there and gives me a wave that looks friendly to his mates, but which I can tell is actually aggressive. *Macho little shit.* I wonder, not for the first time, what the hell he was doing in our house the other day. And with my niece.

As I approach the town, the roads are so clogged with abandoned cars that I leave ours on a grass verge. Music is pumping from the hill, and bright lights, fluorescent green and orange, illuminate the fortress walls. Fireworks explode across the sky, chrysanthemums of incandescent white and iridescent purple. I walk along the beach: the palm trees are lit up with garish green LEDs, their leaves whip in the wind; the damp sand is cool underfoot and a skim of surf freckles my face. Half-naked teenagers are snogging and splashing in the shallows. The sea is black and choppy, snarled with cross-currents; I wouldn't fancy anyone's chances if they slipped in. I can't see Bethany.

On the other side of the promenade is the street leading to the supermarket, and on the corner is the *stazione di polizia*. The windows are sealed with iron shutters. I try the door, but it's locked, just as Amy said it would be. I head up the hill towards the castle, pressing myself through the throng. The music and the boom of the fireworks rattle in my ribcage. Dark alleyways spiral from the main route up to the top of the fort and I try to peer into them, but I'm carried onwards by the mass of people heading for the square.

The piazza is crowded; there's a stiff breeze rising from the sea and most of the Italians are seated, on the steps of the fountain, round the bars and cafes or at long trestle tables. There's a large marquee with a knot of holidaymakers at the entrance; those emerging are carrying plates of chips, roast chillies, focaccia, ciabatta, bowls of shellfish. The air is pungent with fried garlic and there's the greasy smell of cooking oil, seared meat and hot dogs; my stomach rumbles and I realize that, apart from a slice of chocolate cake, I haven't eaten since breakfast. The old men we saw previously are still there, sitting by the giant chess set, drinking Grappa, only now small children weave in and out of the pieces, hiding behind pawns and rooks. There's a carousel with chairs on metal chains swinging out as the ride spins; the children on board scream. Light bulbs above them flash on and off, illuminating the sign on the front: *Lasciate ogni speranza o voi che entrate*. Whatever the hell that means.

I climb onto the stone wall round the edge of the square, trying to ignore the drop of several feet to the streets below. I scan the crowds slowly. There's a West African man selling shells and cheap sunglasses from a tray around his neck. I'm looking for my tall, handsome sister, who has long brown hair, but almost everyone here is dark-haired, and the square is packed.

It's the walk that's familiar: a man with a broad chest and a spring in his step, surrounded by a group of other young people. *Joe?* Could it be Joe? I can't see his face, but as he moves away, I catch sight of the man's dark, curly hair. I thought Joe left early this morning. Had he stayed on?

'Joe!' I yell and wave my arms. 'Joe!'

The man turns towards me, as if he's responding to his name being called, but I can't tell – he might be too far away to hear me. I jump down, and now I can't see him at all. I haven't seen Bethany, either, although I suppose it's not surprising as there are so many people here. I'm about to push through the crowds to see if it really is Joe, when I notice two policemen heading towards me.

They halt, now that I'm no longer a public liability, standing on top of a national monument, and they're losing interest already, but I elbow my way through the Italians and I seize one of them by the arm.

'Please,' I say. '*Prego.* We've lost someone.' I feel a bit ridiculous. After all, Bethany's only been gone for an afternoon and an evening. I have no proof that she's missing, other than her phone, left behind on her bed, and the fact that I can't imagine Bee missing the whole of Ruby-May's anniversary, no matter how cross she was with me.

The older one shrugs, as if to say, *Haven't we all?* The other, the younger one whose sleeve I grabbed, puts his head on one side.

'It's my sister,' I say.

'From here?' He gestures to the square with his chin. 'How old?'

'Thirty-four,' I tell him and the urgency fades from his expression. 'I don't know if she came here. She left our holiday house by *il cavalluccio marino* sometime this afternoon. We haven't seen her since.'

He taps his ear. 'Is loud. We go.' I follow him out of the square and under the lee of the fortress wall. It's only marginally quieter. The older police officer stands a couple of feet away, as if to distance himself, and watches the revellers making their way up to the piazza.

'I am Agente Marco Martelli. My colleague is Agente Alessandro Pianozzi. Tell me what happen. Why you worry about her?' Martelli takes out a notepad and a pen. He's young – younger than me – with grey eyes, dark hair and a thick, bristly moustache. He nods as if he knows the place, when I say we're staying at *Maregiglio*.

I tell him it's not like Bethany to leave her phone behind, or not to tell us where she is. The other officer must have sharp ears because he interrupts, 'She like a drink, a party. She come back.' He gives a lugubrious shrug. 'She is the grown woman.'

Martelli nods. 'Agente Pianozzi is correct, no? It is not an emergency. And you can see, we have many, many people here and on the island, and there is only we two. The *stazione di polizia* is closed. But I say you, if she don't return by midnight and you still have the concern, you call to me. I go to the ferry, I watch the last boat leave – it is one or two of the morning – and then I come to the holiday house. She is not back by the breakfast time, we telephone to the *Carabinieri* in Grosseto. They cannot come any earlier.'

'Who?' I ask.

'The *Carabinieri*. They are the important police. We are only the small town *polizia*.' He hands me his card, points to his mobile number and taps the notepad. 'I have your details, Signor Flowers.'

The older officer speaks to Martelli in Italian and he nods gravely at me and they return to the piazza. They look supremely unconcerned. One of the barmen leans over the heads of the Italians crowded around his counter and hands both police officers an espresso.

30
AMY

She runs to the door when she sees the lights of the hire car, but Nick is on his own. He shakes his head when he gets out.

'I spoke to a police officer,' he says. 'Agente Martelli. He'll be here between one and two a.m. if Bethany doesn't come back before then.'

'What the hell for?' Matt says. 'You Flowers – making everything into a drama. She'll be propping up a bar somewhere.'

'I hope you're right,' Nick says. 'But just in case... have you looked round here?'

'I walked up to the terrace cafe in the vineyard,' she tells him. 'I saw Carlo and his friends.'

'Yeah, so did I.'

'They were about to head to the *festa*. She wasn't with them, and he said he hadn't seen her.'

'Do you believe him? Do you think he might have had something to do with it?'

'Carlo? Not likely, is it? You both saw him in the bar. I'm going to bed.' Matt yawns and kisses Amy on the cheek.

Luca and her dad have already gone to their rooms and the children are finally asleep. She makes a pot of coffee and takes it out to the pool. She lights candles and brings out rugs.

Nick can't sit still. He paces round the house and she hears him calling for Bethany, sees the flicker of his torch skittering through the olive trees.

In spite of her unease and the caffeine, she must have drifted off, because when she looks around, she's on her own, her shoulders stiff. There are voices coming from the kitchen. She runs in. Nick is talking to a young police officer in the sitting room.

'Agente Marco Martelli,' he says, shaking her hand. 'I am sorry about your sister. I hope it is only she is having too much fun.'

The man looks tired; he's pale and there are dark shadows under his eyes. They sit at the kitchen table and the officer listens to Nick describing what happened during the day. Martelli checks the details against what he's already written in his notebook, rubbing his moustache. She notices he has a scar through one eyebrow.

'Is there anything else you can explain me? Anything that is suspicious.'

'Yes,' says Amy, joining the men. 'Our iPad was stolen.'

Nick shakes his head. 'It was here. I found it.'

'Yes, but we'd searched everywhere for it. I'm sure someone took it.'

'And then he puts it back?' Martelli asks. He snaps his notepad shut. 'Your sister is probably having the party. She forget to take her phone. She does not have your number in here,' he taps his head, 'so she cannot call to you. But if she does not come here in the morning, you say me, and I telephone to the *Carabinieri*. It will take them one, two hours to reach here from the mainland, from Grosseto. After she has been missing for the whole day, they will come.' He shrugs. 'Probably.'

Nick is about to protest, but his shoulders sag and he shakes Martelli's hand. They watch the officer drive away, the headlights flickering as the car bumps over the rough track.

'We should try and get some rest,' says Amy.

Nick nods. 'She'll be toasting Ruby-May somewhere,' he says. 'Grieving in her own way.' He pats her shoulder.

Amy stands for a moment, looking into Bethany's room, her unmade bed, the curtains still open, stirring faintly in the breeze. Bethany's clothes are strewn around the room, her sports bra hooked over a chair, Lycra leggings trailing like shed snakeskin. Make-up and bottles of suncream and body oil litter her chest of drawers. Next to her bed is a glass of water, a novel and a phial of blue sleeping tablets. It smells of her perfume and suntan oil, as if she's only stepped out for a moment.

She's spent the past year being angry with her sister: if only Bethany hadn't taken those work calls on a Saturday afternoon; if only she hadn't asked their father to look after their daughter. But Bethany has finally persuaded her that their father does have dementia and that it wasn't his fault. As the police had told her after the post-mortem, it was a tragic accident. Amy has also missed her sister, and this holiday has brought them closer again. She thought Bethany felt the same way. Would she really have gone out and got drunk instead of being here, with her, for Ruby-May's anniversary? Amy finds it hard to believe, and unease and anxiety gnaw at her. She climbs the stairs to their bedroom with an effort. She's so tired she can hardly keep her eyes open, although she doesn't think she'll be able to sleep.

16 AUGUST, ITALY

31
NICK

My heart is hammering in my chest and I only have a moment to wonder what woke me, when the banging on the front door starts up again. I stumble downstairs, stubbing my toe in my haste.

It's Martelli. It's still dark outside and I can't see his expression. I feel as if my bowels have liquefied. There's only one reason why a police officer who had been so uninterested would be back here before midday.

'Have you found Bethany?'

'Can I come in?'

I step back to let him into the sitting room. The shadows under his eyes have darkened to purple and there's stubble across his jawline. The white scar through his eyebrow seems more pronounced.

'She is still missing?'

I give a curt nod. Something curdles in my stomach.

'I have a call about a young woman on the beach near to here,' Martelli says. 'I go, I see her. She look like how you describe your sister: she has the long dark hair, is around one metre seventy, slim.'

'How old is she? Is she English?'

'I do not know.'

'Is she okay? What happened?'

'I think someone has attack her. She is unconscious,' Martelli says. 'I find her lying in the sand. I telephone to the paramedics and they take her to the hospital. She is in the critical condition. I go now, but I come here first, to check if your sister has returned or you have the phone call from her.'

'No, I haven't heard from her. I'll come with you.'

I drag on some jeans and grab my wallet and phone. Matt and Amy must be exhausted: they've slept through Martelli pounding on the door, and there's no sign of anyone else, apart from me. Martelli is waiting impatiently, pacing up and down the drive, the stones crunching beneath his feet.

We drive at breakneck speed along the narrow roads, the wind whistling through the open windows. I feel sick, but I'm not sure if it's fear of what we'll find in the hospital, or being hurled round tight bends in the dark. I clutch my phone in one sweating palm, but I decide not to call Amy and Matt until I've seen who it is. I don't want to worry them even more.

When we reach the town, we pass the supermarket and turn down a small road leading away from the beach and its empty, litter-strewn promenade, to what looks like the start of an industrial estate. Martelli slams on the brakes, leaving the Punto at an angle outside the front of a low, whitewashed building with iron grilles across the windows. It's hardly what I'd call a hospital, more like a glorified doctor's surgery. I follow him in. The waiting room is crowded with men who look as if they've had too much to drink and got into scraps, scrapes or fallen down a flight of steps. Martelli speaks to a nurse at the reception desk and then gestures to me to follow him. We head down a short corridor and into a small ward on the right-hand side, with a single occupant. She's lying on her back and she's very still. With her dark hair spread across the crisp white sheets, she makes me think of Sleeping Beauty.

And then my stomach drops away with a sickening jolt.

It's Bethany.

I stumble towards her, but stop short. There's a bandage round her head; one side of her face is swollen and purple.

'It is your sister, Betany?' Martelli can't pronounce the 'th' in her name.

'Yes.'

Martelli speaks to a male nurse, who unhooks a clipboard with notes that's attached to the end of the bed. He says something to the officer, gesticulating expansively.

I call Amy. Her voice is thick, furred with sleep.

'Nick? Where are you?'

'I'm in the hospital with Agente Martelli. Bethany is here. She's – she's unconscious.'

I wait for the news to sink in. She'll be thinking this is my fault, and she'd be right. If I hadn't lost my temper...

'Oh my God, oh my God. What's happened? Is she okay?'

'I don't know. I'll call you as soon as I know more.'

I should reassure her, or something, but I can't think of what to say. I mean, Martelli said she's in a critical condition, she's unconscious. But telling Amy that won't help.

'I'll call you,' I repeat and hang up.

'*Va bene*,' says Martelli, turning to me. 'It is time to call the *Carabinieri*. They come soon, I hope. The nurse, he cannot speak English. The doctor tell to you what happen. I am sorry, Signor Flowers.' He puts a hand on my shoulder.

'Hang on!' I say, when I realize he's leaving.

'The doctor will say to you,' he repeats, taking out his mobile.

I go over to Bethany and sit down next to her. I'm ashamed at how hard I find this, how hard it is to look at her face, once so lovely, now so altered. One eye is sealed shut, the lid puffed and puce. Her lips are cracked and the bottom one is split. The bandage is wrapped tightly around her forehead and I don't want to think of what it conceals. I take her hand. It's dry and cool. I can't remember the last time we held hands. Nearly twenty years ago, I suppose. Hers looks so small in mine and I have a feeling of slipping, of dislocation; Bethany has always been my big sister: robust, fiery, fierce, strong. Now she seems small and fragile.

The nurse returns with a doctor. He introduces himself as Roberto Virgili. He's in his mid-forties, his hair is threaded with silver and his eyes are light grey. He gestures to me to follow him.

'*Allora*,' he says, once we're in his office. He sits behind his desk, and indicates a chair for me. 'Your sister is found on a beach, near *il cavalluccio marino*. She is unconscious. She has been hit on the side of the head with a rock. We bring her into the hospital this morning and we examine her. We do not know who attack her. Agente Martelli has called to the *Carabinieri*, and a *Maggiore* will come here soon from Grosseto.' He puts his notes back down on the desk and says, 'Your sister may bleed to her brain from this injury.' He taps the side of his own head. 'We have to keep the close look to her, and she may need to go for the CT scan on the mainland. As you can see, Signor Flowers, this is the small hospital. We do not have the equipment we want.'

'What does that mean? If she has blood in her brain?'

'It mean she could have the seizure. Is serious. She can die. Can happen fast, like that.' He clicks his fingers and I wince. 'We hope that her head does not bleed inside from the trauma of the blow, or that the bleed is small. We hope she will recover in a few days.' He spreads his hands and shrugs. 'We cannot tell at this precise moment. Even the CT scan will not help yet; it is too early to say what happen. So we wait and we look. She go to Grosseto tomorrow, if she need the scan. Or she stay here one more day, two days maybe, go home with you, have the scan in England. We must watch, because she could have the seizure at any moment.'

The palms of my hands are clammy and I wipe them on my jeans. I need Amy here, I'm not the right person for this. I don't know what I should be asking. Amy ought to bring Luca with her. He could speak to Dr Virgili in Italian and maybe we'd have a better understanding of what he's trying to say. I'm jiggling my foot up and down; the laces of my Converse are ragged and dirty at the ends and there's a sticky stain on one toe, where Lotte spilt ice cream on me. I push my knee down to stop myself.

'There is something else, Signor Flowers.'

I shrivel inside. I want to tell him to stop, to wait for my sister, because I don't want to hear whatever he has to say.

'When she arrive to the hospital we ask if she has been sexually assaulted,' he says.

I close my eyes and grip the armrests of the chair.

'She is completely dressed.'

I let go and release the tension from my shoulders. I realize I was holding my breath.

'Who found her?'

He shrugs as if this is not important. 'A holidaymaker out for the walk. But,' he continues, 'when we examine her later, we find she has anal fissures. This injury is consistent with the rape.'

I don't want to hear this about my sister. I can't sit still any more. I get up and go and stand by the window. My pasty-white reflection stares back at me.

'I don't understand. You said she wasn't sexually assaulted.'

Dr Virgili inclines his head. 'I cannot say for sure. Because she had the clothes on, we do not check exactly when she arrive to the hospital. It can be she was rape last night, or it was another time, very recent. Maybe she say yes, or yes at first, but it is extremely forceful sexual intercourse. You understand?'

I think I'm going to be sick.

'For now, your sister needs rest. You can see her later.'

I burst out of his office, dragging lungfuls of chilled air. I stand in the corridor and look through the window of the ward at my sister, lying motionless in the bed, her head bound in bandages.

My mobile rings and I fumble to answer it, in case it's Amy.

'Mr Flowers?'

It's a man, with a cultured English accent.

'Yes?'

'I'm calling from The Castle. I'm one of the consultants – Simon Golding – and I picked up your message this morning. Is this a convenient time to talk?'

I can't think fast enough. There's probably some rule about not using your mobile in a hospital unless it's an emergency, and now is hardly the time to discuss my father's next appointment at the Memory Clinic. Golding takes my silence for assent.

'You phoned regarding your father, Professor David Flowers.'

'That's right,' I say. 'But—'

'The receptionist is not here, so I thought I'd call straight away, save you worrying over the weekend.'

'Worrying?'

'Yes. I'm afraid you have the wrong number. Your father has not been to visit the Memory Clinic at The Castle. Perhaps it was another facility near Bristol? There's a BUPA hospital in Henleaze – the Spire?'

'Are you sure? It was about a year ago. He has a note of it in his diary.'

'Well, you're right, he did visit The Castle,' Simon Golding says.

'Oh. Then...' I'm confused. I glance back at Bethany, but my sister is still unconscious.

'His appointment was not at the Memory Clinic. He had, let me see—' I can hear the click of keys as he types – 'yes, there we go, a routine medical examination, and he was pronounced in the best of health for a man of his age. However, if you are concerned about his mental health or his memory in any way, then I'd be happy to book an appointment for him. Or you could call back on Monday to arrange a follow-up medical.'

'I see. What date was the medical?'

'Our records show it was the twenty-eighth of August, just over a year ago.'

'Mr Golding, can I call you back?'

'Certainly. You have our number. We'll be happy to hear from you or your father.'

'Thanks.'

I hang up and look back through the window at Bee. The one person who can explain why my father had a medical and not a mental-health check, and then lied about it, is unconscious in a foreign hospital and may die, because someone hit her on the head with a rock.

32
NICK

The men in the waiting room sit, their faces and hands caked with dried blood, legs outstretched or knees splayed apart. I trip over feet, and a guy curses me; the room smells of alcohol and sweat. I yank open the front door and even though it's still early, the heat hits me like it's solid. I crouch in the shadow of the building, but there's little respite. The temperature and smell, the lack of food and sleep are making me nauseous. I've had five missed calls and several texts from Amy.

'How is she?' Amy asks as soon as she answers the phone.

I explain as briefly as I can what Dr Virgili told me, minus the bit about the sexual assault. 'Can you bring Luca with you? We need someone who can speak Italian.'

'He left this morning to see his family. He said he'd postpone his trip, when he heard what had happened to Bethany, but I told him to go. I didn't want him to miss seeing them – he only has a few more days free before he has to be back for a meeting with his supervisor. He said to say goodbye and he'll see you in Bristol.'

We're both silent for a moment and I can hear Lotte and Theo's high-pitched voices in the background.

'I'll come now. I'll leave the children with Matt,' she says. She's slurring her words, she's so tired. 'It would be too upsetting for them to see her in hospital.'

♜

The blinds are half-open and I can see the glories of the hospital car park: bleached concrete and dusty cars, the sun blinding where it razors off wing mirrors, a metal waste bin piled with Peroni cans. I continue to pace up and down the waiting room, falling over injured men's outstretched loafers, as I drink a warm can of Coke from a vending machine in the corner. It doesn't make me feel any better; my stomach churns. Every time a nurse approaches the reception desk, I hope it's going to be news that Bethany has regained consciousness, but so far no one has called me over.

Our dusty hire car screeches to a halt on the road outside the hospital. A Lamborghini hybrid purrs behind it and stops smoothly in the car park. Two men get out. They're wearing navy trousers with a red stripe down the side, knee-high boots, dark caps and they have a white strap over their pale-blue shirts, which I realize, with a start, is what holds their guns. They arrive at the door to the hospital at the same time as Amy and courteously gesture for her to enter first.

I hug Amy and then step in front of the *Carabinieri*.

'Are you here to see Bethany Flowers?'

'*Si*. Who are you?'

I introduce myself and Amy.

The man shakes our hands. 'Maggiore Gianni Ruggieri, and this is my colleague, Capitano Antonio Biondi.'

Ruggieri has a crew cut, greying at the sides and slightly longer on top, pale-brown eyes and heavy brows.

When we try and go to the ward where Bethany is, the male nurse stops us. There's a heated discussion, with much arm-waving. Amy catches sight of our sister through the window and puts her hand over her mouth. Dr Virgili appears and listens for a moment, then gestures to the *Carabinieri* to go into his office. He takes one of Amy's hands in both of his.

'Signora Flowers. I am sorry. Your sister is still unconscious. If she wakes, the *Maggiore* will interview her and, we hope, catch who did this to her. So now, you wait, or you come back later. Visiting hours are in the evening, but, of course, we make the exception for you – if she regain consciousness, you can see her immediately.'

I steer Amy back to the waiting room.

'Why did he say "if"?' she asks, sounding panic-stricken. '*If* she regains consciousness?

I buy us both lattes in plastic cups from the machine and explain what Dr Virgili told me.

'She could die? We need to get her a CT scan right away. We have to go to the mainland!'

'He says the bleed might not show up yet and he's got to keep her here and observe her. If she needs one, she can travel tomorrow.'

Amy thinks for a moment. 'We've only got the villa until ten a.m. tomorrow, and the ferry, the train, the flights – they're all booked! Who could have done this to her?'

'I'll stay on with Bethany, take her to the mainland if she needs a scan.'

'Signora Flowers?' It's the other officer, Biondi. 'We will take your statement now. You will be next,' he says to me. 'Please. This way.'

Amy follows him into Dr Virgili's office.

33
NICK

It's midday. Bethany still has not regained consciousness. We've come back to the holiday house to try and work out what to do. Matt is googling flights to see if they can change theirs, as well as looking for places to stay. I've been half-watching *Blade Runner 2049* on my iPhone to distract myself. I already know most of the script off by heart: *Pain reminds you the joy you felt was real.*

'It's not looking hopeful,' Matt says. 'There aren't enough flights for all of us to go back later, and I can't find anywhere big enough for six or seven people. There's only one hotel and it's fully booked.'

Dad and the children are watching a DVD, although he's fallen asleep, in spite of the dragons and the explosions. Chloe is curled up on the sofa next to them, her arm round Lotte, looking like a child again. I notice a book, the pages curled back, sticking out from under the chess set. I slide it out. It's Dante's *Divine Comedy.* Luca must have left it behind. I've just started flicking through it when I hear the crunch of tyres.

It's a Lamborghini. I let the two officers in, and introduce the *Maggiore* and the *Capitano.*

'This is Matt Jenkins, Amy's husband and my brother-in-law. My dad, David Flowers; Chloe Jenkins-Yu, Matt's daughter; the kids are his and Amy's: Theo and Lotte.'

'No one else is here?' asks Ruggieri.

He's softly spoken and it's a polite enquiry, but there's something about him – his height, his military bearing, maybe the weapon he's carrying – that makes it seem like a threat. I shake my head, but I add that we also had Luca and Joe staying with us, and why they'd left the island. He nods impatiently – Amy must have told him this already.

'My wife is upstairs,' Matt says.

'Is that a real gun?' asks Theo.

'The *pistola*. We have the Beretta AR70 in the car,' Ruggieri says.

'Cool!'

'Coffee?'

'*Si. Grazie*.'

Amy comes downstairs, her face pinched with worry.

'Do you have any idea who could have done this to my sister?'

'We investigate.'

I put the kettle on and set out the cafetière. 'The photos!' I say. I'd completely forgotten.

'What photos?' Amy asks.

'I saw some creepy pictures of Chloe, when I found her iPad after it had gone missing. I meant to say, but… well, there was the anniversary, and then Bethany disappeared. They looked as if Chloe didn't know she was being photographed, but I wasn't sure. Sorry, I'm an idiot. I should have told you earlier.'

'What were you doing looking at my iPad?' Chloe asks, sitting up and pushing Lotte off her.

'Sorry, Chlo. I saw them accidentally when I found your iPad and I opened it to check it was okay. I was going to ask you.'

'And this is relevant?' asks Ruggieri.

I shrug. 'It's suspicious. Maybe whoever took them might have been responsible for attacking Bethany.'

'Show me.'

Chloe sullenly opens Photos on her iPad and passes it over to the *Maggiore*.

'Who is this?' Ruggieri asks, pausing over the one of Chloe and Carlo goofing around at his farm.

'Carlo Donati,' Chloe says.

'His family rented the holiday house to us,' Matt explains. 'All our dealings with the Donatis have been through Carlo.'

'Did you see him on the day that Betany goes missing?'

Amy starts to speak. 'In the evening, at the terrace bar in the vineyard—' when Chloe cuts across her.

'Yes.'

There's a pause as we all look at her.

'Turn that down,' Matt snaps at the children.

'I saw him in the afternoon. He tried to persuade me to go to the *festa* with him and see the fireworks. I thought about it,' she adds, looking defiantly at Matt, 'but then I came back here.'

'Where does Carlo go?' asks Ruggieri.

She shrugs. 'He said he was going to meet his friends.'

'You did not see Betany?'

'Of course she—' Matt says, but Chloe interrupts again. 'Yeah. I did.'

'You saw Bethany?'

She looks ashamed. 'We bumped into her. She was walking through the olive grove. She told me to go home. I got angry and I shouted at her.' Chloe starts crying, and Lotte gives her a sloppy kiss on the cheek. 'I was going back anyway, and I didn't like her telling me what to do.'

'Christ!' Matt says. 'And you only thought to tell us now?'

'I didn't know she didn't come home or that anything had happened to her! And then, when I found out she'd been... I thought you'd be mad!'

'Leave her be,' Amy says to Matt, but her voice is gentle.

'What happen then?' asks Ruggieri.

'Nothing,' Chloe says. 'Bethany carried on walking. I stayed and talked to Carlo for a bit, and then he walked up the hill to meet his friends at the bar and I came back here.'

'Did Betany say where she go?'

'No.'

'What direction did she take?' asks Biondi.

'Does Auntie Bethany still have a sore head?' Lotte asks.

'Yes, love, she does.'

'That way.' Chloe points in the vague direction of the coast, away from the holiday house.

'What time was this?'

Chloe shrugs again. 'After lunch. Maybe between four and five o'clock. Can I go and see her?' she asks Amy, drying her eyes.

'I'll take you later,' I say.

I hand out coffees to everyone, including my dad, who's just woken up.

'Who are these gentlemen?'

'It could have been him – Carlo Donati,' Matt says.

Chloe's head snaps up.

'He was in the house once,' I say, 'as if he'd been upstairs and he wasn't expecting us to be here. And Dad's journal and Chloe's iPad went missing. Those photos – maybe he was spying on her.'

'Unless she know he takes them,' Ruggieri says, looking at my niece. Chloe flushes a deep pink and looks down at her hands. 'This journal and the iPad are not reported stolen. You say only missing and then you find them?' He turns his flat, hard gaze on me and I nod. 'It is his house. He come to check you are okay – you need anything. Three of you see him the afternoon your sister go missing. It is hard to believe he have the time to attack your sister. What is his motivation?' Ruggieri places his hands together in the prayer position and then pushes them out towards us in a sudden movement: 'Allora. We will speak with him and the famiglia Donati. We think it is most likely that your sister take a walk on the beach. She meet a drunk man, someone celebrating Ferragosto.'

'And that's it? You're not going to—' Amy says.

'We keep looking for the person who attack her, but I warn you, it is difficult. A lot of people here. People on holiday from the rest of Italy. There is no CCTV, apart from two cameras in the town centre. There is only the *polizia* – Martelli and Pianozzi you meet already. Now that *Ferragosto* is finished, everyone leave. When the people go, it is impossible.'

Amy, Chloe and I drive back to the hospital as soon as Ruggieri and Biondi have left.

Dr Virgili is waiting for us. 'She has regained consciousness,' he says, with a smile, ushering us into the ward.

Bethany opens her eyes as we burst in. The whites are bright red and I have to look away for a moment.

'Bee! Oh, thank God!' Amy's eyes fill with tears and she kisses her sister on the cheek.

'Hey,' Bethany says, and her voice is a guttural whisper.

'How are you feeling? What happened?'

Before Bethany can respond, Chloe throws her arms round her aunt, who does her best not to wince. Chloe cries noisily, and Bee strokes her head and gives us a half-smile. I stand about with my hands in my pockets, feeling like a spare part. Bethany's face looks worse than it did yesterday: her lips are swollen around the cut; her eye is so puffy she can barely open it; and the skin below her bandage down one side of her face is a livid red and grape-black. Where her hospital gown gapes, I notice twin bruises below her collarbone, as if a man's thumbs had pressed into her flesh. Who would do this to her?

'I don't know. I don't remember.' She swallows hard. It sounds as if it's painful for her to speak, and not just because of her lip.

'Do you want a drink of water?'

'Yes.'

The nurse helps her sit up and Bethany cringes as he hoists her up the bed.

The cut on her lip reopens and a bead of blood runs down her chin. I pass her a glass of water and a tissue from the bedside table. Her hand shakes as she tries to drink.

'Shouldn't she get her lip stitched?' Amy says.

Dr Virgili examines her face. 'No, is not necessary. No shouting or laughing,' he adds. He smiles at her and deep grooves appear in his cheeks.

The nurse presses a damp cloth against her mouth and indicates that Bethany should hold it there. The doctor takes out a pencil torch and shines it in one of her eyes, then the other.

'Do you have the nausea? You vomit on the beach, before we bring you in.'

'Yes, I feel sick.'

'And do you know what happen to you?'

'She said no, she can't remember,' I interject. I can't stand seeing Bethany struggling to speak.

'Okay, well, she is not – how you say it? – out of the woods. We monitor for the blood clot. For now, we leave you. Pull this cord if you feel bad: your head, you want to vomit. I give you some painkiller. Signor, Signorina, Signora, you must only remain with her for a few moments. She must rest.'

'It looks worse than it is,' Bethany whispers, after the doctor and the nurse have left.

Amy is practically wringing her hands, as she tells Bethany that they haven't been able to change their flights or find anywhere to stay.

'I said I'd take you to Grosseto for a brain scan, or fly home when the doctor gives you the all-clear, so you can go to the hospital in Bristol,' I say.

'If there's any doubt whatsoever, you get her off this island,' Amy repeats to me.

'I don't want to leave you,' Chloe says.

'I'll be fine. I've got Nick to look after me,' Bethany says.

'I should stay with you. Nick can fly home with the others,' Amy says.

'The kids need you, Ames,' I say.

I glance at Bethany and she does a small thumbs up in agreement with me.

After we've been there for quarter of an hour, the nurse comes in and tells us to go. I assume that's what he means, anyhow.

Chloe starts wailing that we can't let Bethany stay there on her own.

I clear my throat. 'Look, why don't you take Chloe for a drink? I'll sit with Bee for a bit, or in the waiting room when the nurse chucks me out, and then I can drive us all back.'

'Yes,' Bethany says. 'You should go out – it's your last night. Party! And you know Nick isn't likely to tire me with his non-stop chatting.'

Amy smiles tightly without looking at me, and the two of them kiss Bethany goodbye. 'I hate to leave you like this, but we'll see you in a day or two, as soon as you're ready to fly home,' she says.

After Chloe and Amy have gone, I wander round the small room until Bethany tells me I look like a caged animal in a zoo and I'm making her feel nauseous.

'A tiger?'

'More like a pygmy hippo,' she whispers and closes her eyes as if, when it's only me here, she doesn't have to pretend any more.

I sit next to her and fidget. I cross one leg over the other and then lean over my knees. I wish Maddison were here; she'd have known what to say. I can't recall why I ended our relationship now. She was nice. Is nice.

'Bee, can you remember who did this to you? Anything about him? Even a tiny detail, a scrap of information could give the police something to go on.'

'The police?' She opens her eyes and tries to look at me.

I move so that I'm in her line of sight.

'Yes. They'll want to interview you, now you're awake. Catch whoever did this.'

'I was walking along the beach. I don't remember anything else. Sorry, Nick.' She squeezes my hand.

'Nothing at all? His shoes, maybe? The colour of his shirt?'

A tear rolls down her cheek and I feel like a complete tool for pushing her. I'm useless at sounding sympathetic or even showing anyone how I feel.

After a few moments I say, without thinking, 'I miss Amy.'

Bethany clears her throat. 'She's only in the bar down the street.'

'I mean, I miss how she used to be. She was always kind, warm. Had time for me. For us. Like, she didn't even ask me anything after Maddison and I broke up, and that's not like her. Sorry. I'm a selfish twat.'

I do know Amy can't be that person any more. Obviously. I wish I hadn't said anything.

Bethany doesn't speak for a few minutes and then she says, 'We all miss our mum. That's the real problem.'

The nurse reappears and speaks sharply to me. When I don't respond, he holds the door open and looks as if he's going to drag me out by the scruff of my neck.

'I guess I've overstayed my welcome. I'll come back in the morning.'

I hesitate at the threshold. I want to ask her why she lied about the appointment she made for Dad at the hospital. I turn back, but Bethany closes her eyes as if she's exhausted. Something vital drains from her face and I remember what Dr Virgili said: she's not out of the woods yet.

17 AUGUST, ITALY

34
NICK

Amy and Matt seem even more tense than usual the following morning, as they attempt to pack and restore the holiday house to some sort of order. I decide to get out of their way and go and see if the *Carabinieri* have made any progress. I take a taxi into town. First, though, I check in at the local hotel – Dr Virgili knows the owner and put in a word for me, so at least I have a room for a couple of nights while Bethany is in hospital. It's round the corner from the *stazione di polizia*, so I walk over. A woman in her fifties is sitting at the reception and behind her I can see two police officers reading the paper, their boots on the desk, paper cups of coffee next to them. A radio crackles and splutters and a bluebottle makes small thumps as it hits the windowpane. There's no sign of Martelli, but I suppose he could be on his rounds or having a day off.

'*Prego?*'

'I'm looking for Maggiore Ruggieri and Capitano Biondi,' I tell her. I say it's in connection with Bethany Flowers.

'*Aspetti qui,*' she says, and heaves herself to her feet.

She knocks on an office door, and a moment later Ruggieri comes out and gestures for me go inside.

'Signor Flowers, please have a seat.'

I sit in front of his desk, or at least the one he's borrowed while he's on loan here. In the strip lighting, his eyes look even paler, and I notice that his fine nose is slightly bent, as if it had once been broken. He looks like Rupert Everett might, if he played football.

'The rest of your family go home, no?'

'Yes, they're heading off later this morning.'

'And your sister – how is she?'

'She needs a brain scan. Look, have you got anywhere? Who did this to her?'

There's a knock and Biondi elbows his way in, carrying three espressos.

I take one of the paper cups and thank him. He pulls a plastic pot of UHT milk out of his trouser pocket and hands it to me, as if he knows I'm not man enough to drink it black.

'We go back to Grosseto,' says Ruggieri.

'What?' I nearly spill my coffee. 'You've only been here twenty-four hours.'

'If it is a drunk during the *Ferragosto*, we have no hope to find him,' the *Maggiore* tells me. 'As I say you before – there is no CCTV, there are no witnesses, only Agente Martelli and his colleague, Pianozzi, on duty; a lot, a lot of people here. But I think, this is not what happen.'

The coffee without the milk is too hot and scalds my tongue. I set the cup down.

'What about Carlo Donati?'

Ruggieri pauses for a moment and then he says, 'I do not think so, no, Signor Flowers. He was with your step-niece, no? And then he walk to the bar on the top of the hill, where he takes a drink with his friends. His mother and father pick him up and drive him and his friends to the *festa* in the town centre. He is there with his family until the early hours of the morning. He has the alibi. He has the witness. He does not have the motive.'

'What about being in our house? Those photos he took of Chloe?'

'*Si*. The boy admit he look to your possessions, maybe move them a little, but he does not steal. He say that he and Chloe take the photo together.'

'He's admitted it? He told you he's been in our house? Looking through our things?'

Ruggieri speaks over me. 'Is his house. No crime has been committed.'

'It's trespass!'

'It is his family's house,' Ruggieri repeats. 'Nothing is missing. He is a teenage boy – looking to you because he is jealous of what you have and he has not. I think he and Chloe have a little...' He makes a gesture with his hands as if he is cupping a flower.

'Flirtation,' says Biondi.

I look from one to the other and open my mouth to protest, but before I can say anything, Ruggieri says, 'We believe that your sister is not attacked.'

'But...' I gape at him. 'She was hit on the head with a rock!'

He crosses one polished boot over his knee and leans back. 'This is what we think too. But it is also the same with a fall. She is drunk, she fall, she hit the head on a sharp stone. There are many, many where she is found, near to *il cavalluccio marino*. She took the Prosecco with her when she left the house. Your sister like to drink, no?'

'She liked a drink now and again – she was on holiday, for Christ's sake! But she's not in the habit of getting drunk enough to fall and hit her head.'

'How do you know? You say you are not with her. We say, she go for a walk to the beach. She drink. She fall. Is simple.' He takes a sip of coffee and leans towards me. 'She is not assaulted. She is found with the clothes. No sign of a struggle. Your brother-in-law, he tell me she drink a lot.'

'Only occasionally,' I say, frowning. 'What about her black eye?'

He raises his eyebrows at me. 'If you mean, the bruise here—' he points to his own eye – 'Dr Virgili say it is from when she hits the head. Sharp rock, it go through the skull here,' he points to his temple. 'The bone is thin, no? The blood go into her eye.'

I'm about to protest, to remind him of the other bruises she has, and then I have a sudden, horrible memory. I'm gripping Bethany, my thumbs digging into her skin just below her collar bone, my fingers pinching her arms, shaking her as I shout, "I will never forgive you!" I swallow uncomfortably. *I made those bruises.*

'Have you thought about the other people who were staying with us? Joe Hart, for instance?'

Traitor.

'You think Signor Hart hurt your sister? She employ him as her personal trainer, no?'

I remember Joe and Bethany had an argument the night before she was attacked, but he's hardly likely to have hit her. *Or did he?* In any case, he'd already left the island early the previous morning. *Hadn't he?* I think of the glimpse I had of the man who looked like him at the *Ferragosto festa*. Was I imagining it, or could it have been Joe? He might have stayed on after he'd left our holiday house.

When I don't reply, Ruggieri shrugs, dismissing me. 'We have to consider all the option. I have the details for the men who stay with you – Joe Hart and Luca Castaglioni. We speak with them on the phone. We know how to do our job, Signor Flowers.'

I feel like a balloon that's been punctured.

'Does Dr Virgili also think my sister simply fell and hit her head? And what about the... the sexual assault?'

'He agrees that it is possible she was not attacked,' says Biondi. I'm surprised at how good his English is: much better than his higher-ranking colleague's. He has an accent, as if he's spent time on the east coast of the States. 'No one tested your sister for blood alcohol levels, so we cannot be certain. Neither did the hospital staff check for semen, because she was fully dressed. The signs of the assault, as you refer to them, could be from consensual intercourse, or an incident that happened a few days ago. But as Maggiore Ruggieri says, there was no indication of a struggle, apart from the wound to her head and some bruising to her arms and chest. There is no evidence she was attacked. If she *had* been hit on the head, it is unlikely now that we will find who did it. Most of the holidaymakers have already left. In any case, she remembers nothing – apart from drinking. And, Signor Flowers, we know that your sister has a history of drinking to excess. We interviewed some of her former work colleagues at the BBC in London.'

The traitorous bastards. Bee once told me she was surrounded by people who'd stab their grandmother to get ahead, but I'd thought she was being overly dramatic.

Ruggieri looks at his watch and uncrosses his legs. 'Signor Flowers, we leave now. We hope that your sister is well soon. If she remembers anything, then you can call to me.'

He gives me his card and holds out his hand. I shake it, because I don't know what else to do, what else to say.

I walk across the road to the promenade, heading for the taxi rank at the far end. Although it's still early, a few Italians have already settled themselves on sun-loungers, angling parasols over their tanned bodies. There's a cool breeze from the sea; any other time, this would beat my usual morning of instant, hunched over a computer screen in a hot, dark studio.

I'm certain Bethany was attacked. Of course it might have been a random drunk, but could it have been someone else? I've got to get this right – bringing us all together on holiday in Italy hasn't worked; my family are still barely speaking to each other. I have to find out who did this to my sister, to us. Plus, I want my sister well enough to answer some hard questions.

If it was someone who knew Bethany, they would have been able to follow her without suspicion. *Joe Hart.* Ruggieri said he'd already eliminated him from his inquiries, but I can't be certain. Was it Joe in the piazza on the evening of the *festa*? And the night before he was supposed to have left, they had a huge row.

When the taxi drops me off at the port, I spot my family leaning against the people-carrier, looking hot and fed up. The ferry hasn't turned up yet – running on Italian time – and there's a jumble of cars clogging the road in the semblance of a queue. Sweat is trickling down my back. I wipe my face with my T-shirt, trying not to expose my scars.

'How's Bethany?' asks Amy, as soon as I approach them.

I don't want to admit I haven't gone to see her yet. 'Just been talking to Ruggieri,' I say. 'The *Carabinieri* are dropping her case. They're probably on the speedboat back to Grosseto as we speak.'

'What? Why? They can't do that!'

'They say she was drunk and fell and hit her head on a sharp stone.' I say it in a sarcastic tone, but my sister and brother-in-law don't react the way I expect.

Amy's face, crumpled with worry, seems to smooth, the way an iron chases the wrinkles from a shirt.

'Oh,' she says.

'Why aren't we getting on the ferry?' asks Theo, scuffing his toe in the sand and sending clouds of dust into the air.

'Wouldn't surprise me,' Matt says.

'I'm bored,' Lotte says. Her cheeks are flushed pink from the heat.

'We'll be going soon.' Amy smooths her daughter's flyaway hair where it's stuck to her forehead.

'Are you kidding?'

'Makes sense. She walked off with a bottle of booze.'

'I can't stand this any more.' Chloe pushes herself to her feet from where she's been slouched against the shaded side of the car.

'I want to get off this island right now. I'm not staying here one more minute!'

'You don't seriously think Bethany really drank a whole bottle of Prosecco? Got so drunk she fell hard enough to knock herself out?'

'What are we doing here?' asks my father.

The Italians, less patient with delays than the British, start to honk their horns. A few of them are milling about in the road, and a cloud of cigarette smoke drifts over us. Theo coughs theatrically.

Matt shrugs. 'Makes sense to me. I'd be plastered if I'd drunk that much. You're right,' he adds in a grudging tone. 'She doesn't normally drink that much, so she's probably not used to it. But she does go for it in a big way when she's stressed.' He looks pointedly at me.

Amy makes a face. 'Bee hadn't eaten anything, and in this heat... It was dark. It would have been easy to slip and fall. In a way it's a relief. How awful if she'd been attacked by someone.'

'But...' I say, and then remember I haven't told them about the sexual assault. The noise from the car horns is making it hard to think.

'That's it – I've had it!' Chloe strides away from us, her straight dark hair swinging down her back. She's in denim hot pants and she looks like a child-woman, simultaneously fragile and fierce, sexy and vulnerable.

'Chloe!' Matt calls after her as she heads towards the dock, where a handful of officials in navy uniforms, lounging on the quay, straighten and smile at each other. One takes the cigarette from his mouth and gestures towards her. It's not clear from this distance whether he's welcoming her or highlighting her salient features to the others.

'So that's it?' I say. 'You're just going to let the police fuck off back to wherever the hell they came from? Jesus, this is your sister we're talking about!'

'Nick!' Amy admonishes me.

'That's a rude word,' Lotte says.

'Two rude words,' says Theo.

Out of the corner of my eye, I notice my father ambling away, in the opposite direction to Chloe.

'Listen, mate,' says Matt. He's not looking at me, he's watching Chloe's progress as she weaves in between the cars. The ferry men adjust their sunglasses and smile, like sharks.

'Dad? Dad!' Amy calls after our father. 'Watch the kids, will you?' she says to Matt.

'Amy! Leave him! I need to get Chloe.'

There's a cheer as someone spots the ferry churning towards us, haloed by a cloud of seagulls, rainbows splintering from the spume.

'I'll fetch Granddad,' Theo says and races after Dad.

'Theo! Get back here! You need to get a grip,' Matt says to me. 'You – in the car, now,' he shouts at Lotte, who bursts into tears and starts screaming at him that she hasn't done anything wrong and it's too hot to sit inside. Matt's face has turned purple as he glances from Chloe, who is now surrounded by a knot of Italian men, to Lotte, who's stamping her foot and refusing to get in the roasting car, and then to Amy, who's running after Theo and Dad.

It's all suddenly become clear to me. Of course Matt would jump at this explanation – that Bethany was drunk and the police were dropping the case. He even *told* the police she was drunk. Because if my sister wasn't attacked by a stranger, or by Joe, who else could it have been? Who else knew where she was or where she might go? I feel as if the smoke and the car fumes are choking me. My sister. So lovely to look at; so unloved. Who else could have done this? Who else hated her? Amy doesn't like Bethany much, after what happened. Has my dad ever shown her any affection? To be honest, it's not like I'm that fond of her. Although maybe I need to work on that. I can't hear properly, as the horns continue to blare.

The heat seems to be making my head reverberate. *Matt.* Matt hates her. He pretty much said she was a *dumb bitch who could print her Drama Studies diploma on a supermarket receipt.*

'For the last time, get in the car,' Matt yells at his youngest daughter. A vein pulses in his forehead. He looks over his shoulder at Chloe, who has her hands on her hips and seems to be lecturing the men standing in front of her, who are nodding and smiling. Any minute now, one of them is going to reach across and touch her bare arm.

Matt grabs hold of Lotte and drags her towards the car. 'Come on! We'll be leaving in a minute. Chloe!' he bellows, and several Italians look from him to his beautiful daughter and back, as if they're at a tennis match.

I tell myself to stop being so ridiculous – accusing everyone in my family, plus my sister's personal trainer, of assault and battery – and jog over to Chloe. I mock bow and offer her my arm, as if I'm in a Jane Austen novel, and fortunately the sharks smile out of the sides of their mouths and my step-niece takes my elbow. I lead her back to the car and hug every member of my hot, sticky family. The ferry pulls away from the harbour, scattering seabirds in its wake. Sunlight winks from the cars on the deck. There's a clear, sharp light on the horizon, blinding in its beauty.

I wipe my forehead as I enter the comforting chill of the hospital and help myself to the water in the cooler by reception.

Bethany is awake and sitting up in bed.

'Nick!' She frowns at me. 'You look like shit.'

'Thanks. Glad I stayed on to check you're okay.' I slump into a chair by her bed. 'You're looking a bit better. Listen, can you remember anything? Anything at all about what happened?'

She looks up to her left as she thinks. The white of her eye is still red, and the bruising round her eye is turning yellow.

'I remember us arguing. I was so mad at you. I took that bottle of Prosecco from the fridge and marched up the hill. I saw Chloe and Carlo and I spoke to them briefly. I told her to leave that little jerk and get back home. She took it exceptionally well. I headed out to the cliff and I walked along there for a while. I watched the fireworks, and then I thought I ought to go back and face the music. I expected Amy would be angry at me for skipping Ruby-May's anniversary, but I hoped I hadn't missed all of it. I decided not to go back the way I'd come, though. I thought it would be quicker to head straight down the cliff path to the beach, the one along from *il cavalluccio marino*. I planned to walk along the sand and up the track to our holiday house. But I don't remember that part.'

'The police are going to drop the case. They say there's no evidence that you were attacked. That you could have fallen and hit your head. Ruggieri says you were drunk.'

She closes her eyes for a moment and doesn't say anything. I can't tell if she's angry or resigned.

'Come on, Bee! I know you. You wouldn't have drunk a whole bottle of Prosecco—'

She interrupts. 'I told them I was drunk.'

'What?'

'The *Carabinieri* asked if it was a possibility, and I said it was more like a probability.'

I'm dumbstruck.

'I hadn't eaten since breakfast. Plus I'd done all those sprints earlier. The alcohol would have gone straight to my head.'

I stare at her. She looks levelly back and she's so calm it unnerves me.

'So you're okay with them heading back to Grosseto?'

'Yes,' she says firmly.

I rest my elbows on my knees and drop my head into my hands. I wait until my pulse subsides. 'I don't get it. It's just... The doctor thought you might have been... raped.'

'Oh. That.'

I whip my head round and look at her in astonishment.

'Yeah. It hurt to sit down for a bit,' she wisecracks, and then she starts crying.

'Bee...'

I grab a tissue and thrust it at her, and then I hold her hand. I can't remember the last time I saw my sister cry. I don't even recall her crying when I fell from the top of the ruin in the garden and everyone was so mad at her, and she was only nine or ten.

She blows her nose and winces at the pain in her head.

'It was Stuart,' she says. She presses the tissue against her lip, which has started bleeding again.

'Stuart?'

'My executive producer.'

'Look, you don't have to talk about this now if you...'

'I've kind of been seeing him.' She glances at me. 'Yes, Nick, of course I know he's fucking married.'

I squeeze her hand. It's not like I'm in any position to judge, given what a shit I was to Maddison.

'Never in public. He wanted it to be a secret. He kept promising that he'd get me back on *The Show*. The exec was a mate of his. So he said.'

Tears are running down her blotched and bruised cheeks.

'So what happened?'

She takes a sip from the glass by her bed, and I hear the slow sound of her trying to swallow the water as if it's solid.

'It was the night before this Italian trip. We were in the studio after we'd finished filming the programme. Drinking a bottle of wine out of plastic cups. Got a bit drunk. And then – oh, you know how I can be. Told him he needed to make me a star. Annihilate Tiffany, the witch. Why wasn't I on *The Show*? He got annoyed. He said, "Bethany, your problem is you're smart without being intelligent, good-looking without being pretty, and approachable in a girl-next-door way, but no one in their right fucking mind would want to be your neighbour." So I said I'd tell his wife. Post a photo on Twitter.'

I shut my eyes to block out the images: plastic cups rolling on the floor, the dregs of wine spilling across the stain-free carpet; Bethany's face smashed into a Formica-topped table.

'The thing is, I did quite like him.'

I swing back round. 'If it was at work, there'll be CCTV of you leaving; a record of you clocking out; the security staff at the back gate – they'd have recognized you. Noticed if you were... upset.'

She shakes her head and then sucks her teeth. 'Not going to do that. His word against mine. End of my career.' She dries her face with the now sodden and bloodstained tissue.

I'm not sure what to say. All the time, this abuse had been going on and I never even knew, because I only ever looked at my sister's Instagram account, instead of actually speaking to her. And even I can see this is really not the right time to ask her about Dad's dementia appointment and why she lied about it. I'll do that tomorrow, I tell myself.

'Nick, get me out of here. I want to go home.'

'But...'

'Come on! The *Carabinieri* have left. I can have a check-up at St Michael's Hospital when we're in Bristol. I'll go mad if I have to keep staring at these four walls for a nanosecond longer.'

This sounds more like Bee. 'Okay,' I say. 'I'll ask Dr Virgili.'

'For God's sake, stop being such a limp dick and just book the fucking flights! If we leave tomorrow morning, I'll have been here for forty-eight hours, and that's enough time to make sure I'm not going to collapse and die of a brain haemorrhage and sue their sorry asses!'

'Glad to see you're getting better,' I say, hauling myself to my feet.

I'm about to take my laptop out of the hire car and go to a cafe that has Wi-Fi so that I can rebook the tickets, when I have a better idea. I grab a taxi back to our holiday house, but instead of turning along the path through the olive grove to *Maregiglio*, I ask the guy to drop me off at the beach. The barman is clearing tables. I go inside the wooden hut and take a ciabatta stuffed with salami and Pecorino. I leave some money on the counter. I almost grab a beer too, but think better of it.

The beach is practically deserted. I suppose most Italians will have gone home, now that *Ferragosto* is over, or else they will sensibly have returned to their villas for a siesta. Sweat trickles down my temples as I slog across the soft sand. The bay is so bright, it's like an over-exposed photograph. I would never have thought I could miss the cold, damp and drizzle of Bristol. I retrace Bethany's footsteps in my mind – up the hill through the olives and then across the hillside and down towards the cliff edge, before she descended to the next beach. If I keep walking until I'm past the headland, I'll come to the spot where Bethany was found.

I'm not really sure why I'm here. To achieve *closure*, as Maddison would say? One minute everyone is accusing a drunk bloke of attacking my sister, and now they all believe she was the drunk. I guess I want to see it for myself. Put my mind at rest. Move on. I climb up onto the flat rocks at the far end of the beach; the heat sears my feet, even through my sandals. The tide is halfway up the sand, lapping at the base of the cliff, but it's low enough that I can climb over the jagged edges. The stone scrapes my toes, drawing blood. I cling to the cliff, my palms burning, and clamber round. I've reached the other beach. It's a thin spit of white sand at the base of the cliffs; a jumble of dead seaweed and sea-bleached plastic, tangled at the tidemark. There's no cafe or sun-loungers, no road down to it, only a crooked path that cuts steeply through the stone down to the shore: the route my sister took. I jump off the rocks and walk a little further. At some point, between here and *there*, is where it happened.

Did someone attack her? A drunk Italian who hated the idea of foreigners on his island? A sexual predator? Joe? Or are the police right, and she simply got drunk and fell over? I squint against the sun. The cliff looks lethal, even if one weren't tipsy. Bethany must have collapsed above the line of brackish debris, or else, when the tide came in, she'd have drifted out to sea and drowned. I shudder at the thought. I scan the ground as I walk. Ruggieri is correct about one thing: the stones here are sharp as needles.

And then I see it. A dull stain on the tip of one. It's my sister's dried blood. I walk over to the edge of the cliff and throw up. It's the heat, making this worse. I can't face the rest of my sandwich and I toss it away. And there, hidden beneath the overhang and half-buried in the sand, is a bottle. I pull it out, surprised by its weight, and hold it up to the light. A cork, originally from a bottle of red – maybe one Bethany found on the beach – has been jammed in the mouth; the stub is dyed burgundy. The sun glows through the thick green glass and, even after two days, the contents hiss slightly.

It's almost full. Bethany had drunk barely a single glass.

So now I know. I stand there, the sun beating down on my shoulders burning my scalp, holding a hot, dark bottle in my hand. My sister was found in the early hours of the morning by a holidaymaker, who called the police. Martelli rang for an ambulance, and the medics carried her on a stretcher round to our beach whilst the tide was still low enough. The *Carabinieri* did not arrive for several hours. She'd been found with her clothes on, so no one had checked for semen; she had a head injury, so

Dr Virgili assumed she'd been attacked and didn't monitor her blood alcohol. When the *Carabinieri* came here, they might not have noticed the Prosecco bottle. Even if they had, perhaps they thought she'd drunk it all, or that it was her second.

But I *know* this is the bottle Bethany took from the house. So now I am certain my sister was not drunk and she was attacked. *I am going to find out who did this to her. I owe it to her.* She wouldn't be lying in a hospital bed if I hadn't accused her of causing Ruby-May's death. I couldn't continue to shout at my ageing father and curse his failing memory, so I took it out on my sister.

I can't help it. I glance back at the bloodied rock. It wouldn't take much strength to push someone, especially if they lost their footing in the sand and slipped: a disproportionate amount of damage for a small amount of effort. Even a woman could have done it. I think of my other sister, Amy, and reject the idea immediately. Of course Amy would have wanted to kill Bethany, if she'd really been responsible for Ruby-May's death, but Amy doesn't have any doubts about her sister. Amy doesn't know that Bethany lied about taking Dad for a dementia test. *Does she?*

I'm not sure what to do now. I need to go back, talk to Martelli, see if I can persuade him to follow this up, in the absence of Ruggieri and Biondi, book new flights, get Bee home. I know, already, that Martelli will give that lugubrious shrug that seems so peculiarly Italian, and I can almost hear him telling me that it is out of his hands.

The gulls screech and fight over the scraps of meat from my ciabatta, and I notice something else. It's small and made of plastic. I pick it up and turn it between my fingers. It's warm from the sun. Another piece of flotsam and jetsam. I put it in my pocket and haul myself up the rocks in the lee of the cliff. As I trudge back across the beach, I notice rust-red petals, shrivelled by the sun, drifting across the sand in front of me – and then I remember when I was last here. A few feet away is the outline of a small grave. Some of the stones and shells have been kicked or knocked, and the mound of sand – damp when Lotte, Theo and I patted it down – has dried and cracked. The lines from the poem Theo read that night play in my mind.

I will lend you, for a little time,
A child of mine...

There's something poking through the top. I walk over and crouch down. It's a hand: a small plastic doll's hand, with fat, chubby fingers, like a child's. I pause and remove my sunglasses, rub my eyes.

For you to love while she lives,
And mourn for when she's dead.

I don't know how Amy has coped, especially when Matt is so emotionally repressed he makes me look like Oprah. I touch the doll's fingertips. They're warm from the sun. I wonder if I should dig her up. Amy had been so upset when she heard we'd buried the doll, but then what will Theo and Lotte think when Pearl rises from the grave? How will that help them understand that Ruby-May will never return?

Ruby-May. Ruby-May. Would I have been happier – would we all have been happier – if she hadn't lived? If we'd never loved and lost, than never loved at all, as some poem I once read at school goes? *Yes*, I think, *yes, I'd be happier now.* But how could I wish away that child's life? Deny her those three bright, blazing years of existence?

I loved Ruby-May, of course I did, I loved her with all my heart. I also loved what she meant: that I was a person capable of being loved, of being responsible, of being worthy of a small girl's attention, and that one day maybe I, too, could become a father and not be a monstrous screw-up like my own dad had been.

As I stand there by Pearl's grave, I have a searing realization: I brought my family here, to this island, to try and put us back together, to make us whole. Instead we're irretrievably broken, with jagged edges and pieces missing. We're like some holiday-house jigsaw puzzle: we're never going to fit together again. I put my sunglasses back on. *My sister lied to me.* Again. She *knew* she wasn't drunk. She colluded with the police. I know now that it's too late for our family. But I am going to find out the truth, no matter what it costs. I'm going to find out who tried to kill my sister. And then I'm going to find out who was really responsible for Ruby-May's death.

PART III

19 AUGUST, BRISTOL

35
NICK

We arrived in Bristol yesterday lunchtime, flying into a damp, grey cotton wool of fog. So much for British summertime. The rain is oddly comforting, though. Bethany slept for most of the journey and when I dropped her off at her apartment, she said she was tired; and no, she did not want me hanging around. There was no point asking why she lied to me; she'd just have lied even more and better. But I will find out the truth. I'm going to take her to have her brain scanned for a blood clot this morning at St Michael's. I'm hoping that she'll feel vulnerable enough to confess, when faced with possible death.

I ring the bell to her flat and I'm buzzed in immediately, as if she's been standing waiting for me. I trudge up the stairs, wheezing a bit. Bethany lives on the top floor, with a view that skims the rigging of the SS *Great Britain*. The door swings open as I reach the landing and a young girl with blonde hair in a straggly bun and a cropped top pouts at me.

'Are you the photographer?'

I'm slightly thrown. 'I am *a* photographer,' I say.

She looks me up and down. I suppose I'm dressed for the part in my saggy jeans and dirty Converse, my retro Adidas top and Gert Lush tee.

'Where's your camera, then?'

'In the studio,' I say, getting impatient. 'Who are you?'

'Holly. I'm the researcher.'

I push past her and into Bee's flat. It's full of people. The sofas have been shoved aside and orange and black cables snake across the floor. There's a camera on a tripod in the middle of the room and the cameraman is fiddling with soft box lights; they droop like flowers on their metallic stalks, the petals gauze and silver. His assistant is fastening a reflector to a stand; the circular gold disc catches and spills the early-morning light across the white walls. There are bouquets of white lilies and roses in glass vases on every surface.

A woman in skinny jeans, a black jacket and Nike Frees strides over to me. She glances at her clipboard as if the answer she seeks will be there and, when she looks back at me, she frowns.

'Are you Martin's assistant?'

'I'm Nick. Bethany's brother.'

'Ah. I'm Jen. It's nice to meet you, but I'm sorry, Nick, this isn't a good time. We're about to start filming.' Her voice is southern, clipped. I'm guessing she's the producer of Bethany's regional programme; originally from London, here because she wants 'the lifestyle' for a fraction of the price you'd pay in the big city.

'Where is Bee?'

'In her bedroom, getting ready, but please don't—'

I walk in without knocking. Bethany is sitting on a chair in the middle of the room, while a man with tattoos covering both arms, and a *Great Gatsby* haircut, is painting foundation on her face. An older man with greying hair is sitting on the edge of the bed, leaning towards my sister, as if he's ravenous and she's a delectable morsel.

'This is my brother, Nick,' Bethany says. 'Jay, make-up artist extraordinaire—' the tattooed man gives a little bow – 'and this is Stuart, my exec producer.'

Stuart stands up and holds out his hand towards me. He's tall, with designer stubble and vintage jeans, a short-sleeved black linen shirt and Paul Smith glasses.

I want to punch him. I grit my teeth and ignore him.

'What's going on?'

'I'm doing a piece on the dangers of booking holidays online.'

Jay moves back slightly to inspect his handiwork. He's made up my sister so that one side of her face is blemish-free, leaving her black eye and bruised cheek, and pinning her hair back to expose the jagged red scar at her temple.

'You're coming with me to get a brain scan.'

She flaps her hand at me. Her nails have been repainted metallic gold, to highlight her new tan. 'I'm fine. Don't fuss. But sweet of you to call in.'

I'm just about to push Jay out of the way and yank Bee to her feet, when Stuart steps in front of her.

'We appreciate your concern, we really do,' he says; his voice is as thick as the toffee in a Twix. 'I promise to take good care of your sister. If she has the slightest sign of a headache, we'll whizz her to the Spire immediately. In fact, Nick – it is Nick, isn't it? – we'll sort that straight away.' He cups Bethany's bare shoulder in his hand. 'It would make a fantastic segue after the piece-to-camera about your experience. As you're doing the voiceover we'll see you disappearing into one of those machines, your brain flashing up on the screen. It'll really heighten the jeopardy.' He swings round. 'Holly? Holly!'

Holly rushes in, a little breathless at being summoned, blue eyes wide as she stares adoringly up at Stuart. He tells her to speak to the Spire, Bristol's premier private hospital, the one that I now remember is in Henleaze, and which the consultant suggested my father might have been to. Stuart wants Holly to organize a brain scan for Bethany. 'Just need access to the MRI or a CAT or whatnot, and a nurse or two. We don't have to *actually* scan her. Tell Jen to arrange it with the crew, right after they've wrapped here. And find a blanket to put round Bee when we're filming her on the sofa. She needs to look like an invalid.'

'Give me a second,' Bethany says, weaving round them. 'I'll walk you out.'

She takes my arm and leads me past Jen, who is barking at someone down the phone, the sound recordist and the real photographer, who is lugging his kit in as we reach her front door.

'How the hell can you even look at that bastard?'

'Shush, keep your voice down. It's going to be amazing for my career,' she says. 'I can do something serious for once. Come on, Nick, don't stuff it up for me.'

'Bethany! He raped you! What are you doing?'

'He's promised he'll talk to the producers of *The Show*.'

I ball my hands into fists, take a breath, count to four. 'You told me you were drunk. You said you weren't attacked on that beach. Which is it?'

'Not so loud! I was drunk, I told you that. But this story sounds better on TV,' she says.

I'm not sure what to believe. 'Dr Virgili said you had to have a brain scan. Have you got a headache? Tell me the truth this time.'

She hesitates for a fraction of a second. 'I've taken four ibuprofen this morning.' She holds the door open for me. 'Call you later, yeah?'

'Bee. I know you didn't take Dad for that dementia appointment.'

'What are you talking about?'

'At The Castle. It's in his diary. When I called them to make a follow-up appointment, they said he'd come in for a medical. You didn't take him to the Memory Clinic.'

'You're an idiot. I don't know anything about him having a medical. I took Dad to the Spire. The one I'm about to go to.'

'For your fake brain scan.'

'Whatever. Like I said, I'll make Dad an appointment when this is all over.'

Now it's my turn to gape at her, but she pushes me out and is about to shut the door when I wedge my elbow in the frame.

'Wait. What was the argument with Joe all about?'

'On holiday? Oh, for God's sake! It was nothing. He asked Tiffany to write the foreword for his book, because he says she's more famous than me. The wanker! Whatever, I'm over it.'

'I thought it was – I thought maybe you'd got together and then you found out he had a girlfriend already…'

'What? Nick, you are so fucking ridiculous. Joe is gay.'

'*Gay?*'

'Yes! Now, will you—'

'I think I saw him. At the *festa*.'

'Probably. He stayed on,' she says. 'Wanted to see the rest of the island and check out the festival, but he pretended to leave, for Amy's sake. Are we done?'

She doesn't wait for a reply, but slams the door in my face. I stand there for a moment, feeling bewildered and stupid, and then go and buy a coffee from the cafe on the waterfront – the same one where I'd bought espressos for Bee and Joe, not all that long ago. It feels cool after the heat in Italy; the sky is the colour of sheet steel, as if it's going to rain. I shiver. I'm convinced Bethany wasn't drunk and that she was attacked, but I don't know why she's lying or what I'm missing. And who the fuck was having sex in the shed, if it wasn't Joe and Bee?

I leave a message for Amy, telling her that Bethany won't go for a brain scan and asking if she'll meet me in Dad's flat.

36
AMY

She lets herself into the flat – she still has a set of keys. The place smells stale: Nick's only spent one night here in nearly ten days, but still, it doesn't look like it did when she lived here all those years ago. She'd been studying and had started dating Matt. Her father had had to return to Somerset every night to look after Nick, once their mother walked out. No more womanizing during the week.

There's almost nothing in the fridge; the milk looks as if it's solidified and there's something growing out of the draining hole at the back. She boils water, pours it all over a mug to sterilize it, makes herself a herbal tea. Blackcurrant and echinacea. *Probably Maddison's.*

There's a battered copy of *The Divine Comedy* on a coffee table. She flicks through it while she waits for Nick to turn up, and sees Luca's name in tiny, flowing handwriting on the frontispiece. She wonders why Nick has got Luca's copy. Maybe Luca lent it to him, but it doesn't seem like the kind of thing her brother would read.

She wanders round the flat, opens one of the sash windows. There was a brief downpour, but now the rain has stopped and the city glitters below her. She climbs out and perches on the stone lintel: she used to sit here, dreaming of life with Matt, her bare toes on the edge, the vertiginous drop below. How she used to love this view: the slow loop of the river, the city centre trapped in its coil, the Suspension Bridge slung across the raw red cliffs and the mud banks below, Leigh Woods and the green hills of Somerset.

It's as if she can map out her whole life from here: the fields and orchards where she grew up, the university her father taught in, the bar where she met Matt, the terraced house that's Chloe's home, the hospital where she gave birth to her children; and, out by the disused railway path on the way to Bath, the cemetery where they buried Ruby-May.

She's not wearing a cardigan and it's chilly at this height. She comes back inside, runs her finger along the books on the shelves, their cracked spines hard to read in the dull light: books on politics, on art, on photography; screenplays and *Star Wars*, comics and comedies; all the lives that have lived here, and the shallow indentation they have left, spelled out in other people's words.

Nick, damp with rain, walks in. The first thing he says is, 'Did you know Joe is gay?'

He looks terrible. His hair is on end and he hasn't shaved. He's pale beneath his light Italian tan.

'Why did you ask me to come here?' she says, crossing her arms, the anger she feels towards him returning in a rush.

Nick says, 'Bethany is lying to us. She was attacked. I know it!'

'This has to stop. You can't go round accusing people of hurting Bethany. You have to accept what the police said.'

'I found her bottle of Prosecco on the beach – the one she took from the house – and it was almost full. She wasn't drunk. She didn't fall.'

'Listen to me, Nick. I spoke to Bethany this morning, after you called me. Even she says you're being creepy and obsessive. She says she *was* drunk. That Prosecco, they sell it all over the island. She could have bought another bottle. The one you found on the beach was probably her second. She went to the terrace bar up on the hill every day; she must have got it there. Please, stop going on about it. The police are right: she tripped and hit her head. And it might not be ideal, but she's using the experience – or a version of it – to relaunch her career. Booking online holidays, the dangers for women on their own in a foreign country, that kind of thing. We need to support her. Let her start over. And you need to deal with the real issue.'

'Which is?' Nick runs his hand through his hair, wipes the rain from his forehead. He's frowning and he reminds her of what he was like when he was six years old.

'Your grief. You need to find a way to deal with your grief.' She blows her nose, wipes her eyes. 'I have to go. Bethany says she doesn't want to speak to you. I only came because she phoned me. Told me to get you off her back.'

'It's convenient for you, isn't it?'

'What are you talking about?'

'That everyone thinks Bee was drunk. But somebody pushed her. She knows who attacked her. And for some reason she's not telling anyone who did it. Why do you think that is, Amy?'

'Nick! You're losing it. I'd suggest therapy, if I didn't think it was a waste of time.'

'She wouldn't tell the police if she loved the person who pushed her. If she could understand why that person wanted to attack her.'

'Are you saying…? Oh my God, you *are*. You're suggesting *I* tried to kill my own sister.'

'No, no! I'm just… trying to think it through.'

'Get a grip. And don't call me until you've sorted yourself out.'

She lets herself out of the flat, dashing away tears of outrage and hurt as she hurries down the corkscrew staircase, past abandoned piles of mail in the hall and out into the rain-soaked street. She pauses for a moment, looking down towards the river, and automatically puts out a hand to stop her smallest daughter from stepping off the kerb, before she remembers.

37
NICK

After Amy walked out, I lie on the sofa and watch Bethany in old episodes of *The Show*, scrutinizing her face for a sign of the abuse she was dealing with, trying to read the lies in her eyes. The sitting room grows bright with light: the sky is washed like a watercolour after today's deluge. I shiver; my clothes are still damp from being caught in the shower on the way to my flat. Something sharp sticks into my butt. I try and sit up, but it digs in further. I slide onto the floor, put my hand in the back pocket of my jeans. I pull out two small, misshapen objects. One is the piece of plastic I found on the beach where Bethany was attacked, the other is the tooth someone had placed on my windowsill in the Italian holiday house.

I sit for a moment, weighing them in my palm, like Anubis. Definitely heavier than a feather. *Somebody is going straight to hell.* I hang my head between my knees, hoping to quell the nausea. I could leave it alone. *After all, no one believes me. Even Bethany is telling me to drop it.*

What would Maddison say I should do? I shake my talismans together, like dice, and put them back in my pocket. I force myself to get up, and I make a strong black coffee. In the cupboard there's an old bottle of apple brandy that Tony, one of Dad's neighbours, brewed. I wonder how long it's been here, in this flat. I wonder if Dad drank it on his own or with... I take a slug and feel the sharp sweetness sing through my veins, and then the caffeine jolts my heart.

I realize, as I take another sip, that when Ruby-May died, something in me died too. I lost the man who'd held that baby in his arms and thought he knew what life was all about; I lost the man I could have been. I drink more brandy and it tastes like something rotten, from the bottom of the orchard in our garden.

Ruby-May is running through the thick grass, long blonde hair catching in the hands of the apple trees; she's laughing. She startles a magpie; it arrows into the sky, the sun shines through its outstretched wings. Ruby-May holds out a bunch of tiny purple flowers in her small fist. Her fingers smell of spearmint. She opens her mouth and green water pours out; skeins of pond weed are tangled in her baby teeth.

It's now or never, I tell myself. I pour the rest of that rancid brandy down the sink.

♖

I sit on the low wall in front of Bethany's apartment block, looking out over the river. I stare through the masts and rigging of the SS *Great Britain*; on the tip of the hill behind the ship is Cabot Tower, dedicated to the man who sailed across the ocean and 'discovered' America. To the left is Goldney Hall, where I imagine my father was once wined and dined when the university held grand dinners for the Ambassador of China and other notabilities. I wonder whom he wined and dined in my flat. His flat. I can even see the roof and the ledge where I used to sit with Maddison. Is Bethany right? Am I blaming my sister because I'm unable to forgive her and I feel sorry for Dad? I hold the black pawn in my palm, roll it between my finger and thumb, feel its grooves and its smooth, spherical head.

I call Amy. I expect it to go straight to voicemail.

'Nick! I told you, don't call me again.'

'Sorry. I'm sorry. You're right. I'm being insane.'

She gives a juddering sigh, as if she's on the verge of tears.

I press on. 'I don't expect you to forgive me right now. Just one thing. I need Luca's mobile number. I've got his copy of *The Divine Comedy*.'

'Really? That's what you're obsessing about now? Okay, I've changed my mind: get some help. Jungian, Freudian, on the NHS, private, bespoke – whatever. You need some serious therapy.'

'I want to know whether to post it to him or not.'

'Nick! Are you even listening? I'm sure it can wait. There's not much point; it'll cost more than it would to buy a new copy. Besides, he'll be back to see his tutor soon.'

'Yeah, well. I'd like to keep in touch with him.'

She makes a clicking sound with her tongue. She thinks I'm a complete fool and that I have more important things to worry about. Anything to get rid of me, though.

'Don't call me again until you're over this,' she says and hangs up.

Amy, though, no matter what she says, is reliable. A moment later she texts me Luca's contact details.

I dial the number, but there's no response. I'm about to give up, when on the ninth ring he answers. I stumble over my words.

'Luca. It's Nick. Nick Flowers.'

I haven't thought this through. *What am I going to say? How do I persuade him to talk to me?*

'Nick. What can I do for you?'

He's cold, businesslike, but then what the hell did I expect?

'I know. I know what you did to Bethany.'

'I have no idea what you say.' He speaks without a moment's hesitation.

Too quick.

'I haven't told anyone yet.'

'Why are you calling, Nick?' he says again.

'How did you know it was Bethany? Something happened on holiday to make you change your mind. You believed it was Dad's fault, just like everyone else, but then you saw something. You were going to tell me! What did you see?'

There's silence, and I wonder if he's put the phone down. I expect him to hang up on me in disgust, just as my sister did. I get up and walk right to the edge of the river, line my toes up with the end of the harbour wall. I look down into the brackish water; weed gently undulates in the current, writhing as if it's alive.

He's breathing more heavily now.

'It was the pills,' Luca says eventually.

'What pills?'

'Temazepam. She was taking the sleeping pills. I saw them in her room – and she give them to your father because he is awake in the night. Do you remember?'

'Vaguely. She offered some to me. But what—'

'On the day that it happen, I work in your mother's old room. I stood up to take the stretch and I look out the window. I see your father asleep in the sunshine. And then I see your sister. She has the blue pill and she give it to him with a glass of water. He swallow it. A little later she come back with a bottle of red wine and she put it next to him. He is still sleeping. She pour wine into a glass and then she do a strange thing. Two strange things. She throw half the wine from the bottle away – she pour it in the flowers! Then she take a little syringe – you know, the purple one that you have with the medicine for children? She suck some of the wine from the glass into this little device and she put a drop on his shirt. She put a drop on his tongue. I say to myself, "This is strange", but I don't think of it again, after what happen to Ruby-May.

'And then we are on the holiday and it happen again. The night before Ruby-May's anniversary, I see her give him the blue pill and a glass of water. And he does not drink, even to take a sip of the champagne with Ruby-May's cake. He tell to me he is on medicine for his heart and he cannot have alcohol. And I think about this all the day, and then I say to myself: if a man cannot drink, but he has a taste for the wine and he is given some, even a little, little drop, that taste will come back, so fierce. When he wake up, he will find the wine and he cannot help himself: he will drink it all.

'Then I know. How could your father tell Bethany he would look to Ruby-May, when he is asleep? Why does he not remember the red wine? Because he did not *choose* to drink it.'

My God! Bethany was looking after Ruby-May. And then she drugged our father after Ruby-May died, to make sure he wouldn't remember. He would literally have had no memory of that afternoon. And to complete her lie, she got him drunk and then she pretended to take him for a memory test.

I look down at an artificial marsh, floating just below me; a coot steps through the rushes and I can smell the sweet, sharp scent of spearmint.

'*Lasciate ogni speranza o voi che entrate.*'

'What?'

'Is something we say in this region of Italy,' he says. 'I don't know what to do with this knowledge. I think, I will ask to Bethany. Give her the chance to tell the truth. I follow her to the beach, I try and talk to her. But she laugh at me. She laugh at me and we are talking about the death of a child – a child I loved more than I love myself! So I shake her. I only want her to say that it is her fault, that she is sorry.'

The coot leaves the haven of the marsh, and launches itself into the open water, breaking the scum of oil that marbles the surface. I can't see any chicks. Maybe they've grown up and left already.

'But she fall, she hit her head. I do not mean to hurt her. I am afraid she die. I panic, I leave her there. Then I hate myself, so I go early to the police station to say them what happen. But I hear one of the officers, Agente Martelli, he pick up his free coffee in a bar and he say they find an English woman on the beach. So I know she is alive and I think, if she tell someone, then it all come out: what I do to her, but also what she do to Ruby-May.'

I feel myself swaying. I take a step back from the water's edge.

'So I go home to my family and I wait. I cancel my flight to Bristol. I tell my tutor I never come back. I do nothing. I sit here and I wait for you or for the police. No one. Bethany say nothing. And now you, Nick. You know the whole truth. It is up to you what you do with this knowledge.'

A couple of swans glide past. The current is choppy in the middle of the river, changeable. They struggle against it and then give up, beating their wings, harder and harder, until they laboriously free themselves from the water and fly downstream. I'd forgotten how noisy swans in flight can be.

'Goodbye, Nick,' Luca says, and the line goes dead.

I turn round and look up at Bethany's flat. She's standing in the window, watching me. I can barely see her face, she's haloed by the brilliance of the studio lights. I slide my phone into my pocket and I wait for my sister.

She walks across the cobbles towards me. The bruise and the scar are livid, where the make-up artist has let them shine through her foundation. She moves carefully, as if she is trying not to jar anything. We stand there for a moment, facing each other. Although the sun is warm on my back, there's a chill wind rising from the water and I shiver. I wonder if it'll rain again. It rains practically every day in Bristol. And I realize that I knew – I knew all along it was Bethany. The sadness is almost unbearable. My own sister.

'Luca,' I say.

'How did you know?'

I hold out my hand. The piece of plastic I found on the beach lies on my palm. It's a tiny black pawn from a travelling chess set.

'I found it on the beach next to a rock covered in your blood. I didn't realize what it was at first, and then I thought it was a coincidence. But it's not, is it?'

She squeezes her eyes shut and winces. I wonder if there is a blood clot, swelling inside her brain, pressing against her skull. How long she has to live. If she's about to die.

'Luca wanted you to admit it. Apologize. He went a little far – he's not naturally a violent man, is he? He didn't mean it to go so badly wrong. But when you cracked your skull open... well, he didn't think anyone would find out it was him, once you were dead. And then you came round and he was in the clear! He hadn't committed murder, and he thought the attack would be blamed on a random drunk, or your own inebriation, because there's no way you'd tell anyone it was him. If you did, you'd have to say *why* a mild, gentle student, a man studying to be a child psychologist no less, would want to kill you. It was a relief, really, when Matt told the police you were probably drunk – so you confirmed it. They dropped the case. Problem solved.'

'I loved her. I loved her! Don't you understand?' Bethany says.

'I do,' I say. 'Just not enough.'

She takes a deep, jagged breath. 'If I'd told Amy, it would have destroyed my relationship with her. How could she ever have spoken to me again, if she'd known it was my fault? I'd never have seen Lotte and Theo or Chloe. You and Dad. Think of our family, Nick, of what this will do to them.'

'You have to tell her,' I say. 'You can't let Dad carry the blame for this.'

'Why not?' she says, standing up straighter, folding her arms. The breeze blows her dark hair back from her face. 'He ruined our lives. His drinking. His adultery. His absence. Why shouldn't he? I think of Ruby-May every day. Every fucking day. There's nothing that I wouldn't give to bring her back. But she's gone. She's dead, and we can't ever change that. We have to think of the future, of each other, of our family.'

'But what you did to him – giving him a sleeping pill, putting the wine out for him, pretending you'd taken him to a Memory Clinic – that was...' I struggle to think of the right word. In the end I simply say, 'Wrong.'

'Do you want to know why? The real reason I did that?'

I swallow. Do I? No, I don't want to hear whatever bullshit excuse Bethany is going to come up with.

But Bethany has never cared what I think. She tells me. She tells me the real reason why she hates our father enough to do what she did to him. When she's finished, she's crying so hard tears drip from her chin. If I were the kind of man who was in touch with his feelings, I'd be fucking sobbing too.

'I'm sorry,' I say. 'That's awful.' That sounds trite. I try again. 'I don't know how you lived with it, all these years.' Nope. No better. I take a breath. This is going to sound callous and I really don't mean to. I lean towards her, but this time I refrain from gripping her shoulders. 'It doesn't change anything. You need to tell Amy – your sister – what really happened. Two days. You've got the rest of today and until tomorrow night to tell Amy.'

Bethany's sadness shifts gear, switches to anger. 'Or what?' she says, coming closer. She's almost the same height as me. My sister stands in a beam of sunlight, her tawny eyes illuminated, pupils shrunk to pin pricks. 'Are you threatening me? *You* won't tell her. It would be the end of our family, and you know it. You haven't got the balls.'

*I can't stay here. I might let her push me into something I'll regret.
Or else I'll kill her.*

I leave my sister standing by the river, and I walk as fast as I can away from the water.

20 AUGUST, BRISTOL

38
NICK

I arrived early enough to see Lotte and Theo before they went to bed. I brought a Lego space rocket for Theo, and a stuffed purple unicorn for Lotte. It was the one I was going to give Ruby-May; it's about time I passed it on to her sister. I bought wine, beer and lemonade; flowers and chocolates for Amy; and a takeaway curry that's currently keeping warm in the oven. I remembered to ask my sister to invite Chloe; I picked Dad up from Somerset and drove him over. Now we're sitting round the kitchen table, eating poppadoms and mango chutney; Chloe is looking at her iPhone and ignoring us.

'What are we waiting for?' asks Matt, pouring us both a beer.

'Bethany,' Amy says, looking at the clock. 'I'll give her another ring.'

I twitch slightly and try not to listen to her call.

'So what's all this about, mate?' asks Matt.

'He just wanted us to get together,' Amy says, smiling at me. She turns away as her mobile stops ringing. I hold my breath, but it's a recording of Bethany's voice; the call has gone to her answerphone.

'Maybe she's in the taxi,' says Amy, sitting down and snapping off a piece of poppadom. She slides her other hand round Matt's neck and they smile at each other.

I swallow and take a swig of beer. Do I really want to do this, just as Amy and Matt seem to be getting back on track? Dad's examining the paintings stuck on the fridge that Lotte and Theo have made, with an expression that looks a lot like contentment. Bethany was right. This will destroy us. All of us.

'Shall we start eating? It's getting late,' says Matt. 'Some of us have to be up early.'

I clear my throat. 'I'll go and fetch her.' Amy and Matt glance at each other. They're thinking I've turned over a new leaf, or some other bollocks. My palms are sweaty and I wipe them on my jeans. 'Why don't you go ahead? Save some for me. For us.'

It's dusk and rush hour has died down, but there's no quick way to reach Bethany's flat from St Andrew's. I drive into the car park behind Bethany's block of flats and pull into her space. I might have missed her. Perhaps she's sitting at Amy's kitchen table right now, eating biryani and spinning our family some tale. I call her, but it goes to voicemail again, and when I ring the bell there's no reply. I imagine her lounging on her white sofa, drinking a flute of ice-cold Cava, waiting for me. She'll say we shouldn't ruin everything by telling them what really happened. She'll tell me I haven't got it in me to do it anyway.

There are no lights on in her flat. I press other people's bells until someone answers, and I tell them my sister's buzzer has broken and they let me in. I run up the stairs: five flights to the top. I pound on Bethany's door. There's no answer.

I text Amy and she replies immediately: No sign of Bee, but the korma is yummy! A x

There isn't a concierge and there's nowhere to hide a spare key in this clinical hall. She hasn't even got a doormat and it's not the sort of place for pot plants. Amy might have one, I guess, but that's not really the point. I'm about to leave, when I try the handle. To my surprise, the door isn't locked. I walk in.

There's the faintest scent of roses. I don't turn on any lights. The street lamps outside, the myriad lights on the hill opposite, blaze through the large, plate-glass windows. I can see the outline of the Clifton Suspension Bridge in a spider-thread of LEDs, the tungsten of Brunel's Other Bridge, lamps glowing on the Grain Barge opposite. The flat is completely empty. I step inside and my footsteps echo on the wooden floors. There isn't a single stick of furniture left. I go into the bedroom. Curtains flutter in the breeze from a window that's open a crack, but there's nothing here, either. Every cupboard in the kitchen is bare.

I call Bethany's phone again, but this time it doesn't even ring, as if the number has been disconnected. I check her Twitter feed and her Instagram account, but the last posts are about her forthcoming programme on the dangers of booking online holidays, and they were posted yesterday. I google her webpage, search for the contacts and find a number for her agent: it's Felicity Pickering of Pickering Productions. I'm not sure she'll answer, but it's a mobile, so it's worth a try.

She picks up on the first ring. 'Yes?'

'Sorry to bother you this late...'

'Who is this?' Her voice is stridently upper-class.

'I'm Nick. Bethany's brother.'

There's a sharp intake of breath. 'I'm surprised you have the audacity to contact me.'

I frown. I've never met this woman before. Unless I did, but I don't remember; maybe at one of Bethany's parties? I must have offended her in some way. Got drunk and said something inappropriate, knowing me.

'Why are you ringing?' she asks, crisply enunciating every word.

'I'm trying to find Bethany.'

'Ah, well, I can't help you there. She's terminated her contract with me. As of this afternoon. Rather abruptly, I'm afraid.'

'I'm standing in her flat,' I say. 'It's empty. I don't know where she is.'

'She didn't tell you?' There's a slight softening of her tone. 'Well, she won't need any of those items where she's going.'

Where is she going?

I must have said it out loud, because Felicity says, 'America. Not sure where; she's given me no forwarding address and she's deleted her email account. I expect it'll be Los Angeles. She always wanted to make it over there. Though, frankly, I think she'll find she spends quite a lot of her time waiting tables.' She gives a bark of joyless laughter. 'Unless that fellow Stuart Linfield comes through with a decent contact for her.'

I thank her and hang up. Even on the way over to Amy's with Dad, the smell of tarka dhal and chicken dhansak steaming up my Vauxhall, I didn't quite believe it. I expected Bethany would phone to tell me I was being an idiot, and Luca was right here with her, laughing at my stupidity, at the joke they've played on me – the ex-child psychologist saying, *Is time to forgive her, no?*

But now I know for sure. I know my sister is guilty of letting my niece drown when she was meant to be looking after her, and then drugging my father and blaming him for her death. And by leaving like this, she's given me a get-out clause. I can simply say that Bethany has gone to LA. We can all chorus: *How rude, how like Bethany to go for a better offer without telling anyone, without even saying goodbye.* And we can watch Dad drink gritty smoothies and eat omega-3s and pretend he's got memory problems, and eventually a part of us will be glad when he passes, because we cannot help but blame him for Ruby-May's death, even though we believed he was ill and his mind was no longer what it once was; and maybe, as Bethany said, we do hold him responsible for our mother leaving and our shit childhoods, and for making us the emotionally stunted adults we've all turned out to be.

Quietly, slowly, we will start to heal. We'll remember Ruby-May with sadness and with joy, but we'll no longer see the world in shades of grey: colour will seep in, as weak as watercolour at first; two, five, ten years later, it'll return in a triumph of technicolour.

Days will pass when we don't even think of Ruby-May, forever frozen at three years old, but still a piece of us, still in our hearts.

I close the door quietly behind me and I walk slowly down the stairs.

But that – that is sentimental bullshit.

I don't want Ruby-May in my fucking heart. I want her here, with me. Alive. And my sister is going to pay for her death.

39
AMY

Amy is clearing away the oily, turmeric-stained takeaway cartons, aware of Matt standing in the hall, jingling his keys impatiently in his hand, while Chloe and her dad sit side-by-side on the stairs, slowly putting their shoes on. Her father, of course, is struggling because of his age, but she's not sure why Chloe isn't keen on going home. Matt is irritable because he's conflicted: on the one hand, he's happy he's had a midweek beer and a curry; on the other, he's annoyed at Nick and Bethany's tardiness, and that he now has to take both Chloe and David home. It'll be after midnight by the time he returns from Somerset, but she still hasn't been able to force herself to make Ruby-May's room into a spare bedroom.

There's a soft knock.

'That'll be them,' she says, wiping her hands on the dishcloth.

'About bloody time,' says Matt, opening the door.

Nick is on his own. He looks odd, washed out. He's done a lot of driving – to Somerset to collect their dad, and back, around Bristol – and he hasn't eaten yet. Either that or it's the street lighting, bleaching his Italian tan.

'So where is she?' Matt asks.

Nick clears his throat and runs his hand through his hair.

'Can I talk to you? All of you?'

'We're right here, mate.' The old aggression has seeped back into Matt's tone.

'Best if we sit down,' Nick says, pulling himself up straight and looking her husband in the eye.

'What's happened? Is Bee okay?' Amy asks.

Nick walks past without answering and stands in front of the oven. He gestures to them all to sit at the table. They're so surprised, they obey. Amy starts getting up again.

'We saved some curry for you. It's—'

He shakes his head. He looks ill, as if he might throw up.

'I've got something to tell you,' he says.

As her brother talks, Amy has the sensation of all the blood in her body draining away, rushing from her head, sinking and pooling in her feet. It's as if she's known, all along, that this is what really happened. Still, the betrayal takes her breath away. A stabbing pain in her chest spreads through her arms, across her back; she thinks she might be having a heart attack.

When Nick says Bethany has gone to Los Angeles and that there's no way to find her, Chloe bursts into tears, as if the enormity of what her aunt has done has just hit her. Matt puts his arm around his daughter and clamps her tightly against his chest. Amy's father looks stunned and grief-stricken, shocked into silence. Matt, though, is loud, livid with anger. She thinks he's going to crush Chloe.

'Why the hell didn't Bethany say anything?' When Nick doesn't reply, Matt asks, 'How did you know? How did you find out? Why didn't you tell us before?'

Chloe whimpers and Matt remembers himself, rubs his daughter's arm and releases her.

Nick looks out of the window. 'Bethany only just told me,' he says eventually. 'The bump on her head – she must have been feeling vulnerable. Guilty.' He puts his hands in his pockets and leans back against the oven as if he's exhausted. 'I told her to tell you. Gave her a couple of days. And this is her answer.'

'This is her answer? This is her fucking answer? To bugger off to America? She should face the consequences. She ought to go to prison for this!' Matt stands up, his chair crashing against the wall. 'I'm going to ring the police. I'm not—'

Amy takes a breath, finds the paralysis has gone. She rises to her feet and puts a hand on Matt's arm.

'Don't,' she says.

He's about to pull away. His face contorts with fury. She can see it in his eyes: he thinks she's going to protect Bethany, choose her sister over their daughter.

'I never want to see Bethany again,' she tells him. 'Leave it. Leave her.'

'I imagine she's suffering,' their father says.

In the silence, Chloe sobs. Matt's knees buckle and he sinks back into the chair.

'I feel as if Ruby-May has been killed all over again,' Amy says.

Nick looks stricken. 'I'm sorry, Ames,' he says. 'I am so sorry. But I thought we should all know the truth.'

She nods. None of them say anything for a moment. She can hear the kitchen tap dripping, the hum of the oven. The curry must have dried out by now.

'But the lengths she went to, to frame Dad. I mean, that's...'

'Evil,' says Matt.

Nick coughs, and glances at his father. 'She did have a reason.'

'Nothing could justify how she treated Dad,' Amy says.

Nick ignores her. 'When Bethany was sixteen she left home—'

'What does this have to do with...' Matt interrupts.

'Do you remember, Dad?'

He shifts uncomfortably in his seat. 'Oh, it was all drama, with Bethany.'

'She went to live in a squat in Bristol with some anarchists.'

Her father tilts his head to one side as he remembers. 'They were masters' students studying on my course,' he says, with the air of a professor correcting his student's grammar. 'Not a bad lot, but it wasn't suitable for a girl of Bethany's age to live with those young men in such surroundings. I went to see her. The place reeked of mice; the kitchen floor had caved in. The whole building had been condemned.'

'You tried to persuade her to come home.'

Amy looks at the poppadom crumbs scattered across the table, grains of rice trapped in smears of mango chutney. She doesn't know why Nick is telling them some story about Bethany. She's finding it hard to focus.

My sister. My sister let my daughter die. She can't think of anything else.

'Bethany wasn't having any of it. We had a huge row. She said some terrible things. But you know how Bee is. Most of it's hot air. Still, it was painful at the time.'

'You spoke to one of your colleagues about her, and he offered to talk to Bethany. In fact he said she could stay in his spare room until she was ready to return home. Professor Paul Williams. One of the senior lecturers. You liked him; he was well respected.'

Our father glances down now at his hands resting on the table, the knuckles starting to swell with arthritis.

'It seemed like a good plan, and it worked – at first. Bethany listened to the prof. He'd always had a way with the students, particularly the female ones,' Nick continues. 'She took him up on his offer and moved into his house in Clifton. It was beautiful. Large rooms, high ceilings, gorgeous Georgian proportions. One of those baths with lion's feet. All the luxuries we didn't have – an endless supply of hot water, an American fridge full of food. He bought her stuff too. A posh dressing gown. A nice frock. A pretty necklace. It didn't worry you at the time that he was in his fifties and had never been married? It didn't strike you as odd?'

It's as if the room has sharpened into high definition: every pore on her father's face is visible, every age spot, every thread vein and stray hair. Amy puts her hand over her mouth and gives a small moan.

'Do you want to tell them what happened?' Nick asks their father.

Their dad clasps his hands together. 'This is wholly inappropriate, under the circumstances. It's not the time or the place. Chloe is present, apart from any other consideration.'

'I know already,' Chloe says, tracing a line through a pool of salt on the table. She doesn't look at any of them.

Matt opens his mouth to speak, but Nick cuts across him. 'He raped her. Repeatedly.'

Her father gives a violent jerk as if Nick has speared him with his fork. He's turned ashen.

'That's somewhat of an overstatement,' her father finally says.

'Dad! She was sixteen. The same age as Chloe. She was a child. She was a virgin. Not that that should make any difference. Professor Paul Williams made her feel she owed it to him. The price of staying in his beautiful flat. The cost of a cheap necklace and a hot meal.' Nick steps forward and places both hands on the table, leans towards their father. 'And you knew. You might have had your suspicions before she even went to stay with him. You'd heard the rumours. Maybe you'd even helped cover up the accusations from his female students. They were silly young girls, and he was an acclaimed academic. You didn't want to lose him from the department. You were Vice-Chancellor at the time. You didn't want a stain on the university's reputation under your guard. But then... then Bethany told you. She *told* you what had been going on. And you still did nothing.'

'It wasn't nothing, Nick,' her father says. 'I took her out of that situation. I put her up in my flat. The one you are currently benefiting from now. Rent-free.'

Matt frowns. 'Why couldn't she have gone there in the first place?'

Amy wipes away a tear and says, 'Because that was where Dad met his women. He might not have been able to stay there for the entire week, after Mum left, but he still used it. He couldn't have his daughter disrupting his affairs.'

'I can honestly say I knew nothing about Paul's alleged indiscretions with any of the students beforehand, or I most certainly would not have agreed to Bethany staying with him.'

'Indiscretions?' Amy breathes the word out. The smell of the spilt mango chutney is so sweet and sickly she thinks it will choke her.

'But you didn't *do* anything,' Nick says. 'You didn't explain to Bethany what had happened. That it was rape. You made her feel it was her fault, and that it was nothing. You told her she was a stupid little girl. And you certainly didn't tell anyone else. Like the police, for instance.'

No one says anything. Chloe is still looking down at the table, avoiding them all. Amy cries quietly.

Her dad unlocks his hands, presses the fingertips together as if he's about to make a point in the lecture theatre. 'It was a different time, Nick. One didn't make those sorts of accusations about one's colleagues. You don't understand—'

Nick bangs his fist down on the table, making them all jump. 'Oh, I understand all too fucking well.'

Matt gets to his feet. 'I think it's time for you to leave, David. And under the circumstances,' he glances at Nick, 'it's probably best if I drive your dad home.'

Nick visibly deflates, as if the toll of telling Bethany's story has sapped him of all his energy. He stands by the kitchen window and looks out over the city spread below them.

Matt pulls his chair out of the way, so their father can get up from behind the table, but he doesn't help him to his feet or steer him by his elbow, as he normally would. After her husband and her father have left the room, Amy looks over at Chloe. She's about to say she'll call Chloe a taxi, when her stepdaughter looks directly at her for the first time that evening and Amy, instead, finds herself asking, 'You knew? You knew all this time?'

Chloe nods. She's blinking hard to stop herself from crying. Amy passes her a tissue and takes one for herself.

'Bee told me. Can I stay here? Please?' her stepdaughter asks. 'I could sleep in Ruby-May's bed?'

Amy hesitates. *It's time. It is time.*

She holds out her hand to Chloe. 'Yes, love, you can.'

PART IV

21 NOVEMBER, SOMERSET

40
NICK

A few ragged leaves still cling to the otherwise bare branches. The pewter-grey trunks of the beeches have a long damp streak, with a greenish sheen on the opposite side from the prevailing wind. Orange larch needles have collected in the corners of the drive, and pinecones pop beneath my tyres. I pull up outside and sit in the car, collecting myself. There is always that moment of dislocation when you return to your childhood home and hold the conflicting dualities within you of yourself both as a child and an adult. *The child inside the man...* That hungry, lonely little boy is still trapped inside me somewhere, or maybe I left him here, wandering in this garden, gathering the courage to climb the ruined cottage by himself; a small ghost, now joined by another child's, only one who never had the chance to realize any of her dreams. *Still not too late to go in search of mine...* I tell myself and try not to wince at my sentimentality.

The house looks as if no one lives here: the windows are dark, the curtains have not been drawn and the once-neat lavender-edged herb garden at the front is dense with ash saplings and long grass. I knock on the door and then let myself in. Amy insisted we all have spare keys. Just in case. Dad is in a high-backed chair by the fire. His hair is uncombed and his cardigan is buttoned up incorrectly. He has a rug wrapped round his lap, but he hasn't lit a fire. He pushes his glasses onto his forehead when he sees me.

'Ah, Nick. What a nice surprise!'

'You invited me.'

'Really? Are you sure?'

'Yup. For lunch. I called you yesterday to confirm. Remember?'

His brow furrows and he looks into the distance. Then he shakes his head. 'I'm sorry, Nick, I have no recollection of that.'

I'm astonished. My father has almost never apologized to me. He pushes himself to his feet, using his fists on the armrests to lever himself upright.

'I'm not quite sure what I'm going to give you to eat.'

I follow his slippered feet as he shuffles into the kitchen. We look in the fridge and the cupboards, and as we accrue a random selection of vaguely edible food, some of which is even within its use-by date – a can of tuna, a packet of no-longer crisp Ryvita, ketchup, frozen green beans – I'm reminded of the ravenous child I once was, scavenging for my supper, coupling unlikely combinations of food: pairing cubes of mandarin jelly with chocolate sprinkles, Cheddar with tinned sweetcorn. And I wince inwardly at how I've neglected my father, now reduced to foraging in his own home, as I once had to.

It's late afternoon on a Friday and I'm bone-tired. Tamsyn and I have been filming at Trebah Gardens in Cornwall all week, for their new website and publicity brochure. The gardens are beautiful, if you like that kind of thing, but the starts have been early, the days long. I left at five this morning to get to Bristol in time to drop off the gear and download the photos and then turn round and head back to Somerset. I'm not sure string beans and crackers are really going to cut it. I find a couple of old but cold cans of Thatchers in the fridge and I pop the top of one, stick the other in my pocket.

'Dad,' I say, as we look at our haul.

He mutters, 'It's not so bad. Not so bad.'

'Dad, let's go to the pub.'

He brightens. 'Good idea, Son. Good idea.'

Now that I'm a bit calmer, I notice how empty the house is.

'Where is everything?' I ask, wandering back into the sitting room.

'Ah, now I recall. I wanted to tell you that I've decided to move.'

'Move? Where? When?'

'I asked Audrey, from the village, to help me pack and sort out… well, your mother's things. It's mostly finished now.' He opens the door to the dining room and shows me neat piles of cardboard boxes. 'I didn't want to involve Amy, but I'll need her help to put the house on the market, find somewhere smaller to live. More manageable.'

'Oh. Well, I guess that's a good idea. What about your flat? I can move out, if you want to be back in Bristol.'

'Too many stairs. You stay there, Son.'

I feel as if the stuffing has been knocked out of me. It's not as if I'll miss this place, but it is our childhood home. There's a small framed photo on top of one of the towers of boxes. I pick it up. It's of Ruby-May, grinning widely, tiny baby teeth, big blue eyes, that tumbleweed of hair haloed round her face.

'Lovely, isn't it? I couldn't bear to pack it away just yet. Chloe gave it to me.'

I set the photo down. I still can't bring myself to look too closely at pictures of my niece.

'She comes here quite a lot, you know,' Dad continues.

'Who?'

'Chloe. On the train and then the bus. A long journey for her. But it's nice to see a young face.'

'Really? Why? Sorry, that sounds rude. I mean, I know you're her grandfather, sort of.'

'Yes, Nick, I am. I am her grandfather. She's been part of our family since she was four years old. She wants to be a journalist. She comes here to talk to me about politics, ask my advice about writing articles, which university she should go to, that kind of thing. Not that I can help her much. It's all changed since my day, hasn't it? Vloggers and podcasts. You could help her, though: give her a masterclass in photography.'

'I'm hardly a master. I spend my day carrying kit and making the coffee,' I say. 'I'm lucky if I ever get to touch the camera. Should have gone to university, like you always told me to.'

I guess Matt must have put Chloe off a career in TV, I think. I look at my watch. The pub will be open now, although it's too early for food.

'You've done well, Son. I'm proud of you.'

I don't know how to deal with a compliment from my dad, so I ignore it.

'Shall we take a turn round the garden? For old times' sake. If you're selling it, I might not see it again. And then we can head over to the Railway Inn.'

'Of course, of course.'

It seems to take an age for my father to lace up his boots, wrap himself in a scarf and a hat, zip up his fleece, try and wiggle all his digits into the correct fingers in his gloves. I fidget and restrain myself from helping him or telling him to hurry up. We walk slowly round the edge of the house. The patio is treacherous: slick with algae, moss growing through the cracks in the paving slabs, and the hedge has encroached so that the glossy laurel leaves nearly touch the walls of the house. It's dusk and it takes a while for my eyes to acclimatize.

'Oh!' I stop abruptly.

'Ah, yes. Did I not tell you?'

'No,' I say. After a moment I pull myself together. 'Good thinking, if you're selling the house. Might put potential buyers off, if they'd… you know, heard what happened.'

The fence and the gate have gone, and there's a flat, muddy patch where the pond used to be. The tyre tracks where a digger has driven over the lawn have sprouted a fine film of new grass.

'Should have done it a long time ago. But the pond reminded me of your mother and the paintings she loved to do. Mind if we sit, for a minute?' His breath rattles in his throat.

I help Dad across the uneven ground to a garden table and wooden seats beneath one of the old perry pear trees. I'm on to the second can of cider and my breath hangs in front of me like a small white soul. A barn owl swoops low across the grass, a soft shadow with a heart-shaped face.

The past few months have been difficult, to put it mildly. Matt and Amy reassured me that I had done the right thing by telling them about Bethany and what had really happened but, of course, it brought it up for everyone, just after we'd achieved some sort of fragile equilibrium. I never told them about Luca's part in it. That's up to him. He's already given up a lot, but it was more that I didn't want Lotte and Theo to grow up thinking that those you love the most aren't who you think they are; that one day a gentle young man might try and kill you.

I feel as if I've lost my sister as well as my niece. None of us have heard from Bethany. I realize, now that she's gone, we made a lot of assumptions about her. My sister's life was so public that if we wanted to know how she was, we never asked her, we simply looked at her Instagram account, or her Facebook page, or watched her on TV. None of that exists now; her phone, her email, her website – it's all disappeared. And obviously those stories never told the truth.

I don't know how to think about Bethany any more: I hate her, but I miss her. I know she was selfish and self-absorbed and shouldn't have left Ruby-May on her own, but I wonder whether, if it had been me, I'd have behaved any differently. We Flowers are all alike, or at least Bethany and I are more similar than I would have admitted before. *Cut from the same cloth*, all that crap.

'I'm glad you've come,' my father says suddenly.

'Hey, are you cold? Maybe we should go in. Or go up to the pub. I could get a blanket...'

'I'm fine,' he says, with his old authoritative brusqueness, but he pats my hand. 'I remember now why I asked you to come. I'm sorry I forgot to buy any food.'

I shake my head, take a swig of cider. 'Don't worry about it. You wanted to tell me you're selling the house. I get it. It's okay.' I stare across the garden, to where the lawn disappears into darkness, the twilight closing in, the woods beyond.

'No,' he says, 'it wasn't that. I wanted to say thank you.'

'For what?' I ask, not really concentrating. Something white falls through the night: the owl must have been perched above the ruined cottage and now it's pounced. Or maybe I'm imagining the thin, high-pitched shriek.

'For telling us about Bethany. I'm sorry, of course I'm sorry, and it was terrible for Amy to have to relive it all over again. But I thought I was going insane: I know I'm growing more forgetful, but really I had no memory of her asking me to look after the child that day. It took a lot of courage for you to tell everyone, but it's repaired my relationship with Amy – and Matt and the children. I'm grateful to you, Nick.'

He pats my hand again. I drink some more cider and feel as if I'm floating.

'I'm sorry too,' he says, 'for what happened to you as a child. I was not faithful to Eleanor. I'm sure you have realized that by now. I drove her away with my infidelity, and because I tried to make her into something she was not: I wanted her to be a wife and a mother. I didn't value her art or her idea of herself as a painter. It's my fault she left, and I'm sorry you had to bear the brunt of it. I was not a terribly good substitute for a mother, to a twelve-year-old boy.'

I swallow hard. I'm not sure what to say, but something heavy has slipped from my shoulders. Perhaps it's time, after all these years, to speak to my mum.

'Thanks, Dad,' I say. 'But it's not really me you need to apologize to.'

'Oh?' he says, and looks at me from beneath his thick eyebrows. His hand clasping the arm of the wooden chair shakes slightly, the veins raised, the swollen knuckles like small bulbs. It seems cruel to say it, and so I don't.

'You mean Bethany,' he says, turning away, his breath condensing in front of his face.

I nod, my fingers starting to freeze where I've been clutching the cold can.

'Yes,' he says. 'That man' – his voice is filled with bitterness – 'that man destroyed something in her. She was never the same again. I always wished I'd handled it differently. A father should protect his daughter. I did not.'

We both sit in silence and I imagine that he, like me, is thinking about the consequences of that failure in judgement eighteen years ago. I down the last of the cider and rub my eyes.

'Is there still a spare bed in the house or have you packed them all up?'

'I've left your room as it was, Nick.'

'Well, let's head up to the Inn and I can have a pint. I'll stay over.'

'They even do non-alcoholic beer,' he says, and I smile at my father in the gloaming.

I go inside and fetch a couple of torches. We walk through the garden, and the beam clips the outline of the ruined cottage. I pause alongside it, feeling the familiar surge of panic, the sickening sensation I still have in dreams, of falling, of being buried alive. It's shrouded in ivy; a sycamore has grown through the bread oven, the roots like something out of *The Blair Witch Project*. It's much smaller than it used to be. Half of one wall collapsed on me and, once the rubble had been cleared away, my father arranged for the remainder of the cottage to be shored up and repointed. Apparently there was some Building Preservation Notice that prevented him from removing it entirely.

'Ah yes,' my dad says, catching up with me, 'what a terrible fall you had. You climbed right to the top of the chimney to hang up some decorations for Amy.' He shines his torch to the tip of the ruin. 'You must have been five or six at the time. You'd have done anything for your big sister.'

'What? No, Bethany dared me to.'

'Oh, I know you were scared all right. You were always more cautious than Bethany. Amy had planned a whole pretend tea party in the cottage and had her heart set on stringing up one of those things – what do you call them? those colourful triangles of fabric – right across the ruin.'

'I was with Bethany,' I repeat. 'She was meant to be looking after me and she goaded me into climbing to the top.'

My father stares at me and I'm expecting him to get that confused, slightly out-of-focus look he has these days when you remind him of something he's forgotten. It's as if Bethany's lie has been realized, like a bad spell or a curse. He says, 'You were with Amy. She was beside herself when you fell and were hurt so badly. Bethany told everyone she was with you and she made you climb to the top. She took the blame. And you didn't remember, because you had concussion.'

'That can't be right.'

'I'm surprised you can recall any of it at all. You were out cold. The paramedics had to dig you out from beneath the bricks.'

'But why would Bethany—'

'Bethany was Eleanor's favourite. Your mum was incredibly hard on Amy. Expected her to be like a little adult, look after everyone, be the mother she herself was not. And Bethany was strong. She could shrug off criticism; Amy would have taken it to heart. I suspected, of course, that was what happened. I asked Bethany when you returned from hospital, and she told me not to tell anyone that I knew.' He gives a chuckle. 'Only nine years old and she was already protecting her big sister.' He gives a sigh and starts his lurching walk down the final stretch of the garden path, his boots crunching in the gravel. 'I wish...' he says, but he doesn't finish the sentence.

I stand there for a moment and feel as if something cold has rushed down my throat and expanded in my chest. I'm outraged. *Have I been lied to by both my sisters for all these years?* And – *if they lied about this, for so long and so comprehensively, what else have they lied about?* Then again, my father's memory is shot to shit. Or at least, it is now.

I order the pie and chips, and a steak and salad for Dad; a glass of non-alcoholic beer for him and a pint of IPA for me. We sit near the fire and wait for our food. Dad starts talking to some of our neighbours and I take my pint and go and stand outside. I call Amy, taking advantage of the pocket of mobile-phone signal, since there's none at The Pines.

She answers on the third ring. 'Is Dad okay?'

'Yeah, fine. We're at the Railway Inn. I'm going to stay over.'

'Oh, good.' The tension eases from her voice. 'And you haven't forgotten...'

'About the party? No. I thought I could hang on with Dad in the morning, see if he needs any jobs done, and then bring him over.'

'Thanks, Nick, that would be helpful.'

It's Lotte's birthday party tomorrow; well, one of her parties. This one is only for our family. I'm not sure I could cope with a gang of seven-year-olds high on cake.

I take a sip of my beer. There's a thick half-moon, a blunt thumb-print; and a skein of cloud drifts across it and glows briefly. I don't know how to say it, so I blurt it out.

'Dad says you were with me, when I fell off the top of the cottage and nearly died. Not Bethany.'

There's a pause and I can feel Amy readjust; something in the way her breathing changes.

'I'm sorry, Nick. I should have told you, but honestly I haven't thought about it for years.'

'So it's true?' I say, tilting my head back and letting my breath crystallize in front of me.

'Eleanor said she was leaving. She was going to go that afternoon. I was trying to keep you occupied, so you wouldn't notice or get too upset. I planned a tea party in the cottage. I thought it would be a distraction, and Mum said we could have cake and orange juice...' Her breath hiccups. 'But then you fell. I was so upset. I'd wanted it to be a special day for you, in spite of what was going to happen. Bethany told Mum she'd been with you. She said she made you climb to the top. It sounded plausible, like something Bethany would do. She didn't tell me beforehand – she just took the blame. You were out cold, so we didn't think you'd remember. Mum was cross with her, but Bee was right: she wasn't half as angry as she'd have been if she'd known it was me. And Mum stayed. For you. She was so worried about you. I know she left eventually and it was awful. It could have been so much worse, though – leaving us when you were only five and Bee was nine.'

I take a long swallow of beer and feel it track an ice-cold line through my chest. The outrage I'd felt earlier dissipates. I reckon I should stop feeling so fucking sorry for myself. I mean, look at Amy, she didn't even get to have a childhood. What kid should know about her father's affairs and that her mother is about to walk out on them, when she's eleven years old? And yet all she thought about was making sure her little brother was okay. As for Bethany...

'Are you okay?' Amy asks.

I clear my throat. 'They've brought our food over,' I say, peering through the misted window of the pub. 'I've got to go. I'll see you tomorrow.'

'Love you,' she says.

'Love you too.'

As for Bethany – what kind of child would take the blame for something like that when she's only nine? Have I made a terrible mistake about my sister?

22 NOVEMBER, BRISTOL

41
NICK

On the drive to Bristol, Dad asks me several times where we are going. I do my best to be a good son and politely, cheerfully say the same thing each time in response: 'Lotte's seventh birthday party at Amy's house.'

And every time he replies, 'But we haven't got her a present!'

I suppose one of us should take him for a check-up at the Memory Clinic. A proper one, this time. I swerve into Toy World in Bedminister and we rush in, then amble around in a slow kind of panic: two men together, looking utterly ineffectual. We're saved by a teenage shop assistant who fires a serious of questions at us and then hands Dad a bumper craft kit that seems to feature a lot of purple, sequins, glitter and some smelly pens. Dad looks at it in bemusement. The guy flicks his long jet-black fringe out of the way and stares directly at me. He's got eyes like marbles, pale blue with swirls of indigo, and the tip of his tongue is pierced with a bolt.

'A doll,' I say, feeling as if my manhood has shrivelled and died in Aisle 3, next to the Barbies. 'But not, you know, a normal one.'

'Not a normal doll,' he says under his breath. 'This way, Gents.'

He marches through the shop, his DMs squeaking, and then grabs something off a shelf and thrusts it at me.

The doll has glossy brown hair and dark-brown eyes and a fierce expression: she's like a plasticized version of Bethany. She's dressed in a swimming costume and Hawaiian surf shorts; neatly laid out next to her is a life-ring, goggles and binoculars.

'Lifeguard,' the shop assistant says, and his tongue ring chinks against his teeth. 'Complimentary dinghy included.'

I hope a doll with a life-saving boat and superhero swimming skills will be a good enough replacement for the one we buried on a beach in Italy.

'Thanks, mate,' I say and notice that my voice has dropped an octave. I turn to my father. 'Dad, I do believe we have age-appropriate birthday presents that we are about to deliver to the intended recipient on time!'

'Must be a first, Son,' he says, smiling at me.

I don't know how Amy does it. One afternoon and I'm smashed. We've been to the park and kicked a football about, eaten ice cream on a bench, in spite of the Siberian wind-chill, built a Lego spaceship, played three different board games, had two meltdowns and spent some time on the naughty step. Matt has now put *Madagascar* on, and we're all slumped on the sofas with cups of tea, the kids on beanbags in front of us about an inch away from the screen. Amy's stuck pizza and garlic bread in the oven and is icing a chocolate cake. It's from a packet mix, she tells everyone, as if she's just failed the Mothers' High-Jump Championship.

I look at Matt to see if I'm meant to reply to this, but he shakes his head and says, 'It'll taste fantastic, love.'

I'm debating whether I can grab a beer, instead of finishing my cup of tea. Chloe trailed round with us all afternoon, barely speaking, but I suppose she does win the Teenage-Girl Prize for Teamwork, simply by being here in body, if not in spirit.

'Hey, have you seen this?' Amy sets down the bowl of buttercream and passes me a flyer.

It's for a boot camp. I'm wondering if Amy is trying to tell me something. I don't think I'm quite ready for press-ups and protein shakes yet. The icing is an alarming shade of blue, and she's pushing small Playmobil figures into it. I glance at the leaflet. It's for personal training in the sun. In Italy. I feel a sort of shudder run through me. Amy puts a water slide onto the cake, then glues a little girl on the top with extra icing.

'Oh, I get it! It's a swimming pool.'

My sister is now pressing red icing-sugar roses round the edge of the cake-pool. I notice the hashtag at the bottom of the flyer: #FitInFive.

'Look on the back,' Amy says. 'Have you seen who's running it?'

I turn the piece of paper over and see the contact details: Joe Hart and Luca Castaglioni. Something clicks into place.

'I must admit I was surprised. Luca giving up being a child psychologist, to go into the fitness industry.' She accidentally smudges blue icing across her cheek. 'Lotte and Theo still miss him.'

It hadn't been Chloe and Carlo, or Chloe and Joe, or Joe and Bethany in the shed by the pool; it had been Joe and Luca. *What else did I get wrong on that holiday?*

Chloe is sitting next to me, still bent over her phone, watching something. I remember what Dad said to me and decide I should make an effort.

'What is it?' I ask.

She looks up, her expression guilty. I want to tell her to chill: I'm not that into *Madagascar*, either. Reluctantly she turns the screen towards me, slips her headphones off one ear. It's some sort of game show – not what I expected her to be looking at. I'm about to shrug and go and get that beer, when I realize. I snatch the phone and yank the headphones from her.

The woman's accent sounds starched, she's so English in comparison to the other hosts and the participants. Her dark hair has blonde highlights, she's incredibly thin and her face looks weird:

razor-sharp cheekbones, yet plump cheeks, and her forehead and eyebrows barely move. She's in heels and has a gravity-defying cleavage. I wouldn't recognize her if I bumped into her on the street.

'She looks good, doesn't she?' says Chloe.

'Are you kidding? She looks awful.'

The show itself is excruciating: the contestants are as thick as planks, their teeth too white, their skins orange.

'What are you talking about?' asks Amy, leaning over the sofa to pass me a glass of wine.

I'm so stunned I down half of it at once. It's actually quite nice, for something that isn't beer or cider.

'Oh my goodness,' she says. 'It's Bethany!'

She looks at Chloe, who ducks her head, letting her hair slide over her face. 'It's an LA game show. I found it on YouTube. She's changed her name.'

The three of us look at the programme in silent horror. I feel as if we're watching a train hurtling towards us, and the cinema audience all know there's a child on the track up ahead.

'What does she call herself?' I ask.

Chloe says, 'Trixie Flora.'

'Jesus H. Christ,' says Matt. 'Sorry, kids.'

'Is this what we've done to her?' Amy says.

I shake my head. Bethany did this to herself. But then I have an image of myself seizing Bethany, my thumbs digging in beneath her collarbone, shaking her as hard as I could as I shouted, *I will never forgive you.*

We have all driven her to this hellish existence.

'Turn it off,' says Matt sharply. 'I don't want you getting upset again, love.'

Chloe reaches over and takes her phone back. She pauses the programme and swipes it from the screen. As she does, I notice her WhatsApp messages. The four of us are silent. In the background will.i.am is singing about being strange and feeling out of place. Lotte and Theo jump up and start dancing.

'I hate her,' Amy says.

'Lion! Jungle!' Lotte shouts, wiggling her hips.

'I miss her,' Amy says.

Dad has fallen asleep and gives a loud snore, which makes the kids collapse with the giggles.

'The pizza is ready.' Amy's voice is faint.

I hit my forehead as I suddenly remember. 'Hey, you know what, Chloe? I've got your birthday present with me.'

'My birthday was two months ago.'

'Yeah. I know. I forgot.'

'That's kind of you, Nick,' says Matt, giving Chloe a warning look, which she ignores.

I get up and hold out my wine glass for Amy to refill. 'Back in a tick.'

I still had the three photos Chloe had taken, which I'd texted to myself when we were on holiday. I'd finally got round to printing and framing one, as a present for her. I go into the hall, where I've left my bag with the picture in it. I'm puzzling over the messages I saw on Chloe's phone. It's obvious she's in touch with Bethany. I suppose that shouldn't be a surprise. Bethany might have chosen to stay in contact with her – after all, they were close, more like friends or sisters than a step-aunt and niece. Or Chloe, with her better IT skills than the rest of us, could have tracked Bethany down. I'm not sure what the message meant, though. Bee had written: Promise you won't tell them!!!

Don't tell who what? Don't tell us that Chloe knows where she is? I doubt Amy and Matt could bring themselves to speak to Bethany, even if they did have a number for her. I turn on the light in the hall and look at the photo I've printed and framed: the selfie of Chloe and Ruby-May. Their faces are squashed together, Ruby-May's blonde hair blowing across Chloe's olive-gold cheeks. They're both grinning. A halo of sun sparks from behind my step-niece's head and Ruby-May's blue eyes are filled with light. I wasn't sure I was man enough to actually print it out; I had to treat it as if it was a work assignment that I'd been asked to Photoshop for Tamsyn. Now I smile back at Ruby-May. I wonder when Chloe took the photo.

I look at the originals on my phone and check the digital data: 15 August, a year ago. I feel my heart constrict.

The day Ruby-May died.

My niece looks so happy – it must literally have been hours before she drowned. I check the time-stamp and yes, it was that afternoon. I wait for the map to load and it's further proof – it was shot on the edge of the woods below the Mendips: our back garden at The Pines. I feel something crawl down my spine. I enlarge the photo and examine the background. Something about it doesn't look right. At the back of my mind I'm also thinking about Bethany... and what she did when I was five years old. I'm conscious that Chloe is waiting for me to bring her birthday present; everyone else is expecting me to hurry back for pizza.

I send Chloe a text. Feeling awkward. Can u come get it. N

I go upstairs and listen for Chloe's footsteps. When she's on the landing, I open the door.

'Why are you in Ruby-May's room? Why didn't you just give it to me in front of everyone?'

She's amused and condescending, in true teenage-girl fashion.

'You're in touch with Bethany.'

'Is that what this is really about?' She taps the mobile hanging over Ruby-May's bed with one finger, sending it spinning.

'Not really, no. Look, I get it. You're close to her, of course you want to keep in contact.'

Chloe tilts her chin defiantly. But then she sighs and says, 'She didn't stay in touch with me, either. I found her online eventually.

She said not to tell anyone, especially Amy, as she'd be upset. Dad wouldn't want me to talk to her, and I don't suppose any of them – any of *you* – want to speak to her. Are you going to tell Amy?' She looks up at me through her lashes.

'Here's your present,' I say.

It's not wrapped and I simply hand it to her.

'Oh!' she says. She snaps on the light.

I blink. Amy and Matt still haven't cleared out Ruby-May's bedroom. There's a duvet with cartoon pigs on it, and some stuffed toys with massive sparkly eyes are lined up in a row on the bookcase. I notice small details: a black patent shoe with a purple heart, small enough to sit on the palm of my hand; a sunhat with a rainbow-horned unicorn on the brim; a Lego rocket with a broken booster.

'That looks just like one I took!'

I force myself to face Chloe. 'It is the one you took.'

'How did you get it?' She glares at me.

'I saw it when I found your iPad at the villa. I texted it to myself. I didn't look through your other photos, I promise.' *Okay, that's a lie...* 'It's just that Photos was open.' *Why the fuck am I apologizing to her?* 'I wanted to print it out as a birthday present for you. Maybe do one for Amy too.'

She shrugs and looks at the picture again.

'Thanks. I like how you've printed it. The colours – kind of super-real. But why are we here, in Ruby-May's room? That's a bit creepy of you. Oh, wait, is it because you didn't want to upset Amy by giving it to me in front of her?'

'I was thinking about where this photo was taken.'

'Your back garden in Somerset,' she says, like I'm an imbecile. She's still annoyed I've taken the photograph without her permission.

'And then I realized there's something not quite right about this picture.'

'Has no one ever taught you how to give feedback? You're meant to be specific, helpful and kind.'

'Well, not *this* photo. This photo is fine. I looked at two others you took at the same time. Wider angle, see?' I hold out my phone to show her, but I don't get too close. 'You're *next* to the pond. There's the fence, behind you. You're *inside*. You can't see the pond in this picture, but it's just below you. The grassy bank you're sitting on slopes down towards it.'

I think of my mother, sitting on that same mossy bank, her thumb hooked through her easel, trapping paint on the ends of her fine, flyaway hair.

I edge past Chloe and shut the door, lean against it. Her eyes widen and she steps away from me. I hold up my hands.

'Five minutes. I want to talk to you for five minutes and then we'll go downstairs and eat that fucking pizza. I'll stay over here.' To be honest, I don't want to be near her. It's for my own safety, as much as hers. I'm not sure I'll be able to control myself.

I walk over to the window, keeping the same distance between us. I imagine sliding my hands around her delicate neck, tightening them, pressing my thumbs into her windpipe... I look out over Bristol. Beams of light have broken through the grey cloud and illuminate a hill in the distance.

'Let me tell you a story,' I say.

I remember a day, twenty-four years ago, and as I imagine it, I create a new memory for myself: of my blonde-haired eleven-year-old sister crying and my dark-haired nine-year-old sister holding her, comforting her, saying that it would all be okay, then turning and running across the lawn and past the pond, to tell our mother a make-believe story about what had happened. Taking responsibility for almost killing her little brother, when she hadn't even been there.

'One summer's day, the day before Ruby-May's third birthday, Bethany was looking after her niece. She noticed she had some missed calls on her phone from her agent and her producer. Bethany noticed that Dad was snoozing, so to be on the safe side she asked *you*, not Dad, to look after Ruby-May. You agreed, and Bethany went inside to make her calls using the landline because, as we all know, the signal is shit at The Pines.'

I glance at Chloe. She's frozen, clutching the framed photograph of herself and her little sister.

'At first, everything was great. You had a fantastic time with Ruby-May. You took some amazing photos of her. She wanted to go and play by the pond, so you fetched the key and you opened the gate and the two of you went in. And you took three more photos. These exact ones, in fact. Maybe you even escorted her back out. Maybe you thought you'd shut the gate. But you got distracted. Perhaps someone tried to phone you or text you, or you were trying to get some signal so that you could upload your photos to Instagram. Perhaps you started filming yourself, back in the day when you still wanted to be an Instagram star. Bethany, meanwhile, was gone for ages. Longer than she said she'd be. And when she came out, looking for you and Ruby-May, you suddenly remembered what you were meant to be doing. Who you were meant to be looking after.'

I wheel round towards Chloe and she shrinks back. I put my hands in my pockets. Better to reduce temptation.

'The Pines has a big garden. You felt safe there. You thought Ruby-May would be safe. You couldn't see her straight away, but you thought: no need to worry, she'll be here somewhere. And so you started looking for her. Bethany did too.'

She searched the ruins of the cottage, tearing her shins on brambles, pushing her head into the hearth and the remains of the old bread oven. She scrambled over the stone wall and ran across the field at the bottom of the garden, frightening the black calves. She tore through

the edge of the woods and splashed down the stream, burning her
arms on the giant hemlock.

'Eventually you found her. In the pond.'

Chloe makes a choking sound. She sits down abruptly on Ruby-May's bed, still holding the photograph.

'Bethany dragged Ruby-May out. She cleared the water weeds from her nose and her throat and she tried to resuscitate her. She broke one of Ruby-May's ribs, trying to start her heart. But you both knew it was too late. Her heart had stopped some time ago. You both knew she was dead. Bethany said she would take the blame. She loved you. She wanted to protect you. She said: *You have your whole life ahead of you. Your dad, your stepmother, your half-siblings, your step-grandfather – none of them will ever speak to you again if they know the truth.* She described how you'd end up on the news. You'd be trolled on the Internet. Your classmates would hate you. Your life would be ruined.'

Chloe is silently shaking her head. I turn away. The urge to smash her head against the wall is overwhelming.

'So you agreed. But then you had a better idea. You said: *Why should you take the blame, Bethany?* It would be the end of *Bethany*'s relationship with her family. As a semi-famous presenter, it would be the end of *her* career. *David is old*, you said. No one would blame him, especially as he's becoming a little forgetful. And Bethany let you talk her into it, because she too wanted to be a star. She too wanted to keep her family around her and her reputation intact. And Bethany, ever since she was your age, has hated my father for not protecting her from his paedophile colleague. You knew the story of what had happened to her and, because you loved your aunt, you hated him too.

'Once you'd both agreed to blame my father, Bethany gave Dad one of her sleeping tablets, and then she put out a bottle of red wine for him. She threw away half of it, so it would appear as if he'd drunk it, and then she used Ruby-May's Calpol syringe to put drops of Merlot on his shirt and his tongue. He slept, smelling the wine, tasting it, and when he woke, he drank the rest, even though it was dangerous because he's on Warfarin. But once a semi-alcoholic, always a semi-drunk, right? You, meanwhile, put the key to the garden gate back in the house. And, only after all of this had been done, did Bethany call an ambulance.'

Chloe's head is bowed. I can see the perfect white line of her parting. I go closer and she cringes.

I say softly, 'You, though, took it one step further. When we were on holiday you thought everyone would realize that Dad didn't have dementia. You wanted to be certain everyone believed Bethany. So you and your friend Carlo started playing tricks on Dad. It was Carlo who was in his bedroom that night, wasn't it?'

I hover over her. She's trembling. I force myself to take a step back and then another. She nods.

'You and Carlo hid his journal and you stole the heart-shaped framed photograph, and then you put them back in obvious places, so everyone – including Dad – would doubt he was in his right mind.'

I swallow. My throat hurts and my head is starting to pound.

'I don't think Bethany knew what you were up to on holiday. And you and Bethany might have got away with what you did last summer, except that Luca had seen her. He'd been looking out of the window of his bedroom that day, and he'd caught Bethany giving our father a blue pill and putting out a bottle of red wine for him. He thought nothing of it, until we were on holiday and he noticed that Bethany took Temazepam to help her sleep. She gave some of her tablets to Dad to stop him wandering around at night. He also discovered that Dad doesn't drink any more.

'The thing is, Luca loved Ruby-May. He loved that little girl as if she were his own. He worked out that Bethany was to blame and that she'd drugged Dad. He wanted Bethany to take responsibility for what she'd done. He tried to force her to tell him the truth. But Bethany wouldn't, because she didn't want to betray you.

'When Bethany realized I'd found out and that I, like Luca, assumed *she*'d been responsible for Ruby-May's death, and she knew that I was going to tell Amy, she decided to leave the country. She left everything she knew and everyone she loved. She did it for you.'

After all, it's not the first time Bethany has taken the blame for someone weaker than herself. I wipe my hand across my eyes. *Oh, Bee.*

'How did you know? I mean, that it was me and Carlo moving his stuff around?'

'There were a couple of photos of the two of you on your iPad. Just teenagers mucking about, I thought at the time. *Flirting* is what the *Carabinieri* said. You were holding a heart against your chest. I only realized later that it was the back of the picture frame – the one that had gone missing. I'd searched everywhere for it. I should have known when it turned up in Dad's jacket pocket – the exact jacket I'd looked through earlier.'

Chloe is crying. 'She didn't deserve it. Bethany didn't deserve to take the blame.'

'What I don't understand is why you're spending so much time with Dad now, in Somerset. You must hate my father, to do what you did to him.'

She shakes her head and tears trickle across her temples. 'I didn't *hate* him. I thought it served him right. Bethany told me about his affairs, how he drove your mum away, how he drank, and then the horrible stuff your dad's friend did to her... David should have looked after her! And he didn't look after you, either. She still feels guilty about it, you know. Leaving you on your own with him. So I thought: why not? Why not let him take the blame? He's retired, he has no life, nothing to lose.'

She takes a breath and shivers. 'When we were on holiday, I went with him to buy bread from the farm because I wanted to see Carlo, and I thought no one would know what I was up to, if David was with me. But I felt guilty. I mean, he's not the way Bethany described; well, not any more. He's like this kind, friendly grandfather. He's *my* grandfather. And now he really is losing his mind, it's like I wished it on him!

'I went to visit him in Somerset when we got back because I felt sorry for him, and then I realized... I realized that he actually loves me. He always has.' She rubs her eyes with her sleeve again and sniffs. 'I'm sorry. I am so sorry.' Almost immediately she starts crying again and I can barely make out what she's saying. 'I *wanted* to tell Dad. I thought maybe then Bethany could come back home. I sent Bee a message on WhatsApp, but she said not to tell anyone. She said I'll lose everything – Dad, Amy, Lotte and Theo. And Granddad. A family. She said the damage is already done, and she's got a new life out there.'

Chloe scrubs at her face with her sleeve, for once in her life unconcerned about the mascara ringed round her eyes, her running nose.

She says quietly, 'It's so lonely at Mum's house. She works all the time. I'm just, like, on my own. I don't have any friends any more. I can't... connect with them.' She tugs at the sleeves of her jumper, wraps her arms around her chest. 'I think about it all the time. About finding Ruby-May... I can't concentrate at school. I failed my GCSEs. I know that sounds like nothing. It *is* nothing, compared to what happened to Ruby-May. What *I* did to – to my sister. And my grandfather. Bethany. Amy. Dad. You.' She looks down at the photo of her and Ruby-May laughing into the camera. 'It was so awful when we found her.' She puts her hand over her mouth and shuts her eyes. She's shaking.

I look away, suppressing the howl that's rising in my chest, trying to block out the image of the small shape on the stretcher, covered by a white sheet. The pond with its surface skin of lilies, pockets of water reflecting the clouds, as if nothing had happened.

After a few minutes Chloe says, 'Are you going to tell?' She looks like a sad, lost child. 'You told everyone as soon as you found out, or thought you knew, it was Bethany.'

I think about Luca saying, *I don't know what to do with this knowledge.*

Bethany was right: if I tell Amy and Matt, they'll struggle to keep Chloe in their family. They will fall apart; Matt won't be able to reconcile his feelings about Chloe with his love for the child he had with Amy. How do you deal with a daughter who lets your other daughter drown? It will ruin her relationship with Dad, when he discovers it was his oldest granddaughter whose idea it was to blame him for the death of his youngest grandchild. If they know, it's going to do more than make Chloe fail a bunch of exams: it'll affect the rest of her education, her future career. And, as Bethany knows better than most, if anyone other than our family finds out, Chloe's life will become a living hell online.

But if I say nothing, I sacrifice my sister. As a family, we will never see Bethany again. And I will have to keep Chloe's secret for the rest of my life. Chloe and I will be tied together, for ever. I lean against the windowsill, rest my forehead on the glass pane. But maybe that is how it should be. After all, she is my niece. I realize I've stopped wanting to kill her. Instead I feel sick: I'm sick with sadness.

There's no help from *Star Wars* today. Of all things, I suddenly remember a line from *Nashville*, where Avery Barkley tells Gunnar Scott: *You can't push that kind of pain away. You gotta own it. Deal with it every day. That's being a man.*

I force myself to turn and face Chloe. She lifts her head, smooths her hair out of her eyes. She holds herself very still, preparing herself for the blow. A part of me admires her bravery. A part of me hates her.

'You'll always carry the death of Ruby-May within you,' I tell her. 'It's who you are now. I guess that's punishment enough.'

I push up the window and let the night air flood in.

'Give me your phone.' She hands it over without protesting. 'Go downstairs. Eat your pizza. Tell them I'll be there in a minute.'

I sit on the windowsill and look out across Bristol. The door closes quietly behind Chloe. Even in the dark, I can see where the bright lights of Bristol end and the green fields of Somerset begin. I think of Luca's book and I wonder if he left it behind on purpose, if he meant me to have it. I recall the last line: *We emerged to see once more the stars.*

I inhale deeply, fill my lungs with the crisp, cold air. I could stay here, I think, right here, until the stars come out, and tomorrow I'll tell Lotte and Theo how I saw all seventy thousand million million million of them. I turn Chloe's mobile over in my hand and open WhatsApp and find Bethany's number. As it connects, I wonder if she'll answer. I wonder what time it is in LA, but then it is the city that never sleeps.

On the ninth ring, she answers.

'It's me,' I say.

'Haaaaay,' she replies, like I'm still her favourite person. 'It's Mr Nick Flowers!'

ONE YEAR LATER, SOMERSET

EPILOGUE
AMY

They bought her a new purple swimming costume for the occasion. It's got a unicorn head with a rainbow horn printed on her tummy, and she was delighted with it. She's wearing a matching purple swimming hat and goggles and, most importantly, as far as Amy is concerned, she doesn't have a life-vest, a float or armbands and she isn't sitting on a giant inflatable horse. She waves at them from the shallow end.

'She looks like a blueberry,' Matt says, and Amy digs him in the ribs.

The coach holds her hand up and blows a whistle, and the children start swimming. Amy sits up straighter, and Nick and Matt jump up.

Theo hops from one foot to the other at the edge of the pool and yells, 'Go, Lotte, go!' His new rash vest that Nick bought him has the Andromeda galaxy swirling across the front, and his bronze medal, looped round his neck, hangs like a UFO in the centre.

It's early August and they've come to the outdoor pool in Street for the village swimming gala. They've set up deckchairs in the grass for the adults, a picnic blanket for the kids. Bethany – the lifeguard doll Nick got Lotte last year – is sitting on top of the coolbox, plastic fists punching the air, silently cheering Lotte on.

'Is she winning?' asks her father.

He has his glasses on, but she doesn't think he can see well enough to make out the purple blob halfway down the third lane that is Lotte.

'Come on, Lotte! You can do it!' yells Matt, in his loudest five-a-side football coaching roar.

It's a beautiful day, warm, but not too hot. The flower beds are lushly planted with hot-pink zinnias and Day-Glo orange canna lilies. A line of swallows twitter on the cables and swoop over the heads of the children in the pool. There's a large ornamental pond, and water lilies, with leaves as big as plates and perfect lotus-like blossoms, coat the surface. It feels as if they're in the tropics instead of Somerset.

Nick chants, 'Come on, come on, Lotte!'

It's the first time she's seen him wearing a vest. The scars running down his arms and snaking across his chest, just visible when he leans forward, are a livid white, but he doesn't seem concerned about anyone seeing them now – not since he and Maddison got back together, anyhow. Maddison's on a shift at the Grain Barge, the floating cider bar where she and Nick first met, and where she still works when she's not making her screen-prints. She's couldn't get out of it, she told Amy apologetically, but she's going to join them in the evening for pizza and a pint of Green Gold over at the Railway Inn.

Lotte is swimming confidently, splashing the girl in the lane next to her with overenthusiastic sculling and kicking. Amy doesn't care whether Lotte comes first or last; she's just thankful that a year of swimming coaching has paid off and her children are no longer frightened of water.

Lotte pulls ahead, and now she's neck-and-neck with one of the other seven-year-olds in the far lane.

'Second place!' yells Theo, and Matt fist-bumps Nick as if their daughter has won an Olympic medal.

'That's my girl!' he says when she runs over, wet and out of breath, beaming at them.

'Did you see me? I was so fast,' she shouts, and Matt picks her up and spins her round, showering them all with chlorinated water.

'Well done, Lotte,' her granddad says, and Nick gives her a high five.

The children fling themselves on the rug and start rummaging through her bags, looking for snacks.

'Where's Chloe? She should be here,' David says. 'She often visits me, you know.'

After he had sold The Pines, he'd moved to a bungalow in a retirement village in Sandford, which was once part of the old railway station. Amy visits him once a week, but it's a comfort knowing that there are carers on-call, who check in at least once a day.

'She's in Zambia, David,' Matt says. 'I've got some photos to show you.' He switches on his phone and thumbs through the pictures, before passing his phone to Amy's father. 'She's doing some voluntary work...' Amy notices him struggling not to say, *Remember?* They've been told by the consultant at the Memory Clinic that it's undermining. Matt thinks it's PC-bollocks, but he's doing his best. 'At a school. Teaching kids English. God knows what she's telling them. Her grammar is shocking and she can't spell for toffee.'

He's proud of her, but they were all taken aback when Chloe failed her GCSEs and then dropped out of the college where she was meant to be doing retakes. She's on a gap year, volunteering for ActionAid. Amy would never have predicted that Chloe, who only last year had spent all her time borrowing Bethany's make-up and posting videos of herself on Instagram, would choose to go and live in a country where most people are without running water, let alone an Internet signal.

In a week Ruby-May would have been five years old. Amy finds it hard to imagine her as a little girl instead of a toddler: those soft, chubby cheeks disappearing, legs folded with rolls of fat suddenly long and lean. Ruby-May has been dead for almost as long as she had been alive. Amy thinks about her daughter every day, and sometimes the pain is unbearable. But a feeling has crept up on her slowly, not quite of contentment, and certainly not of happiness, but perhaps something approaching it.

Matt slides his phone into his pocket and leans over and kisses her on the cheek.

'Shall I get the picnic out, before these locusts eat it all?'

'Thanks. I'll give you a hand.'

'Shame about the no-alcohol rule. I could murder a can of cider,' Nick says, squinting at the sun. 'Anyone want a coffee? Or an ice cream?' he asks Lotte and Theo.

'Nick! We're just about to have our lunch,' she says, as the children scream over her.

Nick winks at them. 'What are uncles for? Want to come with me and choose?'

'I'd like vanilla in a tub,' their father says, and Nick gives him a thumbs up.

'I'll come with you,' Matt says, abandoning his attempt at finding plates and napkins. He ruffles Lotte's hair and the four of them head off in the direction of the cafe, Lotte and Theo shouting out their favourite flavours. Amy has a momentary pang as she remembers that summer two years ago when her children ate nothing but ice cream for the best part of a week. Her therapist would tell her not to be so hard on herself.

She has an urge to turn to Bethany and roll her eyes; to giggle, as her sister, always braver and bolder than she ever was, who would have sneaked a bottle of chilled Prosecco into the park and would, right now, be attempting to pop the cork and pour the fizz into plastic tumblers without anyone seeing. In spite of everything that's happened, she misses her, as if, like missing her daughter, it's hard-wired in her to grieve.

She's aware that Nick and Chloe keep in touch with Bee, but she doesn't ask about her. As far as she knows, Bethany's still in

Los Angeles. She takes out a bottle of 'fake wine', as Matt calls it, and pours her father a glass and then one for herself.

'Thanks, darling,' he says, taking a sip. He makes a face and sighs.

She's about to unpack the rest of the picnic from the coolbox, when she notices Nick's phone. He's left it on his chair. She picks it up, wondering if he meant to leave it or if she should shout after him. He'll be back soon, though, she thinks. She's about to slide it into her pocket to keep it safe, when she sees what's on the screen. He's been looking at an Instagram account: Trixie Flora. Bethany, of course. The profile photo is disconcerting – she can see traces of the sister she once had, beneath this new woman's shiny skin, glossy gold hair, white teeth and small, straight nose. She doesn't want to look at Trixie's pictures – they're a nauseating blur of swimming-pool blues and palm-tree greens, gold chains and designer bikinis.

She takes a breath and a large swallow of the fake wine. It's not bad, and drinking it over the past few months has helped her cut down on the real stuff. In any case, Ruby-May's room has been turned into a spare bedroom – it's where Chloe stayed before she left for Zambia – and that had meant getting rid of the bottle of gin tucked behind *Peter Rabbit*.

But then, in spite of herself, she clicks on the last photo in her sister's account. It's of Bee in sunglasses, a tightly belted coat and killer stilettos striding through an airport with a large suitcase. She scrolls down to the text below and reads:

At LAX! 😎

Taking a break from telly and heading back to Blighty. Thank you for all your support! Love and kisses 🩶

She thinks she's going to be sick. Bethany posted this photo eleven hours ago. Which means, she works out, bile rising in her throat, that her sister will be landing at Heathrow any moment. What the hell does she want? Is she on her way here, to Somerset? She drops the phone as if she's been burned.

Matt and Nick are strolling towards her, the children licking Cornettos, the ice cream already melting and dribbling down their chins and wrists.

'You all right, love?' asks Matt. 'You look a bit pale. On the hard stuff already?' He smiles, seeing her glass of non-alcoholic white wine.

She doesn't know what to say – how to express in words the sense that this fragile peace they've all been reaching towards is about to be shattered.

Her brother passes a tub of vanilla ice cream to their father.

As if it's contaminated, she silently gives Nick's mobile back to him. He looks from her to the screen.

He knows, she thinks. *He's already seen it.*

He takes her hand and his palm is hot, his fingers cold, from where he's been holding the ice creams.

'Can't ever get these pesky tops off,' her dad, says, fumbling with the lid and the tiny, plastic spoon embedded in it.

'I'll help you, Granddad,' Lotte says, handing him her leaking cone to hold.

'What is it?' Matt asks, frowning.

Nick squeezes her hand. 'Bethany. She's on her way. She wants to see us again.' He gets up and she follows his gaze towards the ornamental pond and its armour-plating of water lilies. 'It's time, Amy.'

Amy stands too and reaches for Matt. She's afraid he's going to explode, but her husband pulls her into his chest, cups her head in one hand. She can feel the beat of his heart echoing in her own body. Lotte and Theo are kneeling by her father's feet, concentrating fiercely as they lick their ice creams. And it's as if there's a third child sitting between them, a child with long blonde hair that gleams in the summer sunshine. She's wearing a swimming costume, an old one of Lotte's. She's lost some of her baby teeth and her face is slimmer, her legs longer. Amy notices her bracelet glittering on her thin wrist: a tiny silver unicorn on a thread of coloured beads that Lotte made for her, and on her lap sits Pearl, her doll, naked apart from a purple ribbon round her neck. Ruby-May turns and smiles at her mother.

'Yes,' Amy says. 'It's time.'

ACKNOWLEDGEMENTS

I would, first and foremost, like to thank my readers. All writers say they'd write anyway, whether they are published or not - but if were not for people who love books, we would not have the exquisite pleasure of being able to hold our finished novel in our hands, nor be able to engage with those of you who are kind enough to share our imaginary worlds for a short while. Thank you, particularly to those of you who've followed my thriller-writing journey from the start.

One Year Later is mainly set in Tuscany in Italy, which I love and have visited many times. The island itself, Isola del Piccolo Giglio, whilst fictitious, is in a real location, off the coast of Isola del Giglio. I'm by no means an expert on Italy and have been guided by my friends, Enrico Carsano and Kate Clifford. Enrico has saved me from the perils of using Google Translate, and added an authenticity I would not have achieved on my own. I'm indebted to Paul Whitehouse, who once again has helped me with police procedure, and David Cohen, whose medical knowledge has, as always, been invaluable.

My editors, Sara O'Keeffe and Susannah Hamilton, have given me excellent advice and helped shape this novel. They've been a joy to work with. I'd like to thank the whole team at Atlantic Books, especially Jamie Forrest, Marketing Campaigns Director, and Kirsty Doole, Publicity Manager. Special thanks to Mandy Greenfield, who copy edited *One Year Later* with a light and understanding touch.

A heartfelt thank you to Emma Smith-Barton who, along with Claire Snook, have helped me become a better writer. Special thanks to Claire, who weathered several drafts without complaint. As ever, I'm grateful to my agent, Robert Dinsdale, of Independent Literary, who continues to both support and challenge me to improve.

Thank you to my family: my mother, Rosemary O'Connell, and my siblings, Sheila, Dee and Patrick, their partners, Simon, Ian and Emma, my nieces, Daisy, Jessica and Emily, my husband, Jaimie, and my daughter, Jasmine, and in remembrance of my father, James O'Connell. I'm grateful for such a loving and supportive family. *One Year Later* is, at its heart, a book about the emotional damage families can inflict which, if left unchecked, can continue, generation after generation. I would like to salute all those of you who have come from a dysfunctional family, and are who are doing their level best to become stronger, healthier and happier.

BOOK CLUB QUESTIONS

Apart from the prologue, *One Year Later*, is told from two perspectives – that of Amy Flowers and her brother, Nick Flowers. Most psychological thrillers are usually narrated by a woman – what did you think about having a male perspective? What does it add to the story?

The story revolves around the death, one year ago, of Ruby-May, who drowned the day before her third birthday. Did you believe the characters' recollection of the events leading up to her death?

Were there any discrepancies and if so, did they make you question the portrayal of other events that had taken place in the family's past?

Who did you trust in the novel and why?

The police verdict on the drowning of Ruby-May was 'accidental death'. Did you believe this?

The characters all grieve in different ways for Ruby-May. In what ways did they show how they felt? Do you think it's ever possible to get over the death of a child?

How did you think the children, Lotte and Theo, have learned to cope with the loss of their sister, Ruby-May?

There are three absent characters in *One Year Later* – Eleanor Flowers, the mother, Ruby-May, the dead child, and Maddison, Nick Flowers' ex-girlfriend. How did these characters, who never appear in the current story, shape the novel?

There are two characters who are not part of the Flowers family: Luca Castaglioni and Joe Hart. How did these young men fit into the story?

Sanjida Kay's psychological thrillers feature mothers and daughters. What did you think of the mothers – Eleanor and Amy – in this novel? How are society's expectations of motherhood reflected in these two women's parenting styles?

The settings in *One Year Later* are the family's childhood home in Somerset, Bristol, and a tiny, remote island off the coast of Tuscany in Italy. How did these locations reflect what was happening to the family?

The events that unfold are based on long-held secrets and grievances. Is it ever acceptable to act the way the characters did, given their past histories?

The Divine Comedy by Dante Alighieri is mentioned throughout the novel. How is this Italian poem used to comment upon the events in *One Year Later*?

The novel is ultimately about the emotional damage that families inflict on their children, which is passed on from generation to generation. Do the Flowers family eventually escape this cycle? Is it ever possible to break free from the harm caused by a dysfunctional and emotionally abusive childhood?